" 'BIG' BRO.
Donovan (Donnie)
O'Malley

# OUR YANK

Cover design by Leif Södergren

Cover photo of the author by John Brooke
Oxford photo by Br Lawrence Lew, O.P

ISBN  978-91-979188-1-7

LEMONGULCHBOOKS
www.lemongulchbooks.com

To the memory of
my extraordinarily beautiful,
beloved mother, Marian Jane.

\*

To the memory of my father,
the California heavyweight boxer
known as Red O'Malley.

\*

And as usual, for Keif,
he knows why.

*Also by*
*Donovan O'Malley*

## LEMON GULCH

12-year-old, precocious misfit
Danny narrates his adventures
in a search for acceptance
in "a uncaring world".

A darkly comic moral tale where
kindness is rewarded and evil sternly
punished.

**Gore Vidal:** *"You've found a <u>voice</u>,
I look forward to reading you entire"*

**Solomon Glushak:** *"a book that
starts on a truly melodic minor key
and soars into the idiosyncratic
world with the kind of candor that
few of us dare attempt
...a masterful work"*

Donovan O'Malley

# OUR YANK

LEMONGULCHBOOKS

# 1

"He's here, Miss Pofford!"

"Who's here?!"

"The Yank, Miss Pofford!"

"What Yank?!"

"Your Yank, Miss Pofford!"

"My Yank?

"Yes, Miss Pofford!"

"Well, show the boy in, you Iris! He'll get wet!"

"He is wet, Miss Pofford!"

"Then show him in before he gets wetter!"

"Yes, Miss Pofford!"

Here I stood, shivering in pouring rain before the door of a huge, old three-story house that was to be my home for the next three years. If the world survived the next three years. Or even the next three days. I was just turned seventeen but my passport said eighteen -- they'd made a mistake. I was nervous, tired, and constipated from taking Dramamine for seasickness. As my naval Granddad always said, "An ocean voyage does not regularity promote." I had a bad headache too -- from the constipation. Headaches and constipation always go hand in hand says dear Granddad. As usual, Granddad was perfectly correct.

I had a lot on my mind. First and worst was the Cuban Missile Crisis. But also, being a new student in a foreign school and it was raining like mad! It never rains so hard in Southern California. It made me more nervous than usual. In fact, it was raining so hard I wouldn't have known I was in Oxford if I hadn't seen the sign at the train station. I will add that the station was pretty run-down. Nothing like the new station in San Diego -- and not a palm tree in sight. At least one potted palm in the waiting room would have been comforting.

As I followed my soggy map through the rain toward my new address I tried and failed to spot a single Dreaming Spire in the rainy mist and I knew exactly where to look. I'd learned a lot about them in 'Oxford, City of Dreaming Spires' which I had re-read on the train to calm down. I am an exceedingly nervous guy and my left little finger was already beginning to twitch. A nerve-racking event in itself. Even on a good day. And oh my God! The rain! Would it never stop?! I never liked rain. Not in such excessive quantities.

"Well?!" bellowed that other voice from somewhere deep in this old house. "Well?! Are you going to let our Yank in, you Iris?!"

"Yes, Miss Pofford!" hollered this 'Iris', "I'm about to."

But this 'Iris' blocked the door and glared at me.

"About to what?!" hollered the other voice.

"I'm about to let him in!"

"Then do it! Show some manners, my girl! Will you make him stand out there in the bleedin' rain or will you let our poor, wet Yank into the bleedin' house?!"

"Yes, Miss Pofford."

"Yes what, you Iris thing?!"

"Yes, I'm lettin' him in, Miss Pofford!"

"And take off his coat! He must be wet through!" hollered this 'Miss Pofford'.

Iris stuck her face deep into mine. "Miss Pofford says you're wet!" she snapped!

Yes, I was soaking wet! I thought I might be catching a cold too, as my effervescent vitamin C tablets had run out in the middle of the Atlantic! I'd never in living memory been without my effervescent vitamin C tablets -- not for very long. It could be dangerous. Everyone at home in California knew this. *Everyone.*

As I stood in the pouring rain this smallish, but very muscular, square-shaped woman still blocked the doorway and raked me up and down with her piercing little eyes while she wiped sooty stuff off her elbow then scratched at something in the armpit of her light blue nylon uniform.

"Are you taking off his coat, girl?! Are you?! Are you?! What are you doing, you Iris thing?!" thundered Miss Pofford from deep inside the house.

"I'm taking off his coat, Miss Pofford! He's wet!"

"I told you he'd be wet, didn't I?! Get that wet coat off him before he catches hisself a chill. Get that wet coat off him before he catches hisself a chill!"

"Yes, Miss Pofford!"

But Iris stood her ground, barred my way, glared and made me even more nervous than I already was. To repeat, I am an exceedingly nervous guy anyhow. The rain was pouring harder and harder and I was getting wetter and wetter and wondering if they even sold effervescent vitamin C tablets in England which is what I should have checked before I came here. I suppose I wasn't thinking as clearly as I should. It's a failing of mine – not checking before. But as Granddad always assured me, a most human failing. Bless my dear old Granddad.

Iris finally grabbed my elbow and jerked me right through the door out of the rain and snatched my suitcase and flung it with a huge thud onto an orange and purple-flowered hall rug -- the ugliest rug I had ever seen.

"I heard that noise! What have you done now, you slothful girl?! screamed Miss Pofford from somewhere that seemed like everywhere.

"I set his suitcase down on the floor, Miss Pofford, honest!"

"You threw it, you Iris! I heard! Don't you lie to me, you lyin' little slag!"

"Honest, Miss Pofford, I was gentle as a little white lambie."

"Liar! Is our Yank's coat off?! Have you got his bleedin' wet coat off?!"

"Yes, Miss Pofford."

"Liar!"

"I'm gettin' it off, Miss Pofford. It takes time, you see. As it don't come off easy. As he's wet!"

"I told you he'd be wet, didn't I? Didn't I tell you he'd be wet?! He wouldn't be wet if you hadn't left our poor Yank standin' out in the bleedin' rain!"

"Yes, he would be wet, Miss Pofford, honest he would, as he's

3

walked all the way from the station, ain't he, and it was rainin'! Wasn't it, Yank? Rainin'?"

"Y-Yes," I said, "and it is s-s-s-still r-r-r-raining."

"What'd he say?!" bellowed Miss Pofford, still sight unseen.

"He says 'Yes', Miss Pofford. I couldn't understand the rest, as he stutters!"

"He what?!"

"I said he said 'yes', Miss Pofford! I couldn't understand the rest as he stutters!!"

"You couldn't what?!

"I couldn't understand the rest of what he said as he stutters somethin' terrible!"

"Stutters, does he? Terrible, does he?"

"Yes! He stutters, Miss Pofford! Terrible!"

Then I said, as loud as I could, "I w-walked f-from the s-station in the r-r-rain! That's what I s-s-said!"

"What'd he say?!"

"I think he says yes he walked from the station in the rain, Miss Pofford."

"I told you it was rainin', didn't I?! Didn't I say it was rainin', you I-rees?! That's why he's wet, ain't it?!"

"Well it ain't my fault, is it?!"

"Are you bein' cheeky, my girl?! Are you bein' cheeky my girl?!"

"No, Miss Pofford!"

"Get our poor Yank's bleedin' wet coat off and bring him in! We want to meet him! Get him in here, you I-rees!" boomed this scary Miss Pofford from behind a half-opened door in the hall.

Before I could do a thing, Iris yanked off my wet duffel, tossed it on my even wetter suitcase and pulled me by my dripping sweater sleeve down the dark hallway into a steamy little room lit only by a dim, old fashioned brass table lamp and a television set that was blurting out all the bad news -- and I mean bad news! The Cuban Missile Crisis!

Iris pushed me in front of a very large grey haired lady with huge, magnified wall-eyes behind her thick glasses and an orange knitted scarf over her shoulders. She sat in a purple overstuffed chair and seemed to fill the whole room.

As politely as possible, although I guess it was a very stupid thing to say, I said "I'm r-really s-sorry to d-drip all over your n-nice rug."

"What?"

"I said "I'm r-really sorry to d-drip all over your n-nice rug."

My mother taught me to be polite but Miss Pofford didn't seem to hear me and only glared at Iris and got very red around the neck and I discovered the source of steam in the room. It was coming from Miss Pofford's ears!

"Well, this is him, Miss Pofford, your Yank!"

"Our Yank, I-rees! This here is our Yank," puffed Miss Pofford who turned to three small people I hadn't noticed who were huddled around the television in the darkish room. "Our Yank which has come to us all the way from California."

"He's late," mumbled Iris into her sooty sleeve and hissed at me from the corner of her mouth, "You're late and wet and it ain't my fault."

I didn't think Iris liked me a whole lot though I try to be, I hope, a likable person. But I was too tired and constipated and homesick to find out why just then. I couldn't just ask Iris why she didn't like me. Because maybe she did, in some crazy English kind of way that I didn't yet understand. Anyhow, the English are supposed to be exceedingly reserved with their feelings. They almost never come out and say to strangers what they mean like Americans do. That's what Granddad said Henry James said happened, anyhow, in 'Portrait of a Lady'. But of course that was the Literature of many years ago. So Granddad and I could be wrong.

I guess I'd find out soon enough -- whether or not Iris did or did not like me. I hoped she did. I never liked not being liked. It makes me nervous. More nervous even than I usually am which is upsetting.

"These is our regulars," puffed Miss Pofford from her chair. The redness in her neck had now reached her rosy jowls. She blinked her big, magnified wall-eyes and squinted sweetly at a little curly haired man under an orange lap blanket – they

5

seemed to love the color orange in England -- who was in a wheelchair behind a large old-fashioned typewriter. "This is The Boy," she said, "been with us fifteen years. He don't talk. As he's got the Palsy. Do you, Boy? Talk?"

The Boy grinned and shook his head in a vigorous way that he did not talk.

"He tried to talk once, ten years ago but he got muddled and he ain't tried since," said Miss Pofford, "which is a blessing for all of us. Ain't it, Boy?"

The Boy nodded happily. He seemed relieved that he didn't have to speak. I felt sorry for him. I knew just how he felt because I have trouble that way -- getting words out. Although my trouble is nothing at all compared to his. Anyhow, it's just too darned easy for me to feel sorry for someone. I suppose I go overboard right away when it comes to feeling sorry. I also feel sorry for myself a lot, too. I am so gawky and inappropriate it's dead easy for me to feel sorry for others as I've had a lot of practice and I know how they feel. Which doesn't help anybody at all. As people can get really angry at you when you feel too sorry for them. Sometimes they even hit you as I knew from an unhappy personal experience when I was thirteen. I do not wish to go into this as it would just make me more nervous. But I can't help feeling sorry for people. Particularly when I'm constipated, have a headache and am 9000 miles from home, and homesick. Like right now. My dear, departed Grandma always said that I was extraordinarily sensitive. I think she really meant that I was a mess. But she never have said it because *she* is sensitive too. I miss her.

"This here's The Blind Girl," said Miss Pofford, pointing at a little women with very short grey hair, "Never viewed a thing in her life. Likes to sit round the telly with the rest of us even though she never views nothing. As her hearing is top-notch."

I went overboard for the Blind Girl too and felt sorry for her immediately. It is not easy being so goddamned sensitive. Especially during a Crisis.

Miss Pofford grunted and patted The Blind Girl's arm. "Her name's Gladys and she is seventy years old if she's a day. She lives at Number 13, next door, where you'll be at. Have you, Gladdy, ever viewed a thing in your entire life?"

"Certainly not."

"But your hearing is top-notch, ain't it, dear? Top-notch."

"Definitely."

"Good for you, dear! This is our Yank, Gladdy, which is to live with us. He is a new student at Oxford's famous Rossetti School of Drawing and Fine Art."

Gladys nodded sweetly and extended her hand which I shook politely.

"He's late for his term," muttered Iris.

"Shut it, Iris! -- How long you been with us, Gladdy?"

"Ahhhhhh, Miss Pofford," whined Iris, "you know how bleedin' long she's been with us."

"Belt up, you Iris! Nobody's askin' you for your humble opinions, are they? Did I hear somebody askin' you for your humble opinions?! Did I?! Did I?!"

"No, Miss Pofford."

"Did you hear somebody askin' you for your humble opinions?! Did you, you Iris thing?! Did you?!"

"No, Miss Pofford."

"Then shut it before I belt you one across yer thievin' chops!"

Miss Pofford grabbed an empty, long-necked vase from a table beside her and menaced Iris who blinked and backed away and Miss Pofford flashed me a kindly smile, winked, and set back the vase and sort of looked at me although I'm not sure she was looking at me as one of her eyes was still aimed at Gladys The Blind Girl.

"Before we was so rudely interrupted by our lying little Iris, I was askin' you a question, wasn't I, Gladdy?"

"Yes, Miss Pofford."

"Our Yank wants to know, don't he? How long you've been with us?"

"Twenty years, Miss Pofford, twenty years tomorrow."

"Good for you, dear!"

One of Miss Pofford's eyes snapped back to me "Over in the corner is old Uncle which as you see has slunk away from us."

The oldest man I had ever seen turned his face to the wall.

"Uncle!" shrieked Miss Pofford. Uncle jerked upright, grunted. "Here is our Yank which is to live with us at Number 13, Uncle dear. In the room which is right next to yours. In the basement. In the basement. If Iris has got it tidied up proper! And if she knows what's good for her she had better had! If she knows what's good for her she had bleedin' better had!"

Miss Pofford had a funny way of repeating herself a lot. I guess it was for emphasis. I didn't think it was necessary as she was loud enough to begin with and all that repeating made my head hurt. But it was probably from my constipation and not her fault at all.

"Yank's late!" hissed Iris into The Blind Girl's ear.
"Uncle was here before we ourselves was engaged to look after these premeeses, wasn't you, Uncle, dear?"

Uncle squinted his rheumy old eyes at Miss Pofford and set his jaw and wouldn't say anything.

"Wasn't you, Uncle?!" said Miss Pofford. "Our old Uncle is hard of hearing, ain't he? "YOU WAS HERE BEFORE US, WASN'T YOU, UNCLE DEAR?!"

"Don't know," muttered Uncle and looked away.

"What was that, Uncle, dear?"

Uncle wouldn't say any more but let a loud fart and The Blind Girl went sort of red and fluttered her hands around in her lap and Iris leered and held her nose. Miss Pofford's redness now climbed from her jowls to her forehead and she gave Uncle an exceedingly nasty look then swung back to me. "There's our Nola, too, isn't there? Lives right at the top in a double bed-sitting-room with her old chum, Vera. Number 13, next door, where you'll be at. But Nola don't come down much. It's her knees, you see. Her old chum Vera's got knees too. It's their knees, 'n' it?"

I sort of nodded my head. How was I to know it was their knees? I'd never even met them. But with those bad knees I certainly did feel sorry for them. Grandma had bad ankles. I used to rub them for her and dear Grandma would say, "Andy, my ankles are killing me. You have healing hands. Come and rub my pain away, dear."

I suppose I do have healing hands as her pain always got rubbed away right away. I miss my dear, departed Grandma. When I'm alone I cry when I think about her. Every time. I cry awfully easy. My mother said I'd grow out of it but here I am, just turned seventeen and I am still bawling like a baby half the time. Something must be wrong with me. This is a sad possibility. I try hard not to dwell on it. But anyhow do. It's a shameful admission.

"We like Yanks. Had 'em here for the war, didn't we? I-rees! Fetch our Yank some tea and pink cake!"

"Yes, Miss Pofford!"

Iris jumped to attention and ducked into the hall.

"You I-rees! Come back here, you hor-reeble I-rees!"

Iris stuck her head through the doorway and kind of slouched there. "Yes, Miss Pofford?"

Miss Pofford seemed now to aim one eye at me and one at Iris. "This here is Iris. Come to me a foundling of fourteen. Thirty years ago if I remember correct. Stop hangin' about, girl! Get a move on  and fetch our Yank his tea and cake! Fetch our Yank his tea and cake!"

"Yes, Miss Pofford!" said brawny little Iris and leapt into the hall.

"They said you was to be here today. You start tomorrow they said to say. As tomorrow is Monday. As you're late, ain't you?" said Miss Pofford. "The Rossetti sent us a message by hand that you'd be late for term but Iris read it and the lyin' little slag lost it. Tomorrow. Yes. Tomorrow at half past nine. You're late for term. Ever so late."

I was late because Grandma died early this year and I was worried about Granddad. He was crying a lot. We both were. I think he'd have felt better if I was there. But I couldn't stay there when I got the Rossetti scholarship. Poor Granddad.  I love him so much. My extraordinarily beautiful mother will take good care of him.

Miss Pofford was now watching the television as I answered politely "I've got a kind of s-special d-dispensation to be late."

"You what?"

"I got a d-d-d-"

"Go on, boy, speak up!"

One of Miss Pofford's huge, magnified eyes latched onto me and wouldn't let go.

"I have got a d-d-dispen-sation," I finally blurted out. Words do what they like with me. I don't have a whole lot of control over them. Which is embarrassing. My mother said I'd grow out of it. But I didn't.

"Dispen-sation? A dispen-sation from the Pope hisself, eh?" said Miss Pofford and showed her teeth and looked like she was either laughing or getting ready to. I wasn't sure.

"Well, you and the Pope is late!", she muttered, one eye still glued on me, "Quite late. Term's begun, ain't it? Yes it has. Yes it has."

I thought she sort of smiled but I still wasn't sure. She drifted back to this awful television news where a lot of high-altitude photos of the Cuban missile sites were stuck on a display board that the experts were pointing at with long black pointers. I was very worried about all this as my best friend Tom is training to be a pilot in the U.S. Air Force and he'd be right in the thick of it. He could be placed on emergency duty at any minute and he's only a couple years older than me. Russian ICBMs could be launched at the USA any day now and the world would end then and there. That's what everybody, including Tom, thinks. On top of it all, here I am studying in a foreign country! I must be nuts! If I had ten effervescent vitamin C's I'd take them all right now! A whole damned handful and not even worry about the consequences!

I'd sat down on my own -- on an old, cracked leather hassock though nobody asked me to. It would have been rude to keep standing while everybody else was sitting and very possibly getting a crick in their neck looking up at me as I am six feet, two inches tall and skinny. Re: sitting, wait until all the ladies are seated then sit. Always be polite to the ladies. I always am. Anyhow, that's what my dear mother says. I miss her already and it's only been not a lot over two weeks. It takes almost four and a half days to ride across the good old USA in a Greyhound bus even if you ride all night and all day as there are lots of stops on a cheap ticket. And crossing the Atlantic by ship takes about eight days too. Depending on the weather. And the ship of course. And the icebergs. That wasn't funny. Why did I say it? Because I am socially inept, that's why -- 'a work in progress' -- as they say.

Miss Pofford's living room was sort of like my dear late Grandma's but without all the vases of flowers that Grandma had all over the place. I noticed a small glass case with a lot of little dolls in it. I hadn't noticed it before because it was right beside the television set from which I had mostly averted my eyes because The Crisis news just went on and on. But at this minute the news was taking a station break for the weather. More rain! I guess you could have called this small glass case a 'Dolls of All Nations' exhibition as there were so many little dolls in national costumes and little uniformed soldiers too, patriotically holding up their countries' flags in their tiny hands. This reminded me of my little 'Uncle Sam -- Symbol of America' doll that I've had since I was a child. Though I didn't like to call it a 'doll' as a boy doesn't have dolls. I preferred the words 'Uncle Sam figure' -- my 'Uncle Sam figure.' He was tiny too and he also carried the American Stars and Stripes and I did feel sort of proud until this made me think of the coming atomic missile war. I suddenly felt my left little finger almost spinning in my pocket. I nearly cried then and there out of sheer homesickness and excessive interior terror. I suppose all this was because of tiredness and constipation and the lack of water-soluble vitamin C. However I'm glad I didn't cry as it would not have been an auspicious beginning at my new address. I must control this serious flaw of mine.

Miss Pofford had a lot of vases too. But there weren't any flowers in them. Maybe she only used them as handy weapons against Iris. Not funny, Andy! My dear Grandma really loved flowers! If we had let my Grandma loose in this steamy little room it would have been blooming like early Spring in two shakes of a lamb's tail. I love flowers too. Not always. But often.

When my allergies aren't playing up.

I suddenly got very hungry. Even though I was constipated. I guess these two conditions can go hand in hand too -- when you're seventeen and your self control is not what it's meant to be. I'd have to work on that. My self-control. I'd be older soon, hopefully -- depending on The Crisis. I couldn't stay seventeen forever and still be in my right mind. Seventeen seems to have too many personal complexities that require growing out of. Pronto!

Suddenly that old fashioned typewriter started to type and made me jump and I looked over and saw 'The Boy' pecking out something slowly with one finger -- like I myself type, when I type, which I don't. Not often. Not yet. But when I do, I intend to learn the proper way -- with all my fingers. But he couldn't help it, The Boy. One finger was all he would ever have at his disposal. I could have cried on the spot. I almost did. The strain was terrible. This is a problem that continually demands my sad attentions.

Anyhow, The Boy nodded over at me and as nobody but him was paying any attention to me -- I got up and went over and read what he was typing: 'hello i am william.'

"Hello, W-William," I said, "I'm Andy."

William gave me an excellent sort of diagonal smile. I like people to smile at me, especially when I am nervous. Anyhow, I smiled right back. I hoped my smiling at him made him feel better too. I felt a little better. Not a whole lot. But better. Just. Then I thought about how awful it would be to be stuck in that wheelchair behind an old, almost foot-tall ancient typewriter and not be able to talk at all and only have the use of one finger and I felt a lot better for me but more sorry for him simultaneously. Tears popped out so fast I knew I would have to wipe my eyes. My hanky was in my duffel's pocket which was in the hallway so I sat there with my eyes leaking like sieves and I finally wiped them on my sweater sleeve -- not a particularly polite thing to do, wipe something on your sleeve, especially from your mouth, nose, or eyes. In this case, on an exceedingly wet sweater sleeve. This was not a pleasant or even courteous experience. I hoped 'The Boy' didn't notice.

"What's your name again?" said Miss Pofford without even turning her head politely away from the television to face me.

"L-Leander Riley," I said as I sat down again on the old hassock and thought that people should at the very least look at you when they are speaking to you. I wished Iris would hurry up with that tea and pink cake as I was getting a little shaky from lack of nourishment and my left little finger was driving me crazy. I was having a devil of a time keeping it still in my pocket.

To make conversation I was just about to tell Miss Pofford the story of my namesake from the Greek myth about Leander, who swam the Hellespont to be with his girlfriend, the high-priestess, Hero. This was a very special comfort to me, the idea that my namesake had done something heroic. It was sort of an obsession, I guess, to calm down with this image, as it also included water and my birth sign is Pisces, a water-sign. I suppose, as dear Grandma used to say, I am too sensitive for my own good. But I intend to do everything humanly possible to grow out of this needless complication. To grasp experience with both hands, 'as it were', as they say in England. However, I am probably a hopeless case. Just now, anyhow.

"Irish, are you?" said Miss Pofford, again not looking at me.

"Irish d-d-descent."

"Since when has the Irish been decent?!"

Pofford let out a horrible screech that made me jump. She swung around to me and I saw she was laughing. I liked her laughing as, at this very minute, I was beginning to feel astoundingly homesick. This was my first time outside of the good old USA except when I went with Tom to Tijuana, Mexico, just over the international border from San Diego, to buy cheap Puerto Rican rum and leather sandals with rubber-tire-tread soles. Tom had an excellent smile and of course he really liked me as he was my best friend. Which made me think that when people smile at you in a certain way it means they really like you. So if Iris didn't like me, at least Miss Pofford did. She was the Boss. Maybe she could force Iris to like me? No! This is definitely not right. I am not a damned facist! If someone likes you they should like you because they like you and not because someone forces them to. Why do I think such dumb thoughts? This is a sure sign of immaturity. I am so primitive!

"Leander Riley, eh?"

"A-Andy."

"They said you was to be here today. You're late. Gladdy, what's tomorrow?"

"Monday, Miss Pofford. I have lived at Number 13 for twenty years come Monday," said The Blind Girl.

"Good for you, Gladdy," said Miss Pofford over her shoulder, then, to me "You're late. They says to say to you that you're to start Monday which is tomorrow. What'll we call you then?"

"A-Andy."

Why do people forget my name especially just after I've told them? It makes me feel like I don't matter. Maybe I don't. No. That's just my tiredness and constipation speaking. I do matter. I think. To me, anyhow. I hope.

"Andy it is. I-REES!"

I heard a crash from underneath the floor.

"I-REES! What have you dropped now, you clumsy I-rees?!"

"Coming, Miss Pofford!" echoed from below.

"Where's our Andy's tea and cake, eh?! Where's our Andy's tea and pink cake, eh?! Where are they, eh?!"

Miss Pofford's eyes rotated one by one back to the television and the aerial photos of the Cuban missiles -- and I thought about poor Tom again and how he'd fly right into the thick of it soon and I felt like I had a big rock stuck somewhere in between my stomach and my guts.

"The Spaniards is behind all this!" yelled Miss Pofford at the TV and made me jump again. "That's what I say. What do you say, Andy?"

"Uhhh... The Sp-Spaniards aren't r-really involved in..."

I couldn't get the next words out but I was saved by Iris who sailed through the door with a big wooden tray of tea and large pieces of pink cake and a lot of bread and butter and I was awfully hungry even though it was white bread which my dear mother always called 'gut-glue' and just what my constipation didn't need!

"About time too! you Iris!" said Miss Pofford.

"It ain't my fault, Miss Pofford!"

Iris leapt away as Miss Pofford lunged at her, "Belt up and pour our Yank his tea! Tuck in boy, we've already had ours."

Iris stayed out of Miss Pofford's striking range as she poured my tea and handed me a big piece of pink cake which I wolfed right down and the tea was wonderful. Hot and with milk! I had never had milk with tea in my life. It was like nothing I'd ever tasted. I was starving even though I had not excreted for three days. Regularity is so important. That's what dear Grand-dad always says. He knows what he is talking about too as he was what dear Grandma always called 'An Anal Retentive in the definitive sense of the word'. Granddad always said 'Andy, I am a martyr to my poop which is hard as diamonds set in cement and seldom makes a truly comfortable appearance.' Dear Granddad's exact words.

"Our Iris is in disgrace!" spat Miss Pofford and nearly knocked me off my hassock! "Spent The Blind Girl's meter money at the Bingo Parlor in Little Clarendon street, didn't she, Gladdy?"

The Blind Girl twisted her fluttery fingers together and tried to smile although I could see it was hard for her as she was really nervous, probably a little afraid of Iris too. Like me. I hoped The Blind Girl was never constipated. I wouldn't wish that on anyone. Particularly not a poor blind person. It's funny, when you haven't eliminated for three days you tend to think about it almost all the time. And a whole lot of other things too, of course. Maybe that's just me. Probably is. It is not a healthy sign.

Miss Pofford lunged again at Iris who jumped backward. "Didn't you, Iris, you fat little thief?! Spend our Gladdy's meter money?! Two and bloody six it was, wasn't it? A half crown! Two and bloody bleedin' six! Which must be deducted from her rent again! Which must now be deducted from her rent again!"

I felt uncomfortable with all this screeching and I had no

idea what 'meter money' was but I kept wolfing down all that nice, pink cake and hot tea as I'd only had one chocolate bar since lunch on the train and man does not live by chocolate alone...see how lame you are, Andy Riley, when you try to be funny? Pathetic!

"Is our Yank's room ready? Is it?"

"Yes, Miss Pofford."

"Warm, is it?"

"Yes, Miss Pofford."

"Shillings in his meters?"

"Yes, Miss Pofford."

"You ain't gone and spent 'em all at Bingo? Like you did our Gladdy's?!"

"No, Miss Pofford."

Miss Pofford swung over to me, smiled sweetly and said "You'll be at Number 13. I do both houses you see, as I was engaged many years ago by Ravencroft College which owns these two houses to take care of 'em, you see. Number 12 which is here, and Number 13 which is next door and where you'll be at. Eh?"

"Errrr..."

That's about the third or fourth time she'd told me. She repeats herself a lot. I guess we all do. I certainly do. A lot. I'm exceedingly forgetful. I am in need of a crash course in remembering. They have them back in California. I wonder if they have them here in Oxford? If they do I wonder how much they'd cost. They'd have to be exceedingly cheap before I could partake.

"So you'll be at Number 13, next door, in the basement bed-sitter, right next door to old Uncle's room. I trust our kitchen noises won't disturb you none as there's a 'thinness' in the basement wall, ain't there? Our kitchen is at the other side of the basement wall from where you'll be at, behind the 'thinness.' I trust our kitchen noises will not disturb you none?"

"Errr...n-n-no."

"Good for you, Yank! I-REES!

Iris had sneaked into the hall and was chomping down a big piece of the nice pink cake and its strawberry filling dribbled down the front of her blue nylon uniform.

"What's your name again, Yank?"

For the third time I answered "A-Andy."

"Iris! Stop hangin' about and show our Andy to his new lodgings and be quick about it!"

Now wasn't that nice? I am now 'Our Andy' and 'Our Yank.' I liked that. It made me feel at home. Especially as by now I was even more homesick. If that's possible. However, my left little finger was calming down. Which was a comfort. Possibly due to Miss Pofford's kindly tone of voice to me. She was really not so frightening after all. I liked her. Yes. I now knew that I liked her exceedingly well.

"He'll be wantin' to bath. Hot up the bathin' water!"

"But it ain't his bath day" Miss Pofford," whined Iris gulping down the remains of her pink cake and, "It just ain't".

"You do as I say, my girl, or you'll know the reason why!
"Yes, Miss Pofford!"

Iris dragged me by my wet sweater sleeve from the dark little room, jerked my soaking wet duffel from the orange and purple hallway rug, frowned and flung it at me and was out the door and into the pouring rain with my wet suitcase in her short, brawny arms. I tried to grab my suitcase back because ladies must not carry heavy things. Ladies were more sensitive. Even though Iris didn't seem to perfectly fit the bill, she was definitely a female and should be treated as such. With great deference. On all occasions. No heavy carrying!

17

# 2

I chased Iris in the rain through a rusty iron gate into the tiny front garden of the house next door, Number 13, which was joined to Number 12 on one side and on the other side to a long line of old-fashioned three-story houses that all looked alike. As far as I could see through the rain, all of them were joined together. I had never seen houses like these in California. But if my dear Grandma could have seen this poor little front garden, it would've broken her heart. She loved her own garden, and weeds were always nipped in their buds before they had a chance, she said, to establish themselves. Sometimes I feel like I should be nipped in the bud too. Especially now that the whole world was just about to be nipped, so to speak. Why make a big fool of myself just before everything ends? What a thing to be remembered by! Foolishness! But who would be doing the remembering? This was not a pleasant thought and would not go away. It haunted me. Was I really serious about this thought? 'Know thyself' said Granddad. I didn't. Yet. Maybe never. There wasn't enough time left.

Iris dropped my soaking wet suitcase on the flooding doorstep of Number 13 and yanked a key from her blue nylon uniform pocket and opened the door then handed the key to me. As I followed her down the hall over another rug, orange again, with purple flowers too, a door opened just a crack and a blood-shot eye squinted out at me. What a creepy welcome! Was this the House of Vampires or something?! I could have used another nice smile just then, and maybe a cheerful greeting. I wondered who in the world could be so creepy. To stare out at you like there was no tomorrow. But maybe there wasn't and the bloodshot eye knew it? Sometimes I have an extremely sick imagination.

We went down some very dusty stairs to the basement. My dear mother should've seen this! Suddenly a lot of dogs were yelping and scratching behind a door as we passed. They nearly scared me out of my soaking wet underwear! "That's old Uncle's little black doggies, snarled Iris, "Hush, you little black doggies!"

I was by now exceedingly homesick and I never thought

I could be. I always thought I wouldn't miss anyone except maybe my dear Mother or Granddad or my favourite Aunts: Fran, Graycie, June, and Dot, and my small female Border collie, Tinker. Tom was going to try to come over for a week at Christmas because, as an air force trainee himself, he could get a free military flight. But now, with all this trouble in Cuba, he -- Iris swung open a door. "This'll be your room, Yank."

Now if I ever in my life saw a dark, cold, damp, room this was it. At one wall a gas heater was burning in a shiny, red-painted brick fireplace with roots! Real tree roots, white and powdery looking, that grew right in through the basement floorboard on each side of it. The Rossetti had told me that Miss Pofford didn't usually rent out this basement room after a previous tenant had experienced some unspecified unpleasantness here. But as a favour to the Rossetti she would, and very cheaply too. Which suited me. I was exceedingly lucky to have this room, right in the middle of Oxford and only a few blocks from the Rossetti itself! So who was I to complain? But I did. To myself. Though I knew how very lucky I was I still complained to myself! Sometimes I am a very complex human being and I don't understand myself at all. This worries me. I really loved this room. It was mine! But it was so cold my breath made steam. And what were all these little black boxes that covered one wall? They were making tiny, soft whirring and clicking noises. Little black metal boxes, each with a small piece of paper taped on it.

"You'll bath with us next door at Number 12 as there's no hot water down here at Number 13 as we don't have none," said Iris, who sort of slouched against a wall looking at me like I was a freak or something. "I'm to hot up the water for you, as Miss Pofford says. You're to come next door in one half hour as it takes one half hour to hot up the bathin' water in our immersion tank. You can go through your back door to us as we never lock our back door at Number 12 as it's always open. Mind the nettles. Miss Pofford don't like female visitors in her prem-meeses after ten. Miss Pofford'd be ever so upset if there was to be female visitors in her prem-meeses after ten as she says."

"I-REES!"

19

I jumped and nearly fell against a wall! I thought we'd left Miss Pofford back in the other house but she seemed to be right here in the room  beside us! Her voice, big as life, was booming through my wall!

"That'll be Miss Pofford from the thinness," said Iris and stuck her mouth close to a patch of peeling paint and damp crumbly plaster on the wall just beside a big wooden wardrobe with one door with a cracked mirror hanging sideways off it. "Coming, Miss Pofford!" yelled Iris, her lips nearly smacking the crumbling plaster of the 'thinness', "Coming, Miss Pofford!"

Iris twirled, slammed open my door and sailed up the basement stairs like the demi-god Mercury, with wings on her big, black-shoed feet.

I inspected my new home, peered through the single dirty window into a brick-lined sort of ivy-covered pit -- a 'light-well' I guess you could call it. I saw water gushing down its brick walls into a grated drain at the bottom and looked up and could just make out, over the top of it, the roofs of a row of tall houses across the street and a narrow patch of dark grey sky in the rain. I could also see if anyone was at the front door.

I shivered. Some of that ivy was growing through a narrow gap at the top of the window and was tangled around a couple of the odd, softly whirring, clicking, little black boxes. This was really crazy and did not do a heck of a lot for my peace of mind. To top it off there was, what we call in the USA, an 'easy chair' and the English call, I guess, a 'Morris chair'? At least I think they call it that...but I probably got that all wrong. Anyhow, this chair had only three good legs and the fourth was bent under and half-broken off so that you had to balance yourself in it a certain way or you would fall over. I tried it and wondered why this chair had not been repaired – it needed a whole new leg with a lion's paw specially carved on it which could have been exceedingly complex and excessively expensive. Dear Granddad, who had in his youth been a carpenter before he went into the Navy, would have had a conniption fit – called it sloth of the worst kind that a chair in this sad condition could be utilized by civilized people! I sort of liked it and christened it The Chair.

My dear Grandma and Granddad were very big on Culture and Civilization with a capital "C" et cetera which to them always meant sensitive, intelligent, well-read, people of reasonable means. Grandma and Granddad were all these things except the 'of reasonable means' part. Due to 'bad luck', said Granddad, and 'poor planning', said Grandma. But my dear Grandma, rest her beauteous soul, was now gone. Early this year. As said. How I miss her. I'd better stop thinking of Grandma or I'll blub. I'm a secret seventeen year old bawl baby. It is humiliating!

I forced myself to stop thinking of Grandma and sat on my lumpy bed for a while and tried to mull over my new situation. I am not very good at mulling over situations of any kind so I couldn't and didn't. Which is not surprising, particularly when constipated -- as all your thoughts, all of 'em, flip right back into your regularity dilemma. Anyhow, I smoked three skinny little cigarettes which made me cough. But they would have made me cough anyhow as I'm allergic and occasionally even a little bit asthmatic. I only smoke once in a while because almost everybody else does and I don't want to be the 'odd man out'. Plus I'm stupid. The cigarettes were cheap English ones, Woodbines, that I bought in a pack of ten on the train from Southampton. I had never bought cigarettes in a pack of ten. It's Crazy!

I now had only two British pounds in my pocket. I was running out of money due to not wanting to cash an American Express Traveller's check as I did not wish to carry a lot of cash on the train. Granddad told me that foreign places and persons can be perilous when travelling. He should know as he travelled all over the world when he was in the Navy.

My great, great grandfather, however, had been a United States senator. I come from an illustrious family in decline. That's what dear Grandma always said. This sort of thing, Culture, was very important to my grandparents although, as said, they couldn't afford it. Culture with a capital "C" is always exceedingly expensive in the good old U.S. of A. I believe that Culture is probably very expensive the world over. Although I have read that museum entrance fees in England are very reasonable. Even free in some cases. Such as for students. This is a good sign. As cheap Culture for me is a must! Cheap Culture is de rigueur for us poor, as dear Granddad said. I have had no reason to doubt this.

So now I sit here smoking a cheap, skinny little cigarette and getting extremely homesick. I am also extremely worried about The Crisis. I guess I worry about everything including the Rossetti and whether I'll be as competent here as I was back home. I was voted the best male artist at my high school. The best female artist was a girl named Myrna who was a genius and exceedingly avant-garde though subject to migraine headaches. She briefly worshipped at the shrine of the famous American illustrator, Ben Shawn.

Anyhow, if my Art studies here don't work out I can always go to college back home -- if there is a home to go back to. Do I really believe that there might not be? Sometimes I do and sometimes I don't. I can only completely believe in the coming end of the world for a few minutes at a time. It is too nerve-wracking. Even if it is true. It keeps jumping back into my brain just like the constipation. This is a deadly duo to deal with that I wouldn't wish on anybody. And don't.

Anyhow, I was offered a college scholarship back home too which I felt guilty for turning down. But I also felt that every artist-to-be owes to him or herself some authentic world travel -- although at the time I felt this I didn't know it would be so goddamn nerve-wracking (Excuse me!). So when I got the chance for the Rossetti scholarship I took it. But then I was worried that they might not offer that scholarship at home again if I didn't do well at the Rossetti. So my success at the Rossetti is very important. You would think that with the offer of two scholarships I would be more confident. But all I felt was guilty at turning down the first scholarship and worried I would fail with the second. Dear Granddad always says that guilt and worry make the world go round and maybe he's right. This, of course, is exceedingly worrying.

Then suddenly I heard the tiniest little whirr and click and the bare light bulb hanging in the middle of my cracked ceiling blinked off. Then another tiny click and the little gas heater in the shiny red-painted brick fireplace went off and it got even colder very fast. I don't think I have been that cold since I camped out with Tom in the Laguna mountains, sixty miles inland from San Diego, California when I was fifteen and forgot my sleeping bag and almost froze my butt off until Tom invited me into his. But I had my effervescent vitamin C to fall back on then. Which was a comfort. So was Tom. He really was!

I heard clomping on the stairs. It was Uncle -- I could hear him muttering to himself -- and his dogs barked.

"Belt up, you hairy bitches!" yelled Uncle, "Belt up you puking bitches!" He let a very loud fart and slammed into his room. Somehow I could hear everything as though it was right in the same room with me. The dogs kept barking until I heard a swat and a yip and they were quiet. Then, more clomping on the stairs and my door banged open having not even been politely knocked on first. It was Iris.

"Your bath is waitin', Yank! Miss Pofford'll be ever so upset if you don't bath now as there is others as are waitin' to bath after you. Bein' that it's their proper bath day for these others and not for you as it's only special bath day for you bein' that your bath day is Tuesday which is day after tomorrow as Miss Pofford says."

Iris grabbed a furry looking grey robe that was slung over her shoulder and tossed it at me. Luckily I caught it as I am a reasonably good catcher some of the time. But, I hasten to add, only when I concentrate. I was always the last to be chosen for the baseball team at Phys-Ed classes in high-school. I was not puzzled by this as it was undoubtedly due to the fact that besides not being able to catch well, I could never hit a ball with a bat either. This resulted in my pretending to have a badly sprained ankle and going off with my good friend, Eddie, who also pretended to have a badly sprained ankle. We both hated organized sports as we were, both of us, rotten at them. I have always thought it was exceedingly unfair that those of us high school students who were especially rotten at organized sports were made a spectacle of by coaches who felt that everybody should be able to hit a home run or make a touchdown at football or run a mile without falling right on their butt! Which, of course, is a nearly impossible feat for people like Eddie and me. Besides, I could swim! But in swimming pools only, because I was once knocked down and sucked under by a monster ocean wave and skinned my knees up something terrible on a nasty nest of barnacles. But swimming in pools was still swimming and I was a very good swimmer. But my school unfortunately didn't have a swimming pool.

Eddie and me, with our fake sprained ankles, phony-limped to a hill just behind the school during Physical-Education hour and always ended up sitting on a certain rock 'resting' said ankles and watching a colony of big, black ants that Eddie had discovered. Either I or Eddie would sit there and hum our favourite parts of George Gershwin's Rhapsody in Blue or An American in Paris – which first got me interested in studying Art in Paris. But Oxford was even better as they spoke English which is always exceedingly helpful with communications of every kind, everywhere. It also had to be admitted that Oxford was hitchhiking distance from Paris as well as possessing The Dreaming Spires, which I have yet to see as it is still too misty and rainy. And the classical drawing training at the Rossetti was meant to be second to none and teeming with famous experts and artists as instructors and graduates who had achieved great success in the Art World. And the immediately adjacent Ashmolean Art Museum had Leonardo da Vinci and Michel-angelo drawings you could hold in your hand! They were in plastic envelopes of course! The Ashmolean also had one of the most important Pre-Raphaelite collections in the world! All available to us students to study!

"Miss Pofford says you was to have this bathrobe as it belonged to the dead gentleman before you in this room which died." said Iris interrupting my current series of comforting European ruminations. "Double pneumonia," added Iris, "He was dead as a doornail, stone-dead. He was just layin' there in your bed, with his head layin' on your pillow, his eyes wide open and crusted over with goo and starin' at the ceilin' like a dead fish out of water." I jumped, of course, when Iris wacked the pillow on my bed for emphasis. Sudden loud noises and motions were anathema for me! "Miss Pofford was ever so upset!"

And so was I! Sometimes I felt like a fish out of water even if I was a pretty good swimmer. "Th-thanks," I said, carefully folding the robe and tucking it under my bed pillow. I was still shaky, hopefully from the cold and not my scary nerves. But I was afraid it was the nerves. Anyhow, I preferred to skip Iris's sad chapter of my ravaged, fish-eyed, stone-dead predecessor but was exceedingly grateful for the robe because as I had packed a behemoth amount of art materials including a very large set of sable watercolor brushes my dear Granddad bought for me, there was not enough room in my suitcase for my own bathrobe. And even a posthumous bathrobe with a gruesome history was most welcome .

"Why is it so dark in here?!" blurted Iris. I jumped again!

"The light w-went out."

"Why did the light go out?!"

"I d-d-don't know."

"Didn't you insert no shillings nor sixpences into your electric meter box?!"

"Wh-What electric m-m-meter box?"

"Your electric meter box, that's what electric meter box!" Iris aimed her nose up in the air, sniffing in the dankness. "Why is it so bleedin'cold?! Miss Pofford'd be ever so upset!"

"The heater w-went off."

"Heater?! What heater?! What heater's that?!"

I pointed. "Over th-there."

"The gas fire? You mean the gas fire?"

"I guess s-so."

"Didn't you insert no coins into your gas meter box?! Insert no shillings or sixpences into your gas meter box?!"

"Wh-What's a gas meter b-box?"

"Them little meter boxes up there on the wall! Them little black boxes! Can't you see all them bleedin' little black meter boxes on the wall?! They're the gas and electric meters for each bed-sitter in this whole house except for Uncle which has got his own in his room. Can't you see them meter boxes on your wall?!"

"Y-Yes, there they are!" I said, attempting to control my twitching little finger in my pocket while pointing directly at the softly buzzing, clicking little boxes and their taped bits of paper as I hoped to placate Iris.

"You got to insert shillings or sixpences in 'em don't you? Or they stop, don't they?"

"If you s-say so, Iris."

"Then you shouldn't use 'em so much then, should you?"

"I j-just got here. I've h-hardly used them at all and I d-don't have any sh-shillings anyhow."

"Electricity don't grow on trees!"

"N-No, Iris, I'm c-certainly c-certain it d-d-doesn't," I said, soft as a little white lambie to charm her. But she only made a sour face -- I was now sure that she didn't like me. She fished two sixpences out of her blue nylon pocket. I knew they were sixpences because they're about the size of a USA dime -- I had bought that miniscule little chocolate bar with a little sixpence. From a little machine. It was my experience up till now that everything in this little country seemed to be surprisingly little. Why is everything in England so little? Is it because there is just not enough room for everything to fit in it? I would never, never say this in front of a native of said lovely country as it could be construed as discourteous.

Iris dragged me by my still wet sweater-sleeve to the ivy-vined wall of softly whirring, occasionally clicking meter boxes, said "Meter box money ain't included in your rent. See this sign? 'Insert money here'?"

Iris inserted a sixpence each into the two top meter boxes, the ones with the ivy tangled around them which were mine, as I noted 'OUR YANK' scrawled on one of those bits of paper and taped between them on a struggling ivy vine. Iris wound the coins into each box and with a tiny click the bare electric ceiling light bulb went on and the gas 'fire' hissed. She hurried over and lit it with a huge kitchen match she snatched out of her pocket and said "Meter box money is not included in the rent as

Miss Pofford says -- not after today it ain't. Not in this basement it ain't."

Meter box money was not included in the rent.

Iris glared at me. "Well", she said, "Well?!"

"M-My m-meter m-money is not included in the r-rent. N-not in th-this basement, it ain't."

"*I know that!* It's bath time ain't it? Use the back door and mind the nettles!"

Iris was out my door but stopped at the top of the stairs and called down, "Nettles'll sting your bottom if you ain't careful! Remember! Use the bleedin' back door! We can't have you paradin' about in your knickers at her front door as Miss Pofford says."

I didn't really think Miss Pofford had said that but Iris cackled happily and clomped down the hall before I could say anything. I probably wouldn't have said anything anyhow as I wouldn't want to be a wet blanket and ruin her little joke. Also I couldn't get the words out. I heard the back door slam. And that was that.

I undressed and pulled on the poor, dead man's grey robe Iris had flung at me. I hoped I wouldn't die of double pneumonia too but I thought it could easily happen without effervescent vitamin C. I was feeling really nutty and couldn't get vitamin C out of my head. I suppose, no I knew, I was overtired. I will be perfectly honest about it, this constant rain was getting me down!

I got out my bath-kit. Tom had bought me an incredibly nice one in brown grained-plastic that looked so much like genuine leather that it might as well have been the real thing. So I started up through the dust-balls on the basement stairs -- if I'd had a broom I would have made short shrift of them as Granddad would have said. Poor Granddad, without Grandma. Anyhow I now had to look for the back door and to remember to be careful of the nettles. That's all I needed -- to get stung on my butt by nettles again! Like in the Laguna mountains when I forgot my sleeping bag. Granddad said it served me right, being so forgetful. He is correct, I suppose. But his saying it hurt more than the darned nettles. I always liked my dear Granddad to approve of me in every way. When he didn't I felt 'down in those deeper dumps' as Grandma used to say and which she had experienced during the tribulations of her old age.

My constipation-headache wasn't getting any better and my left little finger was twitching up a storm as I crossed the weedy, nettle filled, little back yard, exceedingly careful of those nettles -- poor Grandma would have literally cried her eyes out at the sorry state of this overgrown, little back yard. All those scary nettles! Granddad once read in a detective story that buried corpses encourage the multifarious growth of certain unpleasant plants on the very ground above them. This probably included nettles and was not a comforting thought. Even if it was only a lot of BS. Pardon my French!

I entered the back door of Number 12 and followed a sign with an arrow and 'Bathroom', up some stairs and found myself nearly freezing outside a door that said 'Bathroom' on a brass plate engraved with a multitude of curlicues. I opened this door which was one small step up.

"Excuse m-me!" I cried out as the tallest naked lady I had ever seen was standing at the wash basin and peering down at me and smiling as she turned towards me. I looked away as quickly as I could but not so quickly that I didn't take in her breasts and beautiful teeth and the triangle-shaped dark patch between her legs. This was the first triangle-shaped dark patch I had ever seen on a lady. I of course slammed the door shut and will now change the subject as my left little finger is playing up something awful due to this unsolicited shock.

However, I always wished my teeth were beautiful too like the tall naked lady's but they weren't. Although they weren't that bad. When I'm a rich and successful artist on the Left Bank of Paris – which I always wanted to visit ever since Granddad showed me a postcard of the Left Bank and my old highschool buddy, Eddie hummed An American in Paris -- I intended to have my teeth fixed up really perfectly. Like Robert Wagner's were in 'Beneath The Five Mile Reef.'

As I calmed down and began to get back my senses I remembered that this naked lady's breasts were also exceedingly sculptural. I wouldn't have minded at all to draw them. In fact I very much wanted to as I didn't have much experience with breasts of any type except my mother's when she breast-fed me up to the age of one year. Although my memory of that occasion is hazy (a joke!). Not very funny, was it, Andy? Well what did I expect -- coming from me? And without any help at all from Mr. Bob Hope's comedy writers! (another failed attempt!)

The bathroom door opened again. "I sneaked in," said the tall, naked lady who didn't seem in a big hurry to cover herself up, and seemed even to enjoy, maybe, being stared at while naked, "I stole a bit of your hot water, love. Hope you don't mind, Won't be a minute."

She smiled beautifully and gently closed the door. And there, glaring up at me half-way up the stairs to the basement kitchen was Iris!

"Well?!" she said, as her round, beady eyes narrowed into slits, "Well?! Are you going to bath or not?! Or are you going to stand there and not bath? There's others as are waitin' to bath after you bath as it's their proper bath day. This is special bath day for you as you're to bath on Tuesday as Miss Pofford says. Don't forget that. Miss Pofford'd be ever so upset if ever you forget that. Ever so upset!"

"Oh, I won't. I'd n-never, n-never ever f-forget that!" I said, hoping to be especially agreeable so she'd like me. I can't help being like this. I know it is completely cowardly and disgusting and a gross weakness in my character. But I can't help it. So, just for good measure I said "I p-promise I will never f-forget my p-proper bath day. Th-That is a s-s-solemn p-promise, Iris."

"Miss Pofford'll be ever so pleased. Miss Pofford likes people doin' as she says."

But she glared at me again. "Well, she said, Well?! Are you going to bath or not?."

"Err...I'm w-w-waiting," I said, kind of backing down the hall so her voice wouldn't be so loud as my left little finger was *really* playing up in the pocket of my dead man's robe!

"Waitin'? Waitin' for what? Waitin' to bleedin' bath?!"

"Err...y-yes. But th-there's a t-tall n-naked l-l-lady in there."

"A tall n-naked what?!"

"A l-l-l-lady!"

"You what?!"

"A naked l-l-lady in the bathroom." I said as genially as I could under the circumstances.

"A lady?! What lady?! What lady's that?! What lady's in there?! A lady?! It ain't her bath day! What bloomin' lady in Miss Pofford's bathroom?!"

When I thought Iris had finished screaming at me I said -- in an exceedingly little voice as my headache was now worse than ever as I had currently still not excreted -- I said: "I d-don't know."

A crash of dishes breaking followed by "I-REES!" sent Iris sailing  down the stairs to the basement kitchen to join Miss Pofford on their side of the notorious 'thinness'. A narrow escape for me as I don't think I could have stood much more hollering. Not just then. Due to headache, general nervousness, twitching left little finger and the terrible feeling of worldwide destruction that was sticking to me like poison-ivy. My sanity was in danger, I was at, I feared, the scary point of no return!

"There's plenty," said a beautiful soft voice right behind me. I turned around quickly and I was instantaneously comforted by the soothing sight of the tall, naked lady! She was dressed now and it made such a difference! She was in a kind of short bathrobe that showed her knees -- which were not at all bad knees for a woman of her advanced age -- she must have been at least forty or even forty-five! She had a big bottle of shampoo in one hand and she was lovely. Really nice. Pretty, too, for her age. For any age. Even beautiful.

"Water. Hot water, love," she cooed, "There's plenty."

She turned and waved at me as she went out the back door. I guess she lived at Number 13 too. I hoped she was careful of the nettles because her short bathrobe wasn't any longer than it needed to be.

In the steaming little bathroom I turned on the tub faucet and got about two inches of lukewarm water that barely covered the bottom of the tub before it turned ice-cold. I guess this was what they meant by 'plenty' in England in 1962.

Anyhow, I had my first bath in my new home in about two inches of lukewarm water but I didn't mind at all because I was in beautiful Oxford, the city of dreaming, though still hidden, spires. And in England, a definitely foreign and slightly scary place while the whole world was perched at the horrific precipice of doom. This was altogether new but not altogether comforting.

But I could draw! I could paint! -- I was pretty good or they would not have let me into The Dante Dominic Rossetti School of Drawing and Fine Art especially on a scholarship as I kept telling myself over and over. My high school Art instructor, Mr. Bateman, believed in me. So for a few minutes I was able to believe in myself. But unfortunately, I guess I wasn't too sure about my state of mind. I'm sure that's what made me so unsure. I think. I could be wrong. If Granddad was here, he would know.

The tall naked lady had a nice smile and a tender, soft voice. She was so nice that for a few minutes I forgot I had a headache, was constipated, nervous, homesick, and was catching a bad cold. But worst of all: I was totally lacking my vitamins and was relatively sure that life on Earth would be coming to a horrifying, abrupt end in the next several minutes. In other words, as my dear Granddad says, we all of us had a lot on our plate.

# 3

I was still thinking about the tall naked lady as I carefully made my way through the nettles back to my basement and that damned bloodshot eye stared at me again. I was cleaner now but a heck of a lot colder and I still hadn't pooped. I was also out of those cheap, skinny cigarettes and I was certain there were two more before I went to take my bath. But the packet was now empty. I had left them on what I had decided would be my work and dining table but they were gone. I smelled their cheap cigarette smoke from the blood-shot-eye's door as I passed by on my way to the tobacconist's. I may be a whole lot of awful things. But I'm not stupid.

"What'll it be?" said the tobacconist.

"Have you g-got American c-cigarettes?"

He tossed a pack of Marlboros on the counter, said "eight shillings."

Cigarettes in California were only thirty-five cents! And fifteen cents on the ship over! Eight shillings I knew by now, just had to be a whole lot more!

"Have you g-g-got anything cheaper? That's about a d-dollar."

"No," said the tobacconist, "That's about eight shillings."

He took back the Marlboros, reached behind him and tossed a packet of ten Woodbines on the counter. "One shilling sixpence for ten."

"And a T-Time magazine and some p-p-potato chips, p-please"

I fished around in my pockets for my English money.

"Live around here?" he said.

"Across the s-s-street, N-Number 13."

"Pofford's eh"?

"Y-Yes."

"Oh. You're that Yank." He smiled, almost laughed. "The one which is late for term?"

"Y-Yes."

"You better watch yourself, old son, the last bloke in that basement bedsitter of yours died of the pneumonia."

"Iris t-told me. I've g-got his b-bathrobe."

"That bathrobe belonged to the bloke before him," said the tobacconist, "He used to wear it when he bought his cigarettes. They carted him off too. Some home or other for lung-rot."

This wasn't something I wanted to hear right now and I stuck my left hand down deep into my pocket to keep my little finger quiet.

He smiled again. He also had a nice smile and I concentrated on that and smiled back. It was soothing. It made me feel like I was an old friend or something. A smile is an exceedingly important thing, says Granddad. Smiles win friends and influence people. Granddad should know. I never saw a guy with so many friends as my dear old Granddad! Anyhow, nice smiles are exceptionally important today because they make us forget The Crisis for a minute. Smiles are particularly nice with all this rain that never seems to let up. Rain is depressing. Smiles help. Especially when you are nervous and depressed in the first place. Not to mention constipated. I know I sound like some kind of crazy, hysterical hypochondriac. I'm not! I'm only nervous and depressed and constipated. It could happen to anyone. 'Good health is like a frightened duck on a pond,' says Granddad, 'it can come or go at any minute.'

"I think I'll n-need some change for my meters too, I said. "May I please have some s-shillings and s-sixpences?"

The tobacconist laughed. "What's the matter old son, Iris lose your meter money at Bingo?" He laughed again. "Well you're in luck, seein' as how it's your first day."

He took back the ten shilling note and carefully counted out five shillings and ten sixpences, handed me a Time magazine from a stand beside the counter and the rest of my change. You'll find your potato chips just down the street. The best shop in town. This side. Five minute walk. We don't do chips. Only crisps."

"Th-thank you," I said and wondered what crisps were. Something to do with over-fried bits of pork? Granddad loved crisps. Or were they called 'cracklings'? Typical me!

The tobacconist was a nice man. I was glad he was just across the street as it wouldn't be far to walk in the rain for my

Time Magazines to keep abreast of The Crisis. Damn it, there I go again! But at least it's only to myself.

"Do you c-carry laxatives?" I whispered, a little embarrassed about such a personal thing.

"Only if they're not too heavy," he laughed, "No. You'll find that at a Chemist's. They're shut on Sundays but the wife might have something to spare. She was poorly a few days back."

He left the counter and returned after a minute with a small packet. "She said you could keep these as your need is probably greater than hers."

Now wasn't that a kind thought! Coming from perfect strangers too. I was sure I was going to like England and I almost began to hope that England was going to like me too. Though I couldn't help wondering who belonged to the sneaky, bloodshot eye behind the door of the room over my digs and who probably took my woodbines. I didn't like mysteries. And I have never liked everything all at once. All at once seemed to be just what was happening now too. In my life and in the world. Everything. All at once. Worrying. Very worrying. Was I always this way? Sometimes I can't fathom my self!

I am happy to report that, due to the laxative from the kind tobacconist's kind wife, I had a satisfying though strenuous, and only slightly irritating bowel movement on a freezing little toilet with an old wooden seat at the end of the ground floor hall. In order to get to this toilet I had to pass that bloodshot-eye which I did on tiptoe because I do not enjoy being stared at from behind slightly opened doors. The eye fortunately was not there just then. Though the knob on my locked toilet room door was jiggled on two occasions as I sat there on the toilet hoping I had not inherited poor Granddad's chronic intestinal complexities.

After my successful bowel movement I felt able to face anything so I didn't bother to tiptoe past the bloodshot-eye door. One should assert oneself. Whenever possible. Though I never did. Though I wanted to. I knew that not bothering to tiptoe would be about as much as I would assert myself in this particular situation. A great failing on my part which I was anxious to grow out of and doubted if I ever would. So I walked firmly, like a young man should. But suddenly, there it was, that eye again, staring at me in all its bloodshot unpleasantness. So up I went. On tiptoes. Damn me! Now how can I respect a person like me?! Anyhow, I usually tried to tiptoe past old Uncle's door so his dogs wouldn't hear me.

As I went to sleep that night I wondered who that eye might belong to. But I was so tired I did not wonder long and I was soon sleeping and hopefully not snoring unpleasantly -- as nobody likes an unpleasant snoring person. Particularly at night when one needs ones sleep. Particularly now. During these trying times.

Suddenly I woke up to the loud barking of old Uncle's dogs then "Belt up, you hairy bitches!" then, again from Uncle, "Who the hell's out there, eh?!"

I could hear every word as plain as if it was in my own room!

"It's just me, Uncle. Gladys. Iris forgot my meter money..."

"Bugger Iris! All right then, girlie?"

"Yes, Uncle."

"How're you keepin', girlie?"

"Just fine, Uncle. We've an American amongst us, haven't we?"

"Yep."

"He seems quite nice, doesn't he? For an American?"

"Had 'em here for the war. Yanks. Four of 'em. Noisy bastards, every one! Here for the war."

"And now it seems we're to have another war, doesn't it, Uncle? Yet another war."

"Four of 'em. Yanks. Noisy bastards."

"My cousin married a problematic one. But our Yank does seem quite nice. For a Yank."

"We'll see, girlie."

"We shall indeed. Goodnight, Uncle."

"Goodnight, girlie."

As I lay there, now wide awake, my door was very gently thumped on twice and, before I could reply, it opened. I saw The Blind Girl as she quietly tapped her way in the very dim light of a street lamp reflecting in my light-well. Gladys made her way past the foot of my bed to the wall of meters and wound in a coin. The meter buzzed and whirred, joining all the other very softly buzzing, whirring meters as Gladys tapped her way out and closed the door quietly and I was soon gently buzzed and whirred to sleep again.

So Andy slept, too tired tonight to worry about the state of the world, too tired even to dream a nightmare. Tomorrow night he would again be fair game. Nightmares occurred during daylight as well, forced themselves on him, blending anxiety with panic and insecurity with sheer terror. He was excellent at dreaming up nightmares, day or night, then trying to talk himself out of them. But tonight he slept, one arm slung over the side of his lumpy, low, makeshift bed made from a small sofa, his curly blond hair sunk deep into a somewhat -- but not a lot -- frayed pillow, the back of his open hand resting on the dampish carpet.

About midnight the soft buzzing of the many meters on his flaking, ivy-encroached wall diminished by one with a nearly inaudible clunk. Not long after, Andy's door again creaked open. A flashlight beam fell, first on Andy's open hand on the carpet, paused there then inched up to his sleeping face. A figure, finding its way in the flashlight beam, swayed uncertainly across the floor to the meters, wound a coin in, then approached Andy. The figure stood for a moment, drunkenly peering down at Andy with two dozy, bloodshot eyes then swayed back to the door, was about to creep away when Andy stirred in his sleep, sighed and cried out. From the door the figure said softly, "What? You all right then?"

But Andy slept restlessly on, flinging an arm about, kicking up the sheet and blankets, apparently not fatigued enough to be free of his midnight horrors. They were getting worse.

# 4

Weak morning daylight seeped through the window from my light-well as heavy clomping down the stairs shook me awake and Uncle's dogs began to bark.

"Belt up, you hairy bitches!" bellowed Uncle who must have swatted at least one of them -- I never knew how many there were, two or three? The dog let out a yelp which made me glad I had slept my headache away. Dear Granddad always said that sleep is the best remedy for headaches and, with that, I am inclined to agree. As ever, wholeheartedly. Thinking of my Granddad always calms me a little bit.

"Here's your tea and toast, Uncle," hollered Iris over the dog-yelping. I heard Uncle's door bang open then --

"Oh Uncle! If Miss Pofford ever seen your untidiness she'd be ever so upset!"

Uncle -- it must have been Uncle -- farted. Because Iris cried out "Ohhh Uncle, how rude! So early too!" and she went on in a really mean and vindictive tone of voice, "No butter for you today as the Yank gets it all as it's finished as there ain't any says Miss Pofford and the Yank just came from California."

"Bugger California!" said Uncle. "Bugger the Yank."

"Why Uncle, If Miss Pofford ever heard them words she'd..."

"Bugger Pofford!" said Uncle, "Bugger you!"

Uncle's door slammed shut at the same time mine slammed open, and Iris, singing at the top of her lungs, lurched in with a rattling tray of tea and toast.

> *"Today is May Day!*
> *Hooray for May day!*
> *When birdies sing*
> *And everything*
> *And you ..."*

The breakfast tray crashed to a small, warped table beside my bed.

> *"...And you shall marry me!"*

I shot up in my bed. Iris bent over me and looked extremely serious and poked her face right into mine. I rubbed my eyes and her face was so close my hand clipped her on the nose but her round, flat face didn't flinch, just stayed where it was, too close. I could smell her sweat too. It wasn't the nicest smell I ever smelt -- not horrible, but not the nicest. I'm sure dear Granddad would have had something to say about that but I was too sleepy to think of what it might be. However, thinking about all the things that dear Granddad might have said was, as I said, soothing and I was doing it more and more. There was definitely something wrong with me, I was certain. Was I obsessed? Or was this only an idée fixe? If dear Granddad was here I would ask him. If he didn't know I'm sure he would ask Grandma but... Grandma was gone and Granddad was grieving and I should have stayed longer to comfort him. Damn me! I would have cried then and there if Iris would only leave. But she went on and on with important stuff, I guess, about their breakfast traditions et-cetera, et-cetera.

"Miss Pofford says to say to you that tea and toast for breakfast comes with the room but egg and bacon with breakfast will be one shilling and sixpence. She says to say to you that if you wish to have egg and bacon with your breakfast you're to pay an extra one and six as she says. Due with the rent."

With her face stuck right there into mine she waited for my answer. When I didn't answer right away as I couldn't get the words out she added, "Egg and bacon'd do nicely with breakfast as it's ever so cold outside now as Miss Pofford says."

"And inside t-too," I added with a terrible shiver that did not seem to please Iris at all. I sat back in bed and tried to pull my face out of Iris's but she swooped in even closer and my head thumped against the icy wall behind. "I'd do as Miss Pofford says," said Iris and scowled.

"I'll do as Miss P-P-Pofford s-says then," I said, cowering toady that I am!

Iris grinned. "Egg and bacon it is. One egg? One bacon?"
"Y-Yes."
"That'll do nicely. I'll tell Miss Pofford that you'll have egg

and bacon. One and six extra due with the rent. Miss Pofford'll be ever so pleased."

I nodded.

"Right you are! Egg and bacon! One and six extra due with the rent. Your tea and toast is here on your table which is included." She slammed the top of the warped table with the flat of her hand and my tea slopped out over three pieces of thick, cold toast in a wire holder.

"Miss Pofford'll be ever so pleased you're doin' as she says. Miss Pofford likes people doin' as she says. When I tell her you're doin' as she says she'll be ever so pleased."

"G-Good."

Iris frowned. "Miss Pofford gave you our poor old Uncle's butter for your toast. Butter's finished as they didn't deliver none when they should've. Poor old Uncle was ever so sad as I told him you got his butter."

"G-Good G-God!" I said, "I didn't know! I'm r-really s-sorry! Please take my butter back to old Uncle!"

Iris stared at me like I was a criminal or something to have taken poor old Uncle's butter and said in a very dark way "What's done is done."

The room was freezing and it was still raining. It was like being naked in the Laguna Mountains in winter. I really needed to warm up so I brought the steaming cup of tea to my mouth and was just about to drink when the room shook.

"I-REEES!"

Iris rushed over and put her mouth to the thinness and shrieked: "Coming, Miss Pofford!" And she sang as she flew out the door and up the stairs:

"Today is May Day!
Hooray for May Day!"

Which made me wonder if it was really going to be 'May Day' in an atomic missiles sort of way. Not a pleasant thought for so early in the morning and my first day at The Dante Dominic Rossetti School of Drawing and Fine Art in Oxford!

It really wasn't all that much butter but I decided to give it all to old Uncle right away. So I pulled on my robe and did, and when he'd quieted down his dogs he thanked me and said he'd give it to his puking bitches as it made their hair shiny.

I now sat shivering, mopping up what was left of my tea with a kitchen towel Iris had dropped. Lucky for me the tea wasn't hot or I could have suffered first degree burns. And me just about to leave for the Rossetti if it was still there at nine thirty this morning. 'We are haunted by the spectre of total atomic war' kept running through my head as I dressed. I then unpacked my large drawing pad and new charcoal pencils and a single-edged razor to sharpen them with. But I kept thinking about the spectre of total war and added would I be a failure at the Rossetti and how could I get some effervescent vitamin C as soon as humanly possible?! I know how stupid that sounds! But that's just me and I'm not surprised. I definitely think I'm not the deep thinker that like to I think I am as I always come to this conclusion when I think about it.

Could I hold my own among these British Art students? Today would be my own May Day -- in one way or another. Though I had no idea then that my own personal May Day was only days away and would not be like anything at all that had ever happened to me. My 'gas fire' meter clicked off and I imme-diately began to shiver so I re-opened my suitcase, hunted for something warmer to wear. Something much warmer to wear.

# 5

What a nice young man, thought Irene. She hadn't meant to take most of the young Yank's hot water yesterday afternoon. Irene liked Yanks. Liked them so much she had married one. Actually, two. Well, as good as. The first was called 'Alabama'. She never knew his real name. But that was long over. Was probably over before it began. They were only needy. She and he. Everyone was needy those days during the war.

Irene's second Yank, Sergeant Ricardo Martinez, wasn't needy at all. He was grateful and he proved it. And kind. He was a very special man. What had happened? Don't we learn anything? Bad planning? No planning? No, Irene, it was the war. WW2. Remember?

Irene wondered why this young Yank -- and he was *so* young -- would come all the way to the Rossetti to study Art. Though the Rossetti was excellent for classical training, she knew they had many fine Art schools in America. She'd go there one day. Or would have. If it weren't for complications.

Iris had warned her that the Yank was to bath yesterday but Irene couldn't resist freshening up. Then she and her Jean-Francois spent a breathless night together and had enjoyed a steamy reprise this morning. He had left just now, crept out the front door of Number 13 not three minutes before Iris, with her rattling breakfast trays, came in the back door.

Irene sighed. She needed another bath today too. She liked to be fresh for work and with a touch of hot water, even lukewarm water, her lovely skin took on a -- how to say it? -- a glow, a sheen that belied... She took off her robe and observed herself carefully in the tall, oval floor mirror. Jean-Francois had left two love bruises on her left thigh and a love bite on her neck. She zipped open her makeup kit and rubbed a bit of pancake makeup over the three bruises, stood back, Not bad for a forty-eight year old. Not bad at all. She was lucky. Or was she? She sighed again and wondered how it might all end. She knew precisely where and very nearly when. But not quite how.

Iris put down her empty breakfast trays and slouching at the door of Number 12's basement kitchen, said, "He's to have egg and bacon tomorrow."

"Who is?!"

"Why, the Yank, Miss Pofford!"

"What Yank?!"

"Your Yank, Miss Pofford, which come yesterday, Miss Pofford! Honest!"

"Yank? Yank?! Had 'em here for the war. Four of 'em. Noisy bastards. What about 'em?! What do they want now?!"

"He's to have egg and bacon."

"That'll be one and six, due with the rent."

"That's what I told him, Miss Pofford, didn't I? Egg and bacon, one and six."

"Due with the rent. Uncle got his breakfast?"

"He wasn't happy with no butter for his toast."

"Because you lost the bleedin' butter money at Bingo."

"Awww, Miss Pofford..."

"Shut it! The Blind Girl ate?"

"Yes, Miss Pofford."

"Mr. Lemmington got his breakfast?"

"Mr. Lemmington says the Yank stayed too long on the loo, Miss Pofford. Mr. Lemmington says he tried to enter twice. He says he almost had a accident as the Yank stayed too long on the loo."

"The Yank's got a perfect right to stay on the bleedin' loo, don't he?! He just came all the way from California, didn't he? He needed to, didn't he?!"

"Yes, Miss Pofford."

"Well there's an end to it! Mr. Lemmington paid his rent?"

"No, Miss Pofford. He's to give you four bunny-rabbits he shot yesterday behind his Uncle's vicarage. "

"Only four? Any fowl?"

I guessed I'd be warm enough. I had on two sweaters, two pair of socks, and my duffel coat which I nearly caught on fire. I'd hung it close to the gas heater -- I mean gas 'fire' -- to dry it out. Sort of a stupid thing to do. Then Iris brought me a big black umbrella Miss Pofford had loaned me so I wouldn't get my drawing pad wet in the rain. This was such an extremely moving gesture! But I didn't have the time to cry. I would thank her later. I crept up the basement stairs so Uncle's dogs wouldn't hear. In the dark hall I turned to see if the Bloodshot Eye was at the door and I tripped over something soft. It was four dead rabbits! Four poor little dead rabbits tied together by their feet! I could have vomited! Someone had obviously been torturing the poor little tykes. Not a good sign. I wondered if Bloodshot Eye was involved in this atrocity and wouldn't have been surprised if he or she was!

As I fell my drawing pad and pencils poured out of my large unzipped leatherette portfolio and were scattered all over the awful orange and purple hall carpet and I was on my hands and knees trying to gather them up when two ladies came roaring down from upstairs without looking where they were going! The first lady, who was very small, tripped right over me. I grabbed her just in time so she wouldn't fall and hurt herself. But the second lady, who was exceedingly large, grabbed my arm so tight it hurt. Really hurt! She had a 'grip of steel' as Granddad used to say about a naval buddy of his that he used to arm-wrestle with. It soothes me to think of my dear Granddad in these times of danger, surprise and despair.

This second lady who was just as tall as me pulled me right up from the floor like I was a rag doll or something! She put her face down into mine just like Iris does. This, in itself was a very unpleasant habit! "Watch where you're goin'!" said this second lady in a rough, unpleasant way. Watch where I'm going?! I thought, but I smiled anyhow, in an exceedingly genial manner, as per usual with me.

"I'm Charlie," said the large, second lady. "This is Regina."

"Hellew," said Regina in an extra refined voice like you hear in English movies on TV, like the way beautiful Phyllis Calvert spoke in Madonna of the Seven Moons. 'Awfully pleased to meet yew.'

Then Charlie grabbed Regina and pulled her down the

43

hall. As they were going out the front door Charlie turned and frowned at me. What had I done? -- only tripped over four abused, dead little rabbits that almost made me vomit and that weren't even mine and shouldn't have been on the floor in the middle of that darkish hall in the first place! I now had two English enemies, Iris and Charlie. Although I think Regina, the pretty one, liked me. I am certain  they were middle-aged. At least thirty-five. The both of 'em!

Irene took a custard tart from her bag, removed it from its wrapping and took a bite, munched. She was reclining fabulously, she assured herself, in her semi-comfortable chair, reading Lady Chatterley's Lover. That shortish bathrobe in which she'd surprised Andy had been replaced by a red silk, ankle-length kimono. It was special. A gift from her long gone Yank, Sergeant Martinez. Her "second almost husband". She would remember him always with a terrific sense of loss. It never went away, never would. Sergeant Martinez had confiscated the fabulous Japanese kimono during the American occupation of that defeated country. He'd also given her a necklace of perfectly matched, natural pearls -- definitely not the cheaper, though still very valuable, 'cultured' kind. For some crazy reason, she had been able to hang on to these treasures through thick and quite a lot of thin. The pearls were safe in a secret place in her room. Kept there for the day she needed to wear them...or whatever.

Irene had no family, no heirs. No real friends even, only acquaintances. The war had taken care of that. She'd moved about a lot, couldn't stay put. There was too much happening in wartime. Then it was too late. Her Jean-Francois wasn't really a friend. Not in the friend sense. He was a screw. An excellent one to be sure. She wasn't complaining. Not at her age. Now she'd have been quite happy with a kiss. A loving kiss. On the lips, on the forehead, on her sodding elbow! Any damn where. So long as it was sweet, gentle and loving. That sort of kiss never seemed to come her way now unless she tried terribly hard to get it and she didn't do that anymore. So beggars mustn't be choosers. But Jean-Francois was a very different kettle of fish.

This could be problematic. Worrying, this.

Irene took another bite of custard tart. One day soon, she knew, British bakers would finally wake up and realize that sugar was no longer rationed and their custard tarts would be sweeter -- entrenched wartime habits were hard to break. She was the past-mistress at breaking habits and she ought to know. Usually her broken habits were unsuitable men. A small carload. But she reasoned early on, that breaking these habits offered an alternative that was not a notable improvement. Oh, leave off, Irene! She winced, turned a page in her book. Today she felt every single day of her forty-some years. It shouldn't be happening so quickly. Someone was cheating her. Irene laid down her book, laughed softly, said "God? Dearie? Is it you?"

# 6

The Dante Dominic Rossetti School of Drawing and Fine Art wasn't as big as Andy had imagined it although the main studio room was immense and had excellent natural lighting. It was housed in a wing of the Ashmolean Art Museum. Its light-catching windows were huge and through them Andy could see the splendid Ionic columns of the entrance to the Museum as well as the Randolph Hotel and Oxford Playhouse directly across Beaumont Street. He'd brought a small but comprehensive map and was beginning to learn street names. You never knew when information would come in handy -- as in seeking shelter for an enemy bombardment evacuation. Andy often perused atlases and encyclopaedia in search of 'information.' This also calmed his nerves, especially when his ridiculous left little finger was twitching. As it was, furiously, just now.

He had hung his wet duffel on a rack in the cloak room with the many other duffels and was glad he'd brought it because nearly everybody else had one. It made him feel more secure -- he preferred not to stand out in the crowd particularly in some foreign place where he didn't 'know the score'. Particularly with World War III pending.

Andy had never seen a duffel coat before Granddad found his own in the attic and gave it to him. You didn't need them in Southern California. It had a hood too! But Granddad's duffel smelled heavily of mothballs, especially when wet. Andy had hoped the smell would be gone by now. It hadn't and it made him queasy. He hoped none of the other students could smell it but was certain they could. Maybe he shouldn't have brought it after all? Maybe this smelly duffel coat was more of a hindrance than an advantage? He felt 'gauche'. Yes, that was the word! He felt gauche and he didn't like it. But he was aware he felt it. Did that make him a little less 'gauche'? There was a 'modicum' of comfort here. Kind of balanced itself out.

"That's the American! His name is Leander! Can you believe it?! I saw it on the list." Marcella was embarrassed to have spoken so loudly to Alasdair, the smallish, plumpish young man who sat beside her. They were sharpening their charcoal pencils with single-edged razor blades as they waited for the appearance of the model. As Andy approached, Marcella got a better look and half-hoped he had heard her. He had.

"Does she think I'm deaf?" muttered Andy into his two super-bulky sweaters and pocketed his twitching little finger to quiet it down.

Marcella had extremely short hair, too short, thought Andy, who was now sharpening his own new charcoal pencils. She had very white skin -- no tan at all -- she looked like a ghost and she was impolite, even 'brazen', Granddad might have said, and Grandma would have added instantly, that you shouldn't speak about people like they weren't in the room. Was Andy being too harsh? Was it only some quaint English custom to speak about people as though they weren't in the room? The English had, he thought, a plethora of odd customs that might seem rude to the average foreigner, especially to this foreigner -- himself. Andy, however, must not allow himself to be offended and must study their ancient rituals and learn to respect them. Andy knew he must always be very open-minded. Judge not, lest ye be judged was a favourite saying of Granddad's. Almighty God's as well.

Mr. Bateman, Andy's British-American really excellent high school Art instructor, and a talented artist himself, had encouraged Andy to apply for the Rossetti scholarship. Had helped him choose the best examples of his work and had photographed and made slides and had even written a strong recommendation to the Rossetti Master. After many months here he was, Leander Riley, the winner of an American place.

Andy had not yet noticed the intense attention he was getting from Sheila, just two drawing boards to the right of him. Sheila was a rich man's daughter with 'money of her own' from her late grandmother. But Andy, even had he noticed her, wouldn't have thought her rich at all. Sheila might have owned a Rolls-Royce but she certainly didn't dress expensively. Andy, of course, wasn't to know any of this. He hadn't met her yet. But he would. She'd see to that.

Rich people always wore expensive clothes where he came from. If they were women, always had on a lot of jewellery, especially gold bracelets that clanged like Sylvia's, the rich girl back in Art I, his freshman year in high school. Her father owned an important meat packing company and Sylvia brought candy bars and heavily sugar-iced cupcakes with marzipan fake cherries for everyone in the class every Friday and was very popular. Andy couldn't remember if her popularity came before or after the candy bars and cupcakes.

It was different in America. Rich men always drove Cadillacs or Lincolns or Chryslers. Or maybe a classic Rolls-Royce like Mr. Bateman's, if they were British, or car connoisseurs. Mr. Bateman insisted that he was devoted to his classic 'motorcar'. It was like 'a much loved pet' and was 'crucially essential to his well-being' and he set aside two whole days each month for washing, seasonal polishing and attending to all its needs right down to its gleaming hubcaps.

Andy gazed around the very large room at the others setting up their easels and drawing boards. Their clothes seemed extremely warm -- had to be because the room was cold. There were bulky sweaters like his and thick tweed skirts and heavy wool stockings and heavy corduroys like his. A few students even wore wool fingerless gloves. But, subtract the winter clothes and they looked just like any other art students Andy had ever seen in the fortunately Mediterranean climate of Southern California. And several of them weren't even fulltime Art students but studied all sorts of subjects in the many other colleges of Oxford University.

Andy sneezed -- was glad, no, overjoyed, he'd taken two recently purchased effervescent vitamin C's -- and patted the trusty tube of tablets in his pocket. The 'chemist' was just around the corner. 'Chemist' he thought. He'd expected to find long tables of test tubes and Bunsen burners and mortars and pestles where they mixed a 'plethora' (he loved that word!) of prescriptions on the spot, rather than the usual American drugstore fare of endless stacks of packaged pills and potions and a white marble-countered 'Soda Fountain' from which he feasted on banana splits and thick, freezing milkshakes and vanilla sodas and root-beer floats and hot fudge ice cream sundaes -- and even bacon, lettuce and tomato sandwiches -- those wonderful 'BLT's! You could get BLT's everywhere as well as tuna-salad and 'Devilled egg' sandwiches!

Andy suddenly ached for what he had left behind across a continent and an ocean -- nearly half a world away. But he felt proud of himself to have finally ventured this far from home -- dangerously idiotic, as it turned out! Though he was, in a farfetched, accidental way, heroic. He kept that thought. It comforted. But only a 'modicum' -- he liked that new word too. They used so many more over here.

However, the comfort was fleeting. His throat was raspy and getting sore. He would take another vitamin C at the first break to avoid, possibly just in time, being forced to join, at their tuberculosis sanitariums, the few surviving tenants of his frigid basement digs. And as dear Granddad advised, always expect the worst and you'll never be disappointed.

Andy wished the tobacconist hadn't told him about that other fatality of his own treacherous digs. Andy was far too young to die. At least to die in that way. Of course, the other two victims were older than he. There was comfort in that. For him if not for them. Though he and the whole living world were soon to be ashes and only an anxious memory. Remembered by whom? There it was again! This was another matter altogether and was a reality he only *partially-embraced,* this *end-of-the-world-scenario.* How he and Granddad had warmed to that word, *scenario!* Everyone was now suddenly living amidst a *new-and-terrifying-scenario.* There was *no-escaping-it! Partially-embraced* was such a splendid phrase too -- and here was another -- *conveniently-appropriated* from his Granddad. These delicious phrases offered distance from the *utterly-unthinkable* that was *rapidly-becoming* the *inescapably-probable.* Andy and Granddad dearly loved their little phrase games which they often *utilized-interchangeably* on a *plethora-of-profoundly-irreducible-subjects.* And, almost best of all, *as-it-were* which had such a learned ring to it!

Andy and Granddad were bookworm pals. They spent whole summer days together playing Scrabble and devouring books and sandwiches and iced tea. Andy sometimes wondered whether, had his own father survived WW2, they would have been such loyal pals as he and Granddad.

Andy heard raised voices and looked up to see that the rude Marcella was now having a small altercation with another girl over a vacant easel. The other girl was loudly telling Marcella that Marcella was not really serious about drawing, and was 'lollygagging' as Marcella was actually reading classics at Lady Marian Hall and did not care a 'fig' for drawing from the nude model. Therefore, this other girl maintained, the vacant easel should be rightfully hers, a bona fide, conscientious student of Art. Marcella protested that art was for the masses and she was mentally of the masses. The other girl, whose name Andy learned two hours later was Sheila, was considerably taller than Marcella, and said "Not bloody likely, m'lady" and *forthwith-successfully-commandeered* the vacant easel. *As it were!*

Irene laid down her novel, took a bite of custard tart, patted her lips with a tissue. She rose, applied fresh lipstick, removed the red kimono and carefully examined her naked body. The makeup over her three love-bruises was still intact. She threw open a door and grandly walked the three steps to climb the modelling platform where she towered, gloriously naked yet again, directly over Andy who instantly cut his finger on the single edged razor with which he was sharpening his third, new charcoal pencil.

"We must stop meeting like this," stage-whispered Irene, and winked.

Andy gulped, sucked at his bleeding finger and turned as red as Irene's recently doffed kimono.

"I'm Irene, love. You're Andy. I believe we met recently? housemates are we not?"

Irene thrust her hand at him. Marcella, who had just relinquished that easel and was again watching Andy, giggled. Sheila glared. First at Irene then at Marcella. Andy, choking on his words stood, and reached to shake hands for his very first time with a tall, naked lady. "You b-borrowed..."

"Borrowed?"

"M-My hot…"

"Stole, darling, stole! The original hot water thief, that's me!"

"M-My hot w-w-water," Andy finally managed, and tried to smile.

Irene smiled warmly back and arranged herself on the draped, not half so comfortable chair as the one she'd recently vacated in her changing room.

"You'd better put something on that cut, love, before it goes septic. And could you aim the electric fire directly at me, Andy? Right up me legs? And switch it on? I'm perishing with cold!"

Andy, bright red, complied. He understood this. He had been cold since he first set foot in England.

"Gracias," said Irene, who'd learned it from her long ago Sergeant Martinez. She looked about. The guest instructor for the day, a well known British artist, had not yet arrived.

"Well, my little chickens," she said, expertly taking her pose from last week's sitting for those who were involved in long-term, more comprehensive drawings or paintings, "let's get to work."

About forty students, squinting, sized up Irene in their various ways, and put their newly sharpened charcoal pencils or turpentine-smelling brushes to paper or canvas. Andy was relieved that the unwelcome attention paid him had faded and he was in his element again, drawing. His left little finger, bless it, had momentarily stopped twitching. What luck that little finger wasn't on his drawing hand which was now stinging from the cut! He always remembered to thank God even for little favours as requested by dear Grandma.

He hoped to know, much more than hoped, by the end of the day how he compared to his fellow students. He was worried. He had seen several paintings as the other students set up their easels. They were excellent, exceptionally observant and compositionally highly accomplished. There were extremely high standards here. Could he achieve them? Had the Rossetti's scholarship committee made a mistake choosing him? The work he'd seen was everything he knew his own must strive to be, had to be! Particularly now, his first day. Would he be laughed out of the Rossetti? It wasn't impossible. Nothing was these days. This last week especially. Was it to be the last week for humankind? He shuddered, stifled a sneeze and continued to worry.

Fortunately, his constipation was a thing of the past. Atomic missile warfare had only very briefly played second fiddle to his 'constipational complexities' and *proportional-thinking* was being slowly re-applied. But how he missed his Granddad!

Andy had now taken, altogether, three effervescent one-gram vitamin C tablets and felt a little better and not quite so homesick. But he was sneezing inordinately and didn't wish to even consider a bad cold. There was too much going on and if he allowed it, his mind would again become a merry-go-round of sheer, cowardly terror. He needed his Granddad and could not understand why he had heard no one else speak of what should be a horrifying world threat! Were they trying to be polite? Were they not worried? Were they ignorant of their common peril? It may have been at the other side of the Atlantic, but these were their American cousins!

Andy buried himself in his drawing. Irene winked at him again. He reddened again, awkwardly winked back, and was soon lost in his work and as much at peace as he ever got. But peace at the easel was quickly diminishing! Irene was a terrifically difficult subject to draw! She was a sensational model so why was he botching it?! Botching the very first test of his prowess in a foreign place and before all these talented people! Even if she was the first naked woman he had ever seen, let alone, tried to draw! Was it because he liked her? Who couldn't help liking such an open, charming person? But now, without exception, every charcoal line he had set down seemed stiff, ill-observed and amateurishly inept!

Drawing was simply a matter of observation Mr. Bateman had said. Why couldn't Andy 'observe' today? One must see properly, precisely, before one draws. It's all there for the seeing if you just open your eyes. Drawing was simply the business of seeing. Finding the line and following it. If you cannot find the line and follow it you are damned and doomed! Every man had his own tragedy and this, it seemed, was his!

Andy clenched his teeth, told himself he could conquer his fears, his crippling shyness, his chronic lack of complete confidence and judgment, and his need to quote in his head the comforting words of others who had real opinions of their own, i.e. his own dear Granddad; his extraordinarily beautiful, beloved Mother; his deceased Grandma; good old Tom, and, of course, his benefactor, Mr. Bateman, not to mention his four, witty, favorite aunts. Andy needed to put something in that space that should, but did not yet, contain himself. Drawing was, had always been, a safe harbour from all the immature confusions hammering to enter his head. He now tried his old device -- crazy as it seemed, even for him -- that he was his mythical namesake, the heroic Leander, secure on land and forever to avoid that fatal last plunge into jealous Aphrodite's vindictive, watery tempest. But Andy also knew he was a severely limited Leander with severely limited real faith in himself and lacking a high-priestess, 'Hero', who loved him. Was that what was wrong with him? It had to be more complicated than that.

He had hoped he could hold his own at the Rossetti but his doubts mounted. Why was life so competitive? Such a battle?! Was it him? Probably! He coughed, wiped his running nose with a hanky, coughed again, wiped his nose again. Now he was side-tracked, damn it! Damn him! The Crisis thundered back. Now he couldn't stop thinking about the crazy Crisis, thinking about his whole family, wiped out! Thinking about Tom flying a shiny jet directly into it and being instantly atomized. And the rain, the rain! Would it ever stop raining?!

He stared at the humiliating attempt on his huge drawing pad and coughed again. Why was he such a nervous wreck at seventeen when life should have been one great howl of post-adolescent, innocent, joy?! Why was he so screwed up? He re-wrapped the small bandage around his razor-injured finger -- he kept a packet of these for just such small injuries -- and shoved his left hand into his pocket to hide that twitching traitor, his rampant little finger. Irene looked down at him from her posing platform, wondered what was wrong. This troubled boy was catching cold? Was that it? Or something worse? His cellar room was surely a death sentence. She'd help him somehow. He needed a paraffin fire -- a kerosene stove, her years-ago-own-two Yanks had called it -- they'd used them in their tents in week long training exercises. She'd had one herself in that not so distant wartime past. A brief phone call would suffice. She had once been a regular visitor to Andy's awful cellar -- Iris had, over some minor tiff, continually neglected her meter boxes and the meter money was included in her rent. She would help poor Andy if it was the last nice thing she ever did. Was it the mother in her? She smiled, liked the thought. She was the right age to mother the boy.

# 7

I was very deep into my third drawing of Irene and having insurmountable problems with it when suddenly everybody was jumping up and cramming themselves into their duffel coats and wool scarves and somebody came up behind me and gave me a push and I was so tense I almost yelped like one of old Uncle's dogs! And I turned around to see and she was beautiful! She stood there in a ratty old fur coat comically tapping her foot. The coat's elbows were nearly worn right down to the unlucky animal's stiff, bare hide. If I'd known then that she was rich I would have been exceedingly surprised.

Somehow, in California, it is very important if somebody is rich or is not. Don't ask me why. I guess it is the things they can buy with all their money. Or is it the other way around? -- maybe it's the things they don't buy that is important. What does that mean?! I don't even know what I mean!

Irene smiled, winked yet again and disappeared into her changing room.

"Well?" said this beautiful girl. "Are you coming to coffee or not?"

Suddenly here I was at the Playhouse Bar across the street from the Rossetti buying coffee for this girl whose name I had just now discovered was Sheila and that her father could buy and sell Marcella's father in a trice. I now knew she was rich as she had talked a lot about the 'horrid responsibilities' of a great deal of money and how well she was handling it -- even though most of it seemed to be her father's money. I thought about a lot of money for a while and could not think of a single thing 'horrid' about it! Maybe this wasn't so different from California after all? I never thought handling a great deal of money could be a problem in any way. If I was ever lucky enough to get the chance I knew exactly how I'd handle it. I'd buy a yacht for my dear Granddad who had always spoken of wanting one. I'd buy a new house for my beautiful mother – with a huge swimming pool because she had won a solid gold speed-swimming medal as a girl of fifteen and I'd buy a jet plane for Tom to practice his flying in his spare time.

I guess we have the importance of money drummed into us until we are old enough to drum it into ourselves and a little later, I guess, into our children. I looked forward to having children, a lot of 'em. And money too. It seemed that no matter what you wanted to do, money was required by the bucketful. But what did I know? Granddad always said a fool and his money are soon parted. He should know -- he was soon parted from his more times than he cared to remember. My dear, late Grandma would readily testify to this, and often did. I know there's a lesson here but since I'm not a fool (at least not a complete one) and I don't have any money anyhow, it didn't apply to me and I was safe from bankruptcy for the moment.

I hadn't thought about The Crisis for a half hour. I felt grateful to Sheila for this -- for this concentration on the importance of money, for this precious moment of forgetting. I wished dear Granddad was here. I would ask him what he thought about Sheila. He'd had international experience with women of all ages and nations. Though I wasn't sure he had ever had an affaire de coeur with an English woman. That's what he called them, affaires de coeurs (sp?).

The floor in the Playhouse Bar was swarming with students sitting on the thick, dark blue carpet smoking and talking and drinking coffee. The Playhouse Bar served drinks in the intervals during evening performances and Saturday matinees, and coffee the rest of the time. And it was crowded! I've always hated crowds. Especially if they were all smoking. My asthma could play up at any minute. I was certain I would not be coming here very often. I myself, smoked -- a couple of cigarettes now and then didn't seem to bother me. But this room was so smoky you could hardly see across it. Well, maybe not that smoky. Too smoky for me, anyhow. In aces.

"I owe you, love," came from right behind me. As usual, I am easily startled and jumped. Embarrassing! It was Irene. She looked breathtaking standing there with all her clothes on! Muy ("very" in Spanish) distinguished! She smiled and stuck out a small, white paper bag. "One custard tart. I was going to have it with my coffee but I'm cutting down or my unique bone structure will disappear and I shall be out of a job!"

Irene threw her head back and laughed a really pleasant laugh as she stuck the paper bag in my hand. "Not to worry, Irene," said Sheila, who was right beside me, "Sheer bulk is becoming."

"Becoming what, dear?" smiled Irene.

"Errr," said Sheila, "fashionable. It's err...easier for us poor students to draw."

Irene certainly wasn't easy to draw for me! And Sheila was anything but a poor student! Anyhow, I had no idea what they were really saying. I think it is called repartee because it was fast and not always complimentary, at least not from Sheila. But this was England, the home of Oscar Wilde -- even though he was Irish. Which I knew because I was Irish too. A lot of me, anyhow. Grandma had read all his plays. I had read three. I loved their highfalutin language. I need to laugh a lot more than I do.

"I thought you deserved a bit of nourishment, love, living in your damp cellar," said Irene. "Men have died there!"

She laughed again and I knew I liked her a lot. Even though it was not pleasant to be reminded of the double deaths in my digs. There was something about Irene's laugh that grabbed you right in your stomach – something sweet and friendly and calming and, well, I guess, honest. Besides my dear mother and dear grandmothers -- both of 'em -- and Aunt Graycie, Aunt Fran, Aunt June, and Aunt Dot, she was the nicest, most honest older woman I had ever met. And she looked even better fully clothed!

"Our Yank lives in a cellar?!" said Sheila, looking right into my eyes as I handed her a coffee. I sneezed and she splashed the sleeve of her shabby fur coat and said "Oh Shit!" and wiped the sleeve on her other sleeve and at that very minute a tall, extremely beautiful red-haired girl sitting on the floor near us screamed and jumped up and ran out of the room. I'd been noticing her and somebody had been whispering in her ear. I wonder what was said to make her scream and leave so fast?

"That was Wendy," said Sheila, "our professional martyr

enjoying another mini-tragedy."

As I didn't know that martyrs could be professional I let it drop but I said, "She's at The R-Rossetti too?"

"Yup," said Sheila.

"Poor child. She seemed so upset." said Irene. "She's such a lovely and so very talented girl."

"A moot point," said Sheila who took a great slurp of coffee and wiped her chin with her sleeve. For a rich person she did not seem to have rich manners. You must never wipe your mouth on your sleeve. It is an elemental rule of etiquette -- in public anyhow, unless you could sneak it. I knew immediately in my heart, that the beautiful, red-haired Wendy, the 'professional martyr', wouldn't be caught dead wiping her mouth on her sleeve. She seemed to have --  even as she screamed and rushed out -- she seemed to have 'Class' in the way she reacted. She was what Granddad would have called a perfect English rose. I am emphatically inclined to agree with dear Granddad.

My God, I'm babbling. It's a problem with me. Too much trivial stuff keeps roller-skating around inside my skull. I suppose it is my  brain's automatic Anti-Crisis defence system. I sneezed again and wondered if my sneezing was psycho-somatic. Possibly. Probably. Then I sneezed once more. It was embarrassing! And here they both were, talking about me. Talking about me like I wasn't here. And...I guess I wasn't, all of me. Although I should have been. But that's me. So much on my mind. Mostly how my drawing today was lousy! Not to mention the approaching atomic abyss which didn't leave much room for anything else. I didn't want to bore everyone to death about the Crisis. No one seemed even interested enough to panic. I almost began to feel that I was suffering from chronic hysteria. I remember Grandma mentioning the term after she'd witnessed Gregory Peck's hysteria in 'Spellbound' as Ingrid Bergman, his fraught psychiatrist, also hysterical, attempted to get to the root of it all. My dear Grandma was always exceedingly serious about getting to the root of things.  She was a pragmatist.

"Leander needs a paraffin fire," said Irene, "to sit by and be cosy and warm whilst he eats his custard tarts. That cellar room of his is far from luxury accommodation -- I've seen it. I happen to know from personal experience that all Yanks aren't million-aires. I married one. Two actually. There were so many during the war."

"Yanks, tarts, or husbands?" said Sheila.

"Why, all of us, dear, of course. That's why we Allies won." said Irene, with the very sweetest smile and I was exceedingly glad she was fully clothed. It lent gravitas, as Granddad often said. Irene had gravitas in aces!

"Where were y-your American husbands  f-from?" I asked.

"Somewhere in Alabama, first one -- I didn't know him long enough to get the exact location. We fell in love one night, got married in the morning and he was shipped out the next week. Normandy, but I didn't know it then. Never saw or heard from him again, poor lad. Husband two came from a little town on the California/Mexico border."

"I'm from C-California," I said happily, "Lemon G-Gulch. It's near San Diego. I was born in San Diego but we moved to Lemon Gulch."

"Lemon Gulch?!" squeaked Sheila.

Irene laughed and slapped my shoulder and I almost dropped my cigarette into my coffee as I coughed. She said "Lemon Gulch, dear, that's why your hair is so yellow, isn't it, love? All those lemons as a child."

"I think his hair is yellow," said Sheila, "because he's a craven coward. Fleeing from America, his sinking ship!"

"No one is sinking, Sheila, dear, but what are we going to do with those Russians, Andy?"

I was still thinking about Sheila calling me a coward. It hurt because I knew she was correct. She didn't have to say it. I hardly knew her. Anyhow, I didn't leave California to desert any sinking ship but to go to the Rossetti because I got a scholarship. I thought that was obvious!

"He doesn't like to talk about it," said Sheila, "the Russians."

There was a whole lot more of that repartee going on that I didn't catch but I realized pretty soon that they didn't care much for each other. It began to seem too, that Sheila didn't care too much for anyone. At least it seemed like that by the way she talked about some of the other students. Grandma used to say that if you didn't have something good to say about someone then you shouldn't say anything at all. I have always considered it a good piece of advice and I try to practice it. I kind of wished Sheila would practice it too though I am sure she had her good points and only said unkind things sometimes because she felt scared – like me. I'm sure she must have been worried about the world too -- just now -- and did not dare to talk too much about it because it would upset her. That's probably why she called me a coward. I understood this very well. When I am exceedingly nervous I can easily say things I don't mean. I'm not sure why. Maybe I think it will please the people I am speaking to. Although I make it a rule never to say unkind things about anyone or, as Granddad says, It might all come back and bite me in the ass and I'd be up shit creek without a paddle. Although Grandma always said "bottom" for "ass" and "poop" for "shit". But it amounted to the same thing and was a lot more "cultured".

I have never been a crusader or some fanatical kind of guy who would try to force his will on every one else. I have enough to do just keeping myself in line. Anyhow, I sneezed again and carefully wiped my nose on a hanky that had Granddad's initials on it -- Embroidered with many very artistic embellishes by Grandma. How I miss her! I had to dab my eyes just now but I pretended a sneeze, to disguise it.

We finished our coffees and Sheila had to go to the Ladies' Restroom and Irene had to be back at the Rossetti in time to undress. So I waited for Sheila. It would be exceedingly rude to leave without her as she had been kind enough to bring me here in the first place although it was just across the street from the Rossetti.

I was extremely worried that my Irene drawing was going so badly, even the four sketches I had made of her before I started the more finished drawing. No matter how hard I 'observed' I couldn't get what I saw onto paper. Maybe it was all these strange surroundings and the cold and the rain. After I settled down maybe things would get better. This was a worrying development. On top of everything else too. My drawing ability, until now, was the only thing about me that I could always count on. I began to question whether Mr. Bateman was correct in his high opinion of my work. Just because I was chosen best male artist in the 'Senior Standouts' section of my high school Annual didn't mean I was young Michelangelo! What a stupid thing to say! Know thyself, Leander Riley! For Christ's sake! And leave the excellent Mr. Bateman out of it!

I am seriously flawed! From top to bottom. Or as I would rudely say -- but only to myself -- "ass". For shame, Andy! Anyhow, sneezing and pondering my rapidly deteriorating confidence situation, not to mention my incipient cold, I stood outside the Playhouse Bar entrance on the second floor where the air was not so smoky. Then this dark haired guy came right up to me and stuck a business card in my hand and asked me to write down my address on it as he had something for me. He looked a little like my best friend Tom though Tom has red hair. I thought I remembered him from a little earlier at the Rossetti that morning when he seemed to be looking at me and nodded in an exceedingly welcoming manner. He spoke with a kind of French accent and said his name was Yves and I thought he was probably with some kind of student organization that welcomed new students. We have a lot of these in the USA. So I wrote down my address and handed it to him and he handed me another card and left just as Sheila came back.

"What did he want?" she asked.

"I d-don't know," I said and sneezed. "Probably from The W-Welcome W-Wagon." I added and sneezed again.

"The what?!" she said.

"The W-Welcome W-W-Wagon." A k-kind of American custom. They welcome new students."

"How charming. Even if they don't like them?"

"Y-Yes, of c-c-course!

"Never heard of it."

# 8

I'd done a little sightseeing and shopping after class -- not much, because of the rain. So it was dark when I got back to my digs and here was a 'paraffin fire'! Irene had arranged it through a good friend of hers called Jean-Francois. There was a note. It didn't cost me anything because Jean-Francois had this extra one that I was welcome to have as long as I liked. In the USA we call them kerosene stoves. I already knew how to trim their wicks and light them as I had learned in an 'atomic survival' class in my sophomore year in high school. Jean-Francois had also left me more kerosene in a can with a special spout to fill my 'paraffin fire's' tank! What a kind, thoughtful thing for Irene to arrange. My room heat would now be doubled and possibly even almost comfortable.

As I was lighting the wick on my new paraffin fire, a tiny pebble was thrown down the light-well against my window. I went to the window and looked up. There was Sheila! In the rain! After sneezing twice I went up and let her in as a big, fancy limousine was just pulling away from the curb and she pointed to a large, wrapped parcel beside her and grinned mysteriously. I picked it up and we came down the basement stairs to the barking and yelping of Uncle's dogs and I threw open the door to my basement room and trying to be funny I announced "Ta-Da!" It didn't sound at all funny, just stupid, because I was too embarrassed to say 'Ta-Da' quite loud enough and it just fell flat. But Sheila, with a big, sweeping gesture like an actress said in a very loud voice, "The Hanging Gardens of Babylon it ain't!" and motioned to the tangle of ivy that had wrestled its way through the window gap and wound amongst the upper-most meter boxes. Including my own. And we laughed! Then it seemed like she looked at me in an exceedingly steady way with her eyes straight into mine and she winked again. These English women seemed to wink a lot. In America we call it flirting. Anyhow, I was still laughing and I winked back and she looked at me in that intense, steady way again. I wasn't used to being looked at in any steady way by anybody but my best friend, Tom. So I just kept laughing and she just kept looking.

Anyhow, I finally stopped laughing and she stopped looking and I set her big parcel on my work table and she threw herself into The Chair and it flipped sideways and threw her on the floor!

"Jee-sus! I'm getting you out of this fucking hovel before we both go mad!" she said as I helped her up.

My gosh! I thought, what does she have to do with where I choose to live?! Then she ripped off the parcel's wrapping and there stood a small portable radio-phonograph which she called a radio-gramophone. "You look like you could use a bit of entertainment, Andy. God bless Daddy's chauffeur! It's pissing! Or hadn't you noticed?"

I said I certainly had noticed but she didn't seem to hear me.

"Got a towel? Got anything to play?"

I had brought only one record with me. A going-away present from Tom, 'The Mellow Four', a very popular, close-harmony singing group. Tom and I used to play their records and harmonize with them, often for whole evenings. I once sang in a church choir, so did Tom, which is always a help. Anyhow, I gave Sheila my bath towel to dry her wet hair.

A few minutes later I was upstairs on the first landing heating water for our two coffees on a filthy old gas stove that would have made my mother shudder and God only knows what Grandma would have said. Bless my dear Grandma and God rest her soul. I wish He would rest mine too. Sometimes. Not in the same way, of course. That might be construed as a death wish I think. I don't mean to sound scary. A little too 'Hollywood' Granddad would say. A bit 'cinematical' he would tease me. It was just a stupid, humorous remark, my 'death wish'. I've got a million of 'em. None of them very humorous and plenty of them stupid.

Sheila had put on my record and it drifted up the stairs and made me exceedingly homesick again...

*When I'm gone, my love*
*There will come a day*
*You may sigh and say*
*He travelled to a star*

*Why did he go so far?*
*Was it just to be*
*So far away from me?*

This made me so homesick that I cried. Standing in front of that filthy, greasy, old stove, heating water, I cried. Probably some kind of delayed reaction trauma plus my *awful* drawing of Irene. It kept coming back. I couldn't get it out of my mind. I guess today had been too much, me being so high-strung and all. Flighty, my beautiful mother once called it. Too many things were happening at once -- this was a problem of mine. I was worried about my family and Tom, and my dog, Tinker, and the end of the world which nobody else seemed particularly worried about. At least not as worried as I was. My cold wasn't helping either. Though the gift of the 'paraffin fire' was an authentic beau geste which means a 'beautiful gesture' in French and I would thank Irene and her Jean-Francois just as soon as was humanly possible. I intended to thank Sheila profusely, too, for bringing over a phonograph which certainly qualified as another beau geste. This made my eyes start dripping again – they always do with beau gestes, as beau gestes are rare and exceedingly moving for me. Oh, and I forgot to include the umbrella that Iris said Miss Pofford said I could keep as the preceding inhabitant of my digs would not need it any more. One must never under-value a kind, beautiful gesture from a fellow human being. Even if one did not deserve it. Which I certainly did not. Me, the yellow coward from Lemon Gulch, deserting the sinking ship! Sheila was right and I was glad she was down those basement stairs in my room and couldn't witness my horrible, bawling weaknesses. I'm such a sissy! But not all of the time. I hope. And as hope springs eternal I couldn't very easily screw up eternity! But if I could, I would! Inadvertently, of course.

My Grandma who was of Irish and German descent, always said the Irish were a bunch of sentimental bawl-babies. I cannot dispute that as I, myself, cannot hear even one verse of 'Danny Boy' without blubbing. My extraordinarily beautiful mother says my dead father was that way about 'Danny Boy' too. So I guess Grandma wasn't far from wrong. She also said that I had just enough German in me to get me into trouble and just enough Irish charm to get me out. But I couldn't see any thing charming about me at all in my present bawl-baby state.

Then I suddenly began missing Grandma! It struck me like a bolt of lightning! I missed her so much that I sobbed out one more horrible, loud, big, gulping, snuffling, sissy sob, which must have flooded the whole house! Fortunately, nobody heard it but Uncle's dogs. They started yelping something terrible and Uncle yelled "Belt up, you hairy, bitches!" and I could hear Sheila laughing downstairs in my room. This made me feel better. At least somebody was laughing. Then I sneezed and Sheila yelled up the staircase "Am I to get my coffee or not?!"

"C-Coming!" I yelled just as the coffee water boiled over and I sneezed about six more times. That door on the hallway opened a crack and the bloodshot eye stared out at me. I wondered if that eye had seen me sob. This was super-embarrassing. Then the eye disappeared and its door closed. If the eye hadn't seen me I wondered if its ear had heard my super-sob. This wasn't a perfect way to behave on my second day in a totally foreign country. A psychiatrist was needed. Pronto -- as they say in my birth place, sunny San Diego, which is just north of the Mexican border. That's about all the Spanish I know except for being able to sing all the words of 'Adios Mi Chapparita' ('Goodbye to you, my cowboy sweetheart' roughly translated). I had learned this touching song when I had a crush on my High school Spanish teacher, Rosa Flores, who brought her guitar to our Freshman Spanish class and strummed and sang it with such wild emotion that I never forgot it! She seemed much moved when I burst into tears before the class when she finished. She gave me an A+ that semester but broke my heart a few months later when she ran away with Miss Cody, my History teacher.

I have also learned a few French phrases from dear Grand-dad who learned them, as a sailor, from an exceedingly kind lady who lived in picturesque Pigalle in 'Gay *Paree.*' Dear Granddad always called it 'Gay *Paree'* because that is how it is pronounced in the admirable French language. My dear Grand-dad is an extremely eclectic gentleman.

So here I stood, hammered by my past, at the sink in this beaten up old 'kitchenette' on the first landing. I had found a couple of dirty cups that were in a filthy cupboard that looked like it hadn't been opened since WW2. There I go, thinking about war again. It's a sickness but hard to avoid given the crazy current circumstances. Particularly with nervous young people like myself. I washed the cups with a huge old bar of discoloured soap that looked as old as the house and had little specks on it of an indeterminate nature. I set the cups on a rusty tray with that greasy kettle which I promised myself to thoroughly cleanse before I required it again and went down the basement stairs balancing the rusty tray very carefully. As I passed Uncle's door his dogs barked again and I guess he swatted one as I heard a yip and a yap before it quieted down. I did not like to be the cause of a poor dumb animal's suffering and always walked as quietly as possible by Uncle's door. Unfortunately his dog's traditional, barking habits seemed to be exceedingly firmly established.

The Mellow Four's music was still playing as I returned. But I didn't see Sheila though I heard her giggling. I set down the tray and turned to take a small jar of instant coffee powder from my shopping bag in the wardrobe and Sheila yelled "Surprise!"

There she was, stark naked, half-hidden under the bedclothes and two pillows on my lumpy little bed! Another naked woman! Two naked women in one day!

My mind just stopped! I forgot about Tom and The Crisis and the Rossetti and my awful drawings and England and California and my nasty cold. All I could think of was I need at least two grams of effervescent vitamin C ! So I sneezed and grabbed my toothbrush glass and the tin tube of C and shot up the stairs to the sink and filled the glass and dropped in two C's. I needed a few minutes to think. While my C fizzed and my left little finger twitched like an angry cat's tail, I thought. A lot.

I returned down the stairs hoping Sheila had taken a hint and put her clothes back on. She hadn't. There she just sat, her pretty pink breasts exposed, naked in my bed smiling at me and giving me that scary, steady look that she had before. I knew she was completely naked because she'd laid her clothes and underwear on my work table. I guess this is what you might call the 'direct method'! I was stymied! I know this is a big fat cliché but my heart actually seemed to be beating in my throat! After what seemed a very long minute I said "Sorry it's instant, your c-c-c-coffee," and she said "Hardly instant!" and grinned and was even prettier. I guess you could call her beautiful even if she was naked. But I couldn't call her anything as I couldn't get a word out. It was worse than ever!

I spooned in the coffee powder and stirred up two coffees and set one for her on my warped bedside table beside the 'Radio-gramophone'.

"I love your music," said Sheila. "You can keep the radio gramophone."

"Oh, n-n-n-no!" I finally managed to say.

"Oh, y-y-y-yes." she laughed.

"I c-c-c-couldn't."

"Of course you c-c-c-can! I'll make Daddy buy me a new one. One of those stereophonic thingies. So it's settled. You must."

"I'll just b-b-b-borrow it, okay?" I was almost choking!

"Okay, darling, if you must."

Shit! She'd just called me darling! She had no right to call me darling just because she was reclining naked in my bed! I had not asked her there! I certainly had not formally requested it by any personal word or gesture or any action whatsoever. At some other time in the future if and when our relationship had matured to the 'especially dear' category I might have inquired politely: 'Darling would you care to disrobe and slip into my bed?' Or something very like that -- maybe a little bit more casual. I'd never really thought out a matter like this. Obviously, I could not think of the appropriate words just now. 'Darling' is a very special word to me and should be used only as an intimate address to those we hold especially dear. Sheila had met me this morning. How could she possibly hold me especially dear when she'd only known me for a few hours? All I could do was sneeze six more times. I counted them and hoped my left little finger would stop twitching by the time I'd stopped sneezing. It didn't.

I guess I didn't really think it would as I know my little finger like the palm of my hand.

Sheila went on: "I knew at once you were American before you'd spoken a word. Your trousers were miles too short and exposed your white, sports socks. And your wooly didn't sag the way it ought. I've got a Marks and Sparks wooly that's so long I use it as a nightgown."

"W-Wooly"? I asked.

"Pullover! A sweater, darling!" She laughed and took a swig of coffee and did absolutely nothing to cover up her beautiful bare breasts and went on: "Just taking the mick. I usually sleep in the altogether. Starkers. Like now. But I'm far from sleepy. Far from. How 'bout you?"

"I am c-coming down w-with an exceedingly bad c-cold," I was at last able to say. I sneezed one more time to prove it and took a swig from my own coffee and wondered what taking the 'mick' and 'Marks and Sparks' and 'starkers' were all about? I knew that Irish men were often called 'Micks' in the USA but 'taking them?' Taking them where? Or maybe deceiving them? Was this a veiled insult to my Irish descent? Were these really serious English words? Sheila said "Why did you come here to study Art? Art, of all things, in England? Shouldn't you be in Paris? I thought all good Americans went to Paris."

"Only w-when they d-d-die," I said, nervously though happily repeating what my Art teacher, Mr. Bateman had once told me.

"I beg your pardon?!"

"It's a q-quote. Oscar W-W-W…"

"Wilde. Oscar Wilde. It's not a fucking secret, darling! But why did you come to England?"

I was really rattled. "Because I can s-speak the l-l-l-language."

"Only just, my sweet. Look. Are you coming to bed or not?"

Sheila seemed to be getting a little bit irritated with me. I have this effect on people sometimes, I guess. Especially when they're girls, particularly if they're naked. Though they never were -- as this had never happened before, except with Irene, who is probably in her forties, when she borrowed my hot water

68

and posed nude at the Rossetti.

I have the soul of an artist – as Grandma used to say. My Grandmother was a learned lady who had been to a teacher's training college in Philipsberg, Kansas, as a young woman and taught school for a while and suffered through three major world depressions with six children and nary a scratch on her spirit -- that's exactly how Grandma put it. Bless her heart!

There was a soft knock on my door and I froze! Christ! How could I explain a naked girl in my bed when girls were hardly even allowed in the house – or at least after ten PM though it was now far from ten PM. I couldn't say a word. This is not at all unusual for me. As said. As spoken words and me are often strange bedfellows -- pardon my awful pun! It just came into my head and, of course, knowing me, it was profoundly inappropriate. Anyhow, I just sat there and took another swig of coffee as my door was softly knocked on several more times. Then, after a pause, it inched open very slowly and Gladys, or as she is known, 'The Blind Girl' -- who was certainly not a girl as she had grey hair -- tapped her way with her cane across my room to that very softly buzzing, clicking wall of meters. Sheila's mouth dropped wide open! She had covered her exceedingly pretty breasts with a pillow as the door opened and Gladys passed by. She stared at Gladys who had no trouble finding the proper meter and winding in a coin. Gladys then turned and tapped her way back to the door and paused there. "Goodnight, Andy, dear. Sorry for the intrusion," she said softly, "Mum's the word, and goodnight to your guest, dear, whoever she may be."

"Th-thank, you    G-G-Gladys. G-G-Good night to you too."

The Blind Girl closed the door very quietly after her. Sheila said "Fuck! How did she know I was here?! She's blind!"

"Her hearing is top n-n-notch," I said, letting out all the breath I was holding in my tortured lungs.

"Shit!" said Sheila and climbed out of bed and into her thick cotton underwear and I breathed a whole lot easier. "Shit!" she said again and pulled on her heavy sweater, "We've got to find you a new room. I'll make Daddy put a man on it. Shit!"

"I l-like this room," I said and sneezed. I was feeling extremely dizzy now. I'd felt dizzy from the minute I found her naked in my bed. I wasn't sure if it was from my cold or that she was naked or that she was in my bed. Probably a little bit of all three. I guess feeling dizzy kept me from feeling anything else. Although I probably should have -- felt something else. Though I wasn't sure at all what that something might or should be. Anyhow, by this time I was almost used to seeing naked women as I had now seen two of varying ages in only two days at completely different venues. So I took it -- very nearly took it -- in my stride.

Sheila left. She didn't even finish her coffee. She did not seem happy. But I strongly believe naked girls should not leap into your bed without some firm previous agreement. That was my rule of thumb. I stood firmly by it. Or whatever. It made me exceedingly nervous to have someone in my bed – made my left little finger twitch like there was no tomorrow -- especially when there probably wasn't. This did not improve the situation and I didn't know what to do with people who called me 'darling' after knowing me very slightly for only a few hours then hopped naked and unsolicited, into my bed. Although it had not happened that often – well, hadn't happened at all. There is definitely something wrong with me. Do not ask me what it is. For I cannot tell you. As I do not know.

'I know not what', as Granddad would say, 'would that I did'. Impressive! So British too. 'as it were'!

I took from my shopping bag a couple of little pork pies that were suggested by a knowledgeable local grocer and poured some orange squash syrup into my toothbrush glass and added some water from the kettle to dilute it as was instructed on the bottle. It was exceedingly orange-coloured though it tasted nothing like any orange juice I'd ever had – me being from one of the great orange juice capitals of the world, Southern California. We even had a whole county named Orange! Then I remembered that, for dessert, I still had the custard tart from Irene. Although it had been knocked around in my duffel pocket it was, fortunately, still in its bag. This innocent little mashed up

70

custard tart made me feel very happy as it was a bona fide beau geste. The radio-phonograph from Sheila was also a beau geste. Three beau gestes, including the paraffin fire, in one day. No, four beau gestes, including Miss Pofford's black umbrella. The laxative from the tobacconist's wife, however, was yesterday. I must pay these people back somehow! This made me feel better and I thought about it even more as I ate the two little pork pies and saved the custard tart for "afters" as they say in this country.

Then, comforted by eating the little pork pies, and the happy thought of the custard tart to come, and the many gestes, I began to study the drawings of Irene I had done that day. They were even more awkward and stiff then I remembered them! They seemed to be drawn by some exceedingly mediocre beginner. I felt like crying but my first day's drawings at the Rossetti were so horrifically bad they only made me more mad at myself. But it was more than that. Maybe my ability had suddenly evaporated?! Like when my voice changed not all that long go and I stopped wetting my bed. This was new and strange and excessively worrying! My work today did not express even a bit of Irene's inner beauty. She was beautiful inside and out. Her friend Jean-Francois sounded like a nice guy too. She told me after class that he was a car mechanic. There was no question that they were exceedingly philanthropic, the both of them. Yet here I was, after only two days in 'Old Blighty', well on my way to becoming a foreign failure! But what difference could it make? We'd all be dead by next week at the latest. Or maybe even tonight. Jesus! I hope not! I am sorry I thought that! Due to my thoughtlessness it would now be difficult to sleep.

I noticed that the razor cut on my right index finger was now a little red. Though it did not hurt much, just a little sting now and then. I would have to be more careful when sharpening charcoal pencils. Then I coughed. Loud and long. A terrible hacking cough that seemed to come from the pit of my stomach. This was a completely unexpected development!

I poured some water from the greasy, old kettle into my toothbrush glass, dropped in an effervescent vitamin C, and made a mental note to wash the kettle thoroughly, soonest. As my vitamin C fizzed and dissolved I heard voices through the thinness. I went closer, still coughing, and put my ear near the wall. Though I have never been a sneaky, eavesdropping type of guy this talk was, I suppose you could say with impunity, intruding into my room so it was therefore 'fair game.' I coughed again.

"Hear him, Miss Pofford, through the thinness? The Yank has got hisself a bad cough," said Iris.

"What Yank?!" said Miss Pofford, "Had 'em here for the war."

"Why, your Yank, Miss Pofford, which come to us all the way from California. He's got hisself a bad cough."

"Well he's in that horreeble basement, ain't he? What does he expect?!"

I coughed some more and could imagine the both of them standing there at the other side of the thinness listening and staring at each other and shaking their heads and Iris maybe scratching at something itching under an arm of her blue nylon uniform.

"As he's poorly, take him some of them sprouts and potatoes and a bit of ham," said Miss Pofford, "free of charge. Nothing due with the rent."

I was exceedingly moved at the 'free of charge' which would result in my fourth beau geste today. I cannot stress how helpful these geste's were. Especially in view of the coming annihilation. I'd been in England two days and I was already getting sick but was thankfully well cared for. Which was a comfort. Of sorts. Given the circumstances.

I wondered for a while what I'd do if Sheila ever got naked in my bed again. Maybe I'd do something if I didn't have a cold. Yes, that was it. Having a cold and worrying about a world war and being over-nervous as I can be about almost everything in general was not compatible with stark naked snuggling. No! It was inappropriate! I think. But I could be wrong. If only I knew how I felt about certain things. Complicated-emotion things. I'm too nervous for anybody's good. Especially my own. Anyhow, because I was hungry and Mother had always said 'feed a cold and starve a fever' I now had Irene's custard tart with another glass of the astonishingly orange, orange squash even though Iris was going to bring me 'some of them sprouts and potatoes and a bit of ham'. My two little pork pies and custard tart had relaxed me so much that I switched on Sheila's 'radio-gramophone' just in time for an announcement that President Kennedy was going to make a speech tomorrow night. Well, this was the very last thing I needed! It brought The Crisis right back in aces! This was too much! The two little pork pies and the tart now felt like big, lead 'sinkers' in my stomach – my maternal grandmother, Bessie, and I used to fish off the end of the Ocean Beach Pier in San Diego and used lead sinkers to keep the hooks low in the water where the fish were. She was a very sporty woman and rode horses and played a ukelele and sang folk songs with such feeling that it used to break my heart. Songs like Red River Valley and Grandfather's Clock and The Old Rugged Cross and Oh, Them Golden Slippers. I miss my maternal Grandma too. She died when I was ten.

I turned off the radio as I did not want to hear any more about war and I just sat there trying to calm down. My lousy little finger was going a mile a minute. If I breathed too fast I was sure I'd start coughing and sneezing again. At least Sheila's scary visit had taken my mind off of everything else for a while. Thank you, beautiful Sheila, wherever you are!

I was about to drop another tablet of vitamin C into my toothbrush glass when I heard a voice coming through the gap at the top of my window where the ivy grew in. "Leandair! Leandair! Are you zair?!" I looked up into the light-well and saw it was the welcome-wagon student and he was waving a large bottle at me. I was not too happy to be receiving visitors just now. Particularly after that frightening announcement on the radio, and, very particularly, as I was coming down with something seemingly virulent that might be readily passed amongst innocent others. Also because President Kennedy's speech, tomorrow night, really had to be something exceedingly serious and it would definitely personally affect Tom as a trainee pilot whenever, whatever, happened. It is common knowledge that even the youngest, beginner-trainee pilots are pressed into dangerous missions during a severe emergency. I have seen enough war movies to categorically stand by that!

My hands were now shaking a little, not to mention said little finger, and I felt I might be on the verge of getting a horrible fever as my forehead felt kind of warm to touch. But here was this guy at my front door. He was welcoming me. So it was extremely important that I be polite and grateful. 'Good manners are the mark of a man' said my Granddad as often as not. But particularly at the dinner table where Grandma insisted on it. And rightly so!

# 9

I sneezed at least four times and went up the stairs and welcomed my welcomer with a welcoming smile. He looked so much like Tom that it made me cough and my hands shake even harder -- kind of another bout of delayed homesickness I guess. As I led my welcomer down the hall the bloodshot eye poked out from behind its door and I almost said 'mind your own business, please', but that would not have been polite. After all, I was an alien here in Bloodshot Eye's own country. Bloodshot Eye might even have been a lady so my behavior could have been doubly inappropriate!

On the basement stairs I sneezed many times and Uncle yelled "Who's out there?! and I yelled "It's Andy, Uncle," over his barking dogs and Uncle yelled "Sleep well, Andy!" and his dogs kept barking and he yelled "Belt up, you hairy bitches!" and I heard a swat and a yip as was their tradition. Then it was quiet. I don't think old Uncle ever smacked them very hard either. Because I know he loved them as I heard him talking very lovingly to them as I passed his door this very evening when I came back from the Rosetti. I think his swats only surprised them. Like I was surprised the first time I heard the 'hairy bitches' bark.

The welcome-wagon student said his name was Yves which I knew already as it was on the card he handed me at the Playhouse coffee bar. He held out a large bottle of bourbon whiskey and said that he knew for a fact that Americans preferred bourbon to scotch. I didn't actually prefer anything as I've only had two strong alcoholic drinks in my life and got sick after each as I was a child. Both incidents were the result of a search for sweet, cherry brandy in a childhood friend's mother's liquor cabinet. His mother was a divorced, lonely alcoholic with exceedingly large, grey circles under her eyes and I felt sorry for her. She bumped into things and fell down a lot and always had badly bruised knees which were exceptionally visible as we very often wear 'Bermuda shorts' in Southern California. She also had great welts on her elbows from falling down, and once, a big blue lump on her forehead. Even at my young age of ten

I went overboard and suffered for her, knowing that, as dear Granddad often said 'There, but for the grace of God, go I.' I wouldn't disagree. I cried nearly every time I visited my friend and his poor inebriated mother only said "Yeah, yeah," when he first introduced me to her. I had absolutely no plans to become an alcoholic or even a moderate drinker, as it would have been difficult, if not impossible in the USA to buy liquor at my age anyhow. Besides, alcohol made me vomit. Especially when I'd had a lot of sweet, cherry brandy.

Yves asked if I had a glass so I gave him my smallish tooth-brush glass which was clean as it had only been used recently for effervescent C. He filled it to the top and handed it to me.

"Welcome," he said, "bienvenue!"

"M-Merci beaucoup!" I said, happy to know that I was correct and he was indeed in some welcoming organization! I drank the whole glass right down. Now, this really surprised me! I have no idea why I drank so much so fast knowing that I would probably be sick! Typical bad judgment on my part! And my 'merci beaucoup' came straight out of nowhere! Possibly a genetic thing as my extraordinarily beautiful mother, while pregnant with me, had taken a course in French at a local evening school and, according to modern scientific thinking, I might well have heard her French lectures while womb-bound, as it were. An exciting thought, n'est-ce-pas?! Just joking. Mother taught me that.

However, the bourbon burned my throat something awful and I thought I might even barf but I felt it could be efficacious for my cough as Granddad's winter coughs were always well served, he said, by a comforting tipple now and again. Suddenly, like lightning, a nice warm glow washed over me proving dear Granddad correct. As per usual!

Yves poured another glass of bourbon for himself and quaffed it and said he wanted to be a writer/actor -- and he named some French guy I'd never heard of named Ka-moo! Then Yves dropped himself into The Chair, nearly flipped over but found his balance quickly and  elegantly. After all he was French! I did wonder, though, how his student welcoming organization could afford so much bourbon whisky for only one student. I also wondered why he was a French welcomer, not English. Though Oxford was a world famous international educational establishment, a British welcomer might have been a little more, well, British. After all, it was England he was welcoming me to!

"Bienvenue," he said again, with another welcoming smile. I was beginning to like him a lot and the 'bienvenue' was a great comfort as my warm glow grew. Yves seemed definitely to be an extremely courteous European and good manners were always highly welcome in the Riley household.

"I am come to ze Rossetti sometimes to learn to draw," said Yves.

I wondered why, if Yves wanted to be a writer/actor, he was studying Art. My welcomer was either a 'renaissance man' or an enigma!

"I sit on ze back of ze room when I come zair. Ze giant naked female make me nervous." Ah! A fellow nerves-sufferer! Not a minute too soon! Though I would definitely not describe Irene as 'giant'. Except for her giant heart!

Yves filled my toothbrush glass to the brim again, downed it himself then filled it again and handed it to me. I was beginning to feel calm for the first time since I left home. I drank down the whole second glass and from that moment it didn't seem like I had a cold at all! Or that atomic missiles were aimed at my head.

I began to feel very friendly. Not just polite. But very friendly. Exceedingly. You could almost say, excessively so. Then Uncle's dogs began to bark and I knew Iris was on the stairs with my sprouts and potatoes and a bit of ham.

"Belt up, you bloody buggers!" yelled Uncle as Iris passed by his door with her rattling tray.

"Why, Uncle!" said Iris, "If Miss Pofford ever heard such words she'd be ever so upset!"

All this yelling and barking, due to the weird, acoustical arrangement of the particular basement seemed to be occurring right in the middle of my digs like some mysterious ancient Greek amphitheatre.

"Bugger Pofford!" yelled Uncle.

"Mon dieu!" whispered Yves.

"Blimey!" cried Iris who crashed in, said I didn't know you 'ad a guest!" and "Oooo! Don't it just smell of whiskey! If Miss Pofford was to smell this smell she'd be ever so upset!" And she banged down my sprouts and potatoes and a bit of ham.

"Mon dieu!" whispered Yves again and filled my toothbrush glass and quaffed it.

"Miss Pofford said to say to you, Andy, that you was to have these sprouts and potatoes and a bit of ham as you're poorly she said to say, at no charge," said Iris and added, "Nothing due with the rent. A gift from the goodness of 'er heart, so to speak, she said to say. Miss Pofford said that."

"P-P-Please th-thank Miss P-P-Pofford for me, Iris," I said or tried to say – things were becoming fuzzy. Then, through the thinness, came a loud but familiar shriek, "I-REES!"

"Coming, Miss Pofford!" shrieked Iris back into the thinness and leapt through the door and up the basement stairs as Uncle's dogs went wild and he shouted at them until they were quiet. Yves handed me another toothbrush glassful. "Who was zat she-devil?!" he asked.

"That w-was Iris," I said, and quaffed the whole glassful and felt so friendly and relaxed that I thought I might even hug my welcomer any minute! I might have hugged beautiful Sheila too if she had been here. Without hesitation! Honest! I might even call her 'darling' too!

"I hate dogs," said Yves.

I wished I could agree with him just to be agreeable and because I felt so warm and friendly but I couldn't. I love dogs! My smallish Border collie, Tinker, is proof of that and I miss her like crazy! I missed all the puppies she'd ever had too! She has puppies at least twice every year. Or at least every time I let her out of the garage when she is in season and the same small, black and white, naturally tail-less dog she always pairs with has shown up. I chase all the others away as Tinker seems to like him best. Her puppies have never been a problem. We have a waiting list for every litter. They are always born without tails and are always black and white and just as smart as Tinker herself. Granddad said we could have made a fortune selling them. But we give them away. And I always hate to see them go.

"D-Dogs have their p-place," I said.

"Oui," said Yves, "Somewhere else."

Anyhow, we didn't have to agree on everything and it was very kind of Yves to bring the whisky. It was yet another beau geste. This made five gestes in one day! Two of them from courteous Frenchmen. I was now exceedingly impressed with the French! Then I sneezed an explosive sneeze and saw stars and wondered if I was about to lose consciousness.

"You are, pear-'aps become under ze weathair?"

"A c-cold I th-think," I rasped, then I realized that to be a proper host I must immediately ask him about himself, as my dear Granddad would have. "W-What s-sort of th-things d-do you w-w-want to w-w-w-write about?" I said with a great effort to properly enunciate each word which only made it worse.

"The Love and the Death. What else can zair be?" he said, lovingly ignoring my alcohol-driven, additional speech difficulties. He then got up and felt my forehead. "You 'ave ze small fièvre."

He rubbed my forehead gently. This was such a kind, soothing, and humane thing to do that it brought tears to my eyes.

"Your eyes," he said, "zay 'ave ze watair ahs well."

Of course I couldn't say that I was so moved that it made me cry. Actually, I couldn't say anything at all. So I just lay back dizzily on my bed and smiled what must have been an extremely goofy smile as I remember my upper lip got stuck on my front teeth which were exceedingly dry, probably due to the drying effect of the whisky. Alcohol is excessively evaporative and almost certainly caused my super-dry front teeth. It was strange though, that all I could think of was my upper lip stuck high on my two front teeth giving what I thought was a Bela Lugosi vampire-effect. It was just like me to get hung up on something nutty like that! By now my head was whirling! I closed my eyes and it only got worse. So I opened them again and saw that Yves had unzipped my trousers and was pulling them right off me. Now how did I miss that?!

"You must be put in ze bed," said Yves, "You 'ave ze bad cold."

How kind! I thought. These French welcoming students really know their stuff! They know how to make a guy feel better! Then he slipped his hand into my underpants and started massaging my dick in the very gentlest way. What could I do? -- spit in his eye?! I really have to admit that although it was exceedingly surprising, it felt pleasant and reminded me of the time Tom and I had masturbated each other in the trunk of his car when our girl friends were smuggling us into a drive-in theatre just before dark. The movie was 'The Young Lions' starring Marlon Brando and Dean Martin although I was not absolutely sure about Dean Martin due to all the alcohol just now.

Anyhow, this massaging of my dick was comforting and I was so homesick I didn't object at all. Why should I? It felt perfectly correct. Considering the circumstances. So little time, so much to do! So much that might remain undone for eternity! I was snockered and I don't have any clear memory of what happened next except that I sneezed three or four times and everything faded to black.

Andy, breathing raucously, slept, and after a short but vigorous interval, Yves patted the sleeping Andy and himself dry with a fine, French hanky, zipped up his own trousers and pulled a blanket over Andy and tucked him in. "Bon nuit," he slurred softly, "Goodnight, goodnight. Parting is of zee such sweet sorrow. But we must say goodbye till it be tomorrow. Or ze day aff-tair." Yves took up the remainder of the bourbon whisky, switched off the light and quietly let himself out of Number 13, Wilton Street just in time to see the moon disappear in a new bank of determined rain clouds.

After at least three hours, one, if not two, very softly whirring, clicking meters on Andy's wall gave up and clicked off. Five minutes passed before Andy's door creaked softly open and a flashlight beam drawn by Andy's rough, septic snores, sought, found and illuminated his flushed, sleeping face.

The figure, breathing out steam in the frigid air crossed

the floor, inspected Andy, shook its head, muttered "poor kid", and moved to the wall where it wound coins into the two silent meters, returned to Andy's now hissing, gas fire, lit it with a long, kitchen match and returned to the door where it – he – paused and cast a bloodshot eye at the loudly rasping, sleeping Andy and whispered, "Everything all right, kid?"

# 10

"YOOOOOOOO-HOOOOO!"

Andy bolted straight up in his bed. It couldn't have been Iris, he checked his watch. Far too early for breakfast.

"YOOOOO-HOOOOO!"

Andy wiped his eyes, felt his head. It ached. It hammered!

"YOO-HOOOOOOOO! Will *anybody* help two damsels in distress?!"

Was it coming from his window? No! It was drifting down the basement stairs and right through the huge crack under his door.

Three floors up, Vera and Nola, the 'two damsels,' swayed on their canes at the edge of the landing outside their double bed-sitter.

"It's disgraceful, Vera, absolutely disgraceful!" cried Nola. "And it's happened yet again -- me and you with our bloomin' knees standin' in the cold! Beggin'! Beggin' for help!'"

"She'll come," said Vera, "She always comes, sooner or later."

"Later, more like," sniffed Nola. "The woman has not a shred of shame!"

"YOOOOO-HOOOOO!" cried Vera down the staircase.

"Us with no heat and these knees!" said Nola.

"Come, dear, we'll play with Harry whilst we wait, said Vera, gently. "He'll have his morning lesson, won't he? Come, dear. It'll pass the time."

Vera hobbled back into their large but frigid double bed-sitter to a covered birdcage and took the night-cloth from it. Nola followed, leaving their door open for a potential rescuer.

"Good morning, Harry," said Vera.

"Good morning, Harry," said Nola.

"I'll put on his lesson, dear."

"Do so, if you must, Vera, but it will be in vain. You know very well these cheap budgerigars seldom speak. I have said this till I'm blue in the face."

"So you have, dear, but we could get lucky today. Today I feel unusually hopeful."

"Yes you do, Vera, and I admire you for that and I wish I had your err..."

"Perspicacity."

"Yes, that too. But we must be practical, love. Oh, I know when you buy 'em they always say they'll talk -- recite the bloomin' Magna Carta but they never do. These cheap budgies never speak. And they never shall."

"Harry will, sooner or later," said Vera, "We've had him for only a week, love. He's settling in. We must be patient."

"The patience of Job it seems." said Nola with an exaggerated shrug.

Vera switched on a turntable, pushed it close beside the bird-cage, set on the disc and turned the volume up to maximum. A very deep and powerful voice, at a dubious turntable speed, boomed out from the ladies' open door and down the stairs:

"HELLLL-OOOOO, BABY! WANT A KISS?!"
"HELLLL-OOOOO, BABY! WANT A KISS?!"
"HELLLL-OOOOO, BABY! WANT A KISS?!"

Harry the budgerigar, terrified, flattened himself against the far side of his cage.

"He'll never speak!" cried Nola, over the deep bass din. "Never! We were duped, Vera!"

"Let's shout again, love. "I'm chilled to the bone."

From his basement Andy heard the rumbling "HELLLL-OOOOO, BABY! WANT A KISS" followed by the women's desperate "YOOOO-HOOOOO! Can anybody assist us?!"

Ever the gentleman, his head hammering with hangover, gentleman Andy the sprang from his bed to the rescue. Throwing on the dead man's robe, he sneezed twice, then again and had a brief, comforting reprise of something not quite remembered but pleasant from the night before. He paused for a moment, wonderingly, allowing last night's indistinct pleasure to sink in, then flung himself up the basement stairs to do his duty. Dear Granddad would be proud of him!

After the three-floor climb Andy sagged, exhausted against the stair rail before the stricken women outside their open door.

"It's Iris again!" cried Nola.

"Yes, it's Iris." added Vera. "She forgot our gas meter."

"It's not the first time," said Nola.

"Nor, I fear, the last," added Vera.

Andy's hangover pounded nails into his temples as a billion determined cold-germs pulsed through his ravaged frame and he waited for death or at least a loophole to speak. Even under normal conditions he required a somewhat longer time to pull his words intelligently together and the repetition of the booming voice of Harry's recorded speech lesson was distracting.

"I'm Andy," he finally managed. "How m-m-may I help you?"

"We've not yet had our breakfast tea and our gas fire's gone off," said Vera, pulling her lavender cardigan closer around her shivering shoulders.

"HELLL-OOOOO, BABY, WANT A KISS?!" continued the recording at its wrong speed-setting.

"It's our knees, you see," moaned Nola.

"It is agony replenishing our meters on our own," said Vera, motioning Andy in as she and Nola arranged themselves wearily beside their cold hearth in their usual fireside chairs. "All these stairs. We live at the mercy of a cruel gaoler."

"And with our bloody knees!" moaned Nola, "It's a bleedin' disgrace!"

"Poor Gladys being blind," said Vera, "had to tap her way down to the basement last night."

"As she is forced to do on many nights, the poor woman! It is disgraceful!" said Nola.

"It simply cannot stand." said Vera.

"HELLL-OOOOO, BABY, WANT A KISS?!"

"I l-live in the b-basement, I can take care of your m-meters."

"Oh, would you, dear?" said Vera. "Would you?"

"HELLL-OOOOO, BABY, WANT A KISS?!"

Tiny Harry had now shrunk so far against the opposite side of his birdcage, that several of his green and yellow tail feathers poked askew through the cage wires.

"HELLL-OOOOO, BABY, WANT A KISS?!" blared his lesson.

"Your r-record is s-set on the wrong s-speed," said Andy and wiped a shimmering splash of cold sweat from his brow, "You've g-got it on l-long-play m-m-mode. It's s-s-seventy-eight rpm, isn't it?"

"I don't know what you're talking about, love," said Vera quickly as she dug deep into her cardigan pockets for shillings. "Nola's son, Dennis, loaned this infernal machine to us. But you must be right."

"Of course he's right," snapped Nola. "Yanks know about these technology things. I did think Harry's lesson sounded peculiar."

"Well, I wish you'd said, Nola. You know I am quite tone deaf".

"HELLL-OOOOO, BABY, WANT A KISS?!"

Nola rose painfully and led Andy to the gramophone. "Do the honours, love," she said, "Let's catch the bull by the horns!"

Andy adjusted the lesson disc to its proper speed.

"Oh that's much better, dear!" cried Nola, turning off the gramophone, "Now it sounds just like my Dennis."

Vera frowned briefly, rose and handed Andy a fistful of shillings. "Our names, Nola and Vera, are sticky-taped on the side of our meters."

"You *are* kind," said Nola.

"Yes, kind," said Vera as Andy smiled, nodded, sneezed, wiped away more cold sweat and started down the stairs.

"They're lovely, them Yankee boys," sighed Nola as she sat by the dormant gas fire with a box of matches ready to welcome the return of heavenly warmth. "So gentlemanly in that tatty old bathrobe of his. Here! Haven't we seen that robe before, love?!"

Vera lowered herself carefully into her chair, "It does seem familiar doesn't it? But he looks poorly, does our young Yank. He could do with a bit of fattening up."

"It's that basement, isn't it?" said Nola, "Last one there died, didn't he?"

"Ummm," said Vera, "It was rumoured that the poor gentleman before him also perished. A paraffin fire is de rigueur at that depth."

"My Dennis has a paraffin fire, has he not? Two, in fact!"

"And your Dennis lives in a basement."

"Vera! That was it! The Yank's bathrobe! It belonged to that poor, wasted, basement gentleman which died!" said Nola.

"And the poor old gentleman before him, dear," added Vera. "It was passed down -- I know this for a fact through the reprehensible Iris -- it was a most unfortunate hand-me-down. That basement is a menace to life itself," continued Vera with an exaggerated frown so that Nola, who was severely near-sighted, might more easily discern and enjoy it.

"But we'd all of us be safer in a basement these days," said Nola, "We're for it now, ain't we, love? The Russian Peril. Pity them poor Yanks."

"We'll win, Nola, sooner or later. We always do."

"The bible says, and it must be speakin' of Russia, that 'The Great Black Bear from the North will sit astride the world.'"

"Not if he's got our knees, he won't," sighed Vera.

"What a smashin' boy," replied Nola, "His name is Leander." Vera's eyes brightened. "The Leander of Greek legend who, against great odds, swam the treacherous Hellespont time and again to be with his one true love, the fair high-priestess, Hero," recited Vera with some conviction and a far away glint to her eye.

"Staggering, Vera, that was simply staggering!"

"Only a school recitation, Nola, dear. I was twelve."

"Well, I'm staggered! It's got my vote!"


Andy stood shivering on the next landing down. His head was whirling. He felt sick. He was certain the excessive drinking was, as Granddad would have put it, the chickens coming home to roost directly in his digestive tract.

Andy made it just in time to the toilet below, slammed in and vomited. His late night visitor's nearly adjacent door opened a crack, the head appeared and nodded sympathetically as his bloodshot eyes squinted and suffered with each noisy ejection from behind the toilet door.

When he was finished, Andy returned to his basement and dutifully inserted the shillings into the distressed ladies' gas and electric meters. He was just falling back into bed as Iris, to the din of barking dogs and Uncle's curses, crashed in with her rattling breakfast tray. "Oh!" she said, seeing the untouched dish of potatoes and sprouts and ham from the night before, "Oh! Miss Pofford'll be ever so upset as you wasted her food!"

"I'm s-sorry. I was drunk. The w-welcome-wagon."

"You what?!"

"N-N-N-Nothing."

"As Miss Pofford says, food don't grow on trees."

"Yes, it d-does," said Andy, "S-Sometimes" -- he was feeling wretched, even a little hysterical, "Apples d-do, oranges d-do, almonds d-d-do, avocados d-d-d-do and-and-and…you f-forgot to put m-money in Vera and Nola's…"

"No classes today?" said Iris, brushing away Andy's accusation and several of his smaller drawings from the little table to make room for breakfast. Andy coughed and said, "I'm s-s-sick."

"I'm not surprised," said Iris, "Living down 'ere in this dampness where better men than you 'ave breathed their last. I wouldn't live here if my life depended on it!"

Andy laughed, became nauseated, so stopped laughing. He agreed with Iris's 'better men than you' but had no idea what to do about it. How could he ever be better when he was getting worse? It seemed he couldn't even draw properly now, at least to his own satisfaction. Everybody, with the possible exception of Marcella, was better than he was. He knew this from the moment he'd set foot in the Rossetti. The other students were brilliant! His own 'gift' had now faded! Andy was terrified. His life needed work that he couldn't provide. Didn't know how!

But how important was his tiny life beside the catastrophe awaiting Humankind? He coughed and found refuge in several more coughs as Iris grabbed up his untouched dinner and warned "Miss Pofford'll be ever so upset!" and exited to the renewed barking and energetic swearing from Uncle's room.

"Miss Pofford'd be ever so upset if she heard such cursing, Uncle," shouted Iris from the hall through Uncle's shut door.

"Stuff Pofford! Stuff you! Where's my breakfast?!"

"Soon, Uncle, dear" cried Iris, "Soon! We gave most of it to the Yank," she lied, "As he's poorly!"

"I-REES!" screamed Miss Pofford, from the thinness.

Andy's door sprung open, Iris rushed in, pressed her mouth to the crumbling, powdery wall and shrieked "Coming, Miss Pofford!"

Desperate, debilitated, Andy sat in his bed wondering if Sheila was ever again planning to throw herself naked into this very bed. Wondering about his own behaviour, wondering what he would do if she tried it. Wondering about Yves -- what exactly happened? Nothing much, of course. Nothing that hadn't happened before. What's a little mutual masturbation between friends? If there *was* a little mutual masturbation. Although Yves wasn't precisely a friend, the French were certainly friendly, generous, openhearted, accommodating and forthright! First a paraffin fire from Jean-Francois then the whisky and a wank, if it was a wank, from Yves. 'A wank for a Yank' mused Andy who had, as Granddad might have remarked, a 'decided penchant' for said. What seventeen-year-old hadn't? thought Andy who liked this new foreign word, 'wank'. And 'wanker' seemed unavoidable here in England. He had heard it twice on the train to Oxford from Southampton and four times, including variations, at the Playhouse Bar during his one and only visit there on his one and only day ever at the Rossetti. Everyone seemed to be a wanker of some sort! Was it to be admired?! He laughed again but he could not stop himself wondering why he was so nervous with Sheila and why it was so pleasant – whatever it was, if it *was* a wank , with Yves, a stranger until yesterday.

The bourbon! That was it. Bourbon whisky was the solution to all unpleasantness in this discourteous and lately extraordinarily dangerous world. Bourbon was the answer. But only if used wisely. In moderation. Alcohol could get out of hand. No! Bourbon was not the answer! Andy had no wish to bump into things, to fall, to bruise his elbows and knees and get large blue lumps on his head. Or to disappoint or frighten his future children. He began to worry seriously about these children-to-be. How would he support them? What would his children's prospective mother think of him even if he weren't an alcoholic? Who would their mother be? She'd end up hating him! Why did he ever get married?! Especially to her?!

Andy wondered too, if he would ever be well enough to go back to the Rossetti, further wondered if he and the Rossetti would exist  tomorrow or the day after or even an hour from now! This, of course, would put cancelled to his future wife and children. All of that terrifying responsibility, instantly atomized. But at what a cost! This, was not a comfort!

Andy's mind was a mess and President Kennedy was giving an important message tonight. A declaration of all-out war? Then it occurred to him – and he was shocked by it -- that he hadn't yet thanked Irene and Jean-Francois for his kerosene stove! What had happened to his manners?! This was how great civilizations began their slow, inevitable  declines, bit by discourteous bit. This was how they foundered. Little things like not holding doors open for ladies, or escorting a blind person, maybe even the Blind Girl herself, across a street, or giving up ones seat on a bus to an old person or forgetting to say 'How very nice to have met you' when taking ones leave of a new acquaintance, particularly a more mature one. Forgetting these finer points of behaviour invited chaos. Chaos could lead anywhere. As it was now quickly proceeding to do in Cuba. Andy was frightened of anywhere. He preferred somewhere. Somewhere nice and dry. Somewhere -- if possible -- cozy and warm. Yes, God, warm, please. Let it be warm again. But not too warm. But warmer, anyhow. Yes. Please, God! If only for a day or two... even if they were the world's very last two days! Please! And let it, for Christ's sake, stop raining!

# 11

It was dark when Irene laid down her book. She was glad she had told Jean-Francois she wasn't quite up to it tonight. The treatment had tired her. Need they have taken so much blood? She needed every last sodding drop of the bleedin' stuff! She laughed. A sense of humour prepares one! Irene had long been prepared. But doubted she was even up to the Rossetti tomorrow. It took a lot of energy and determination to hold a pose properly. Particularly those boring long poses. She loved gesture sketches when the students had only several minutes and a few quick pencil lines, to get the 'feel' of her. She was excellent at posing for these shorter gesture sketches. She had a decided dramatic sense, had once imagined herself on the stage. "Yeah!" she'd once roared in purest Americanese, "the first stage outta here!" and greatly amused her long gone, 'husband', Sergeant Martinez.

Irene laughed. Loud and long. Until it hurt. She winced. It would probably be good to stay home for a while. Jean-Francois could do some minor shopping. Iris could fill in the rest for a few bob. Miss Pofford wouldn't mind. Miss Pofford charged her no rent, often for weeks at a time, when she modelled in nearby towns or hadn't any current posing jobs. Contrary to what Iris said, Irene knew that Miss Pofford had a soft spot for her. Pofford wasn't a bad sort, an excellent sort, in fact, though she did occasionally cuff Iris to keep her in line. It didn't take a scientist to know Iris was occasionally a wild card. Miss Pofford knew Iris better than anyone so who should object? Irene wished she might cuff a few of her unruly blood-cells about the ears, keep them on the straight and narrow.

She sighed, went to her secret hiding place under a loose floorboard, kneeled and lifted out a small black velvet pouch, loosed its drawstring and dropped a fine pearl necklace into her hand. It shone even in the dim light of her room – she used only low-watt light bulbs to save time on the electric meter but also because bright bulbs had begun to hurt her eyes. Fortunately, Iris was behaving herself and had, generously, under severe pressure from Miss Pofford no doubt, regularly fed Irene's electric and gas meters. Miss Pofford knew when Irene wasn't quite up to par. Though she never spoke of it except perhaps 'Off to the Radcliffe today, are we, dear?' when they'd met by chance in the hall after Irene's bath time. Miss Pofford would speak in a warm, caring voice, always in a warm and caring voice of concern. She meant it. Irene knew which people meant it. They were few and far between. She knew when they meant it because she always meant it and she always knew when they didn't.

Irene fastened the pearl necklace around her neck, regarded herself in a hand mirror. Pearls flattered, soft and luminous against her smooth skin. These were natural pearls, superbly matched. She had read about pearls. There was nothing cheap about her Sergeant Martinez. "Ricardito," she whispered, "hadn't a cheap bone in his fine, firm body." She said it again, touching the pearls this time. They were a perfect parting gift of love from her Yank -- who wasn't, any more than 'Alabama' had been, a legal husband. These perfect pearls were indeed the spoils of war, possibly from the same frightened Japanese merchant who had supplied the fabulous red silk kimono. Both gifts were sent by military post direct from Japan. It seemed a miracle she had received them safely. She had lived a charmed life. Until now.

Irene was losing weight too rapidly. She brought a hand to her neck. She was too thin, needed more custard tarts a day. At this rate at least a baker's dozen. But it was a good excuse, wasn't it? To give them away when she felt too ill to eat them. Especially give them to the gawky, yellow-haired young Yank, the one who was poorly just now. The one who needed mothering so very badly. She hoped the paraffin fire was a help. Why were people so drawn to such boys? Innocence attracts, doesn't it? We always want to replace what we've lost -- those used worn-out parts and ideas that don't function anymore? Andy was an innocent. Irene was certain he was younger than he'd admitted to. Or perhaps he'd simply lived a sheltered life? How completely wonderful to have experienced such a thing! She considered this without a trace of envy, was grateful that some people had advantages others only dreamed of.

Had Irene not been a nude model she might have been a saint. Why not both? She liked the idea, glanced again at her reflection, at her magnificent pearl necklace. This gift of love when there was love. Of a sort. What would happen to the necklace? It had seen her through. She settled again into bed, took up her book, decided not, closed it. What was happening to the world? She dropped the book in her lap – what good was Lady Chatterley's Lover to her? She switched on the radio. "Just in time!" she said aloud, checking her wristwatch.

*"Good evening my fellow citizens,"* began the president of the United States.

"Fellow citizens?" murmured Irene with a smile, "Small world, ain't it?"

> *"This government,"* continued President Kennedy, *"as promised, has maintained the closest surveillance of the Soviet build-up on the island of Cuba…"*

Irene switched off the radio, frowned, sighed "Poor Andy", switched on the radio again, lay back, took up the mirror, gazed at her pearls and listened to one of the two men who held everybody's future in the palm of his hand. "But not mine," she whispered, "Not my future."

Vera and Nola couldn't have been more pleased. They sat, gammy knees tight beside the gas fire that had faithfully burned full on, day and night since the Yank sneaked their handful of coins, dividing them equally as requested, between their softly buzzing little meters. Luckily, Iris hadn't a clue.

"I love a cosy fire," said Vera, laying down her book.

"I should say so, love," sighed Nola, "A cosy fire makes the world go round."

"How are you faring?" said Vera, "Just now, dear, this very minute, dear, knees-wise?"

"Toastin' nicely, thank you," sighed Nola, "In Arcady, love, in bleedin' Arcady."

"I'm so glad, Nola. It's a perfect companion, isn't it? There is absolutely nothing like a cosy fire."

"Nothin' on this bleedin' planet," said Nola reaching for the radio. "Dare I?"

"Why not?" said Vera, "We've nothing to lose."

Nola switched on the radio.

*"…but this secret, swift, and extraordinary buildup of Communist missiles," said President Kennedy, "in an area well known to have a special and historical relationship to the United States and the nations of the Western Hemisphere, in violation of…"*

"He's got excruciatin' back trouble," moaned Nola. "Oh, I do feel for him!"

"Poor man," sighed Vera.

"But he's a looker, ain't he, love?"

"I couldn't disagree with that, dear," said Vera, changing the angle of one knee to better catch the healing warmth, "That is a truism if ever there was one. Pity about his back. I'd not wish such infirmity on anyone."

"I, for one, wouldn't wish our knees on anyone, love," said Nola, "And that goes for young Mrs. Kennedy too!"

"I'll second that, dear," added Vera with a smile of deepest understanding. And they laughed.

"It is a cryin' shame, 'n' it, Vera? About the comin' invasion? Hell will break out again. War! War! War! I'm so sick of war I could spit! The last one was enough for me! The bleedin' buzzy bombs was truly enough for me!"

"Terrifying." said Vera. "I lost my livelihood, didn't I?"

"My Dennis said that ever since the Battle of Hastings everything has been going to hell in a handbag! Gone Haywire!"

"How's that, Nola?"

"My Dennis says that the 1066 invasion of Britain didn't make any sense at all."

"How's is that, dear?"

"My Dennis says that both sides of the conflict was of Viking descent and they shouldn't have been fighting in the first place.

They were family, Vera! Family! That's what my Dennis says. Both of them war-mongering kings or whatever, was sodding Norsemen! Didn't they know they were family?!"

Vera again shifted her knees towards the shimmering heat from their now dependable gas fire. "Perhaps they just forgot?"

"That's what my Dennis thinks. Everything's gone haywire!"

"Haywire!" said Vera with some feeling. "Our Yank must feel perfectly awful about this."

"Poor Andy," said Nola. "Poor boy."

"Poor young Andy," added Vera, "Such a nice boy too. So beautifully refined for a Yankee."

*"...I have directed that the following initial steps be taken immediately: First, to halt this offensive buildup, a strict quarantine on all offensive military equipment under shipment to Cuba is being initiated. All ships of any kind bound for Cuba from whatever nation or port will, if found to contain cargoes of offensive weapons, be turned back."*

Andy climbed wearily out of bed, switched off the radio, coughed, poured and mixed a glass of the absurdly-orange, 'orange squash' and dropped two vitamin C 's into it, watched them fizz. His hands shook so much he spilled a bit on his Y-fronts. He wished Yves had left the bourbon. It was relaxing and he needed to relax. He got back into bed, waited for the C to fizz out, and worried. He knew he had a slight fever too. If a world war didn't get him first, this cold or flu or whatever it was, would snuff him out like a 'brief candle'. He loved Macbeth's famous speech but his mother, who was in an occasional amateur production, told him never to say 'Macbeth' to an actor or they would shush him. He asked her why and she said actors thought it was bad luck to say "Macbeth" so they always referred to him as 'the Scottish King!' It was such a beautiful speech too, thought Andy -- Shakepeare comparing reality to actors on a stage. Andy thought this shushing thing was unfair to both Shakespeare and Macbeth. Even though Andy's favourite was

King Lear. Because he had felt so sorry for Cordelia that he cried when he first saw it on television. He wasn't sure, but he thought Granddad and his beautiful mother had cried too. Grandma, who had recently seen 'Spellbound' with Ingrid Bergman as the psychiatrist, didn't cry at all. Grandma was too busy, she said, analyzing King Lear's motives and couldn't decide whether he was a fool or just plain nuts.

Andy was too tired to write a letter home, knew he'd start bawling if he tried. He shouldn't have been thinking so much about Cordelia! "What a bawl-baby you are, Andy!" he said aloud. It didn't help. Nothing would help now. He was doomed at the age of just turned seventeen. He got out of bed again, set his one and only record on Sheila's turntable, switched it on and returned to his bed where he drank down the vitamin C forti- fied orange squash wishing it were at least a full toothbrush's glass of Yves's bourbon.

*When I'm gone, my love*
*There will come a day*
*You may sigh and say...*

Andy pulled the bedclothes over his head and was instantly dozing, his breathing coming in great uneven gasps, punctu- ated by coughs.

*He travelled to a star*
*Why did he go so far?*
*Was it just to be*
*So far away from me?*
*Was it just to be*
*So far away from me?*

Sang 'The Mellow Four' as two wall meters clicked softly and were silent. Simultaneously the record stopped, Andy's bed lamp went out and the gas fire, with a hiss, disappeared. The paraffin fire's wick needed adjusting and it, too, soon gave up its fragile flame. It quickly became bitterly cold as Andy, still coughing in his sleep, slept on.

Several more hours into the rainy night Andy's door creaked open and a flashlight penetrated the damp darkness to capture Andy's restless, sleeping face.

"Poor kid," he whispered as he stuck a few coins into both his and Andy's wall meters and kneeled beside the hissing gas and lit it, turning it up as high as possible. In the dim light of the gas fire he silently opened the front of the paraffin fire, trimmed the wick with his penknife, lit it and moved it closer to Andy's bed.

He disappeared up the stairs, switched off his light, checked that his gas fire was shut off and returned immediately with three blankets, two of which he unfolded and placed over sleeping Andy, tucking them carefully around him. Dragging the crippled Chair closer to the gas fire, he sat, dropped the third blanket over his knees and trained his bloodshot eyes on the rasping, wheezing, sleeping Andy. "Poor laddie" he whispered. "Poor Yank. Poor American child."

# 12

"I-rees! You, I-rees! Where the hell are you?!" trumpeted through the thinness.

"It's a zoo! We live in a fucking zoo!" cried Cyril, His bloodshot eyes wide. "How do you feel? You look horrid. How do you feel?"

"Horrid," said Andy, hardly awake, "W-W-Who are you?!"

"I am Cyril and I live upstairs," said Cyril, jutting out a leg to balance The Chair, "I live directly above you, dear boy. And, damn me, I have gazed furtively at you on several occasions. Twice, I believe, whilst you slept."

Andy winced.

"Largely in the noble cause of meter feeding, of course. Also, I desire to know whom I'm up against. Knowledge is power. But my behaviour can't have been pleasant for you, laddie. For that, my apologies. I've nothing to say in my defence except that I am bored shitless. Do have a heart, dear boy. So you've noticed me?"

"Y-Yes." Andy coughed, sneezed and said "I didn't m-m-mind at all." He was too sleepy to protest and, as always, encouraged new friendships.

"Last bloke here died. Or looked dead. Or was rumoured to be so. Perhaps it was all but an urban legend. One can hope. They took the last poor lad away shivering on his stretcher. It has long been known that your frigid little room is not fit for human life. But as they say, 'location, location, location!' For we are indeed situated dangerously near the feverish, beating heart of this University." Cyril threw back his head and his long, lank hair made an unusual slapping noise that was hard to miss, "But then you're a Yank, aren't you?" He laughed.

"Y-Yes. I know."

"I heard your semi-death rattle last night whilst replenishing my gas meter and spent the night in this hideous chair watching over you. You sounded dreadful. You do make a racket! But I knew you would survive. I'd have done something drastic if I'd thought you were in serious danger. Pa is a doctor. Harley Street, posh end, he's titled but desperately needed something to do with his hands." Cyril laughed. "I'm an 'Honourable'."

"I h-hope s-s-so," said Andy who could think of nothing else to say. Cyril took a long drag on a cigarette, said as he waved it, "I've borrowed some of yours. Sincerely hope you don't mind."

"N-no," n-n-not at all," lied Andy. Was he speaking to a new, and possibly good friend?

"I'd have shouted for help if you were in mortal danger. Incidentally, you're looking somewhat better just this minute. By the way, it's raining. "

"S-S-S-So I've n-noticed," said Andy, glancing at the gushing gutters outside his ivy-tangled window, "it never s-s-stops raining here."

Then, shrieking through the thinness: "There you are, you I-rees! Where the hell 'ave you been?!"

"A zoo!" sighed Cyril, "We live in a freaking zoo. Has Iris read your mail too?"

"Haven't h-had any yet. I've only b-b-been here th-three days."

"Yes, of course. Fled the war zone have we?"

"I sh-should be home."

Cyril, realized Andy was serious, "Yes, quite. Family and all?"

"And f-friends," said Andy and coughed, "and my d-dog."

As on cue, Uncle's dogs began to bark. "Belt up, you puking bitches!" cried Cyril. "Oh, Jesus," he said as Iris bounded through Andy's door with her rattling breakfast tray, "a zoo!"

"Mr. Lemmington! I thought you was here! I brought you somethin' from Miss Pofford! Your favourite pink cakey-wakey!"

"Set it here, Iris, then you may go."

"Right you are, Mr. Lemmington!"

Iris slammed down the cake and Andy's breakfast. "Miss Pofford says to me, Iris, take this cake over to Mr. Lemmington who ain't paid for his brekkies, none of 'em, for three weeks. But take this cake to him as it's his favourite cake she says to me. Well I done as Miss Pofford says and as I seen you wasn't in and I heard voices from below I says to myself, Iris, I says, our Mr. Lemmington ain't in his room but is in the basement with the Yank. So I says to myself..."

"Yet again," said Cyril.

"I says to myself I says, Iris, just you take Mr. Lemmington's favourite pink cakey-wakey down to him as he's with the Yank. So I brought it here as I thought you was here as you wasn't up there, and you was!"

Cyril leered a sickly smile, murmured "Well done, wench!"

Iris glowed, showed a wide row of very large, unusually perfect teeth, "Oh, Mr. Lemmington, Miss Pofford is ever so upset with all them Russians as is in Spain. I says to her, No, Miss Pofford, it's them Yanks which is in Spain and what right have they got to be there?! And she says oh they've every right as they're Yanks, ain't they? Oh, she was ever so upset! The Boy's upset too! As well as poorly! He's drooling! They're all upset as are at Number 12! Poorly as well!"

Iris slammed out but immediately stuck her head in, entered and approached Andy, sticking her face, as usual, uncomfortably close, "That'll be thruppence for the egg, due with the rent. There's no bacon today as there ain't none. You'll have double bacon tomorrow as Miss Pofford says which will be one and three which will make one and six due with the rent. Miss Pofford said that!"

"Iris?"

"Yes, Mr. Lemmington?"

"Begone."

"Right you are, Mr. Lemmington."

Iris coloured, curtsied and moved carefully to the door where she paused, turned, cast a gleaming smile at Cyril, waved her empty tray at him and exited, gently shutting the door behind her.

Cyril sighed, was about to repeat "A zoo," when Iris again thrust her head through the door. "I forgot to say, Mr. Lemmington, that the police was 'ere last night. Miss Pofford turned 'em away as usual and says to me to tell 'em you was poorly in Banbury with your Mum. Which I done."

"My mother thanks you, Iris. And I thank you. You are thus dismissed."

"Right you are, Mr. Lemmington," said Iris and gently pulled the door shut.

"Sh-she's different with you than with m-me," said Andy, gingerly sipping his tea as his right index finger where he'd cut it sharpening his charcoal pencil seemed to be a bit more inflamed and his teacup unsteady.

"I'll have some of that, said Cyril, commandeering Andy's cup, "Helps this loathsome pink cake go down. They've got some cretinous idea that it's my favourite."

Cyril took a gulp of tea and a bite of cake, swallowed, said "Detestable! I eat it only because it's filling and saves buying lunch."

"Why is Iris d-d-different with you, Cyril? So p-polite?"

"Because I am a gentleman. And you are not," said Cyril, noisily scarfing down the last of the 'detestable' cake and with it the rest of Andy's tea.

"But I always try to be a courteous p-person, a good p-p-person."

"Goodness has nothing to do with it." Cyril grinned.

Cyril was joking, of course. Goodness had everything to do with everything! But he, Andy, had recently discovered that he was not good enough. On the other hand being so high and mighty that everyone respected you seemed comfortable. Almost soothing. It seemed to work for Cyril -- at least with Iris. Andy liked the idea. But there was one behemoth flaw -- how could he impress anyone? He couldn't even draw anymore! His 'gift' had flown! How could he show his face at the Rossetti?! He didn't deserve to be there! They'd tar and feather him and run him out of town on a rail! Or worse, even revoke his scholarship! He stared at his right hand. The cut, wrapped finger was throbbing a bit, damn it! His face squinched up, ready to bawl. Andy saw that Cyril was staring at him and he quickly un-squinched and said "So, Cyril, What were the p-p-p-police after you f-for?"

"Passive resistance," said Cyril nonchalantly lighting two of Andy's cigarettes and handing him one, "I am a passive/aggressive Ban the Bomb freak. We chain ourselves together and lie about for hours on tarmac. Bored shitless."

This immediately completely destroyed the English gentleman theory. Is this what gentlemen did? Chaining themselves in public? Andy had no intention of being on the wrong side of the law. He was law abiding, courteous and not a crusader. Crusaders were not liked. Andy couldn't bear that. "Not never, not no how," he whispered to himself.

"What did you say?" asked Cyril through a perfectly blown smoke ring.

"N-Nothing," said Andy, "N-N-N-Nothing at all."

Then Andy coughed, loud and long and felt he was about to vomit up his lungs. Hearing this extra loud cough echo under her floor through the thinness, Miss Pofford from her chair before the telly and yet another Cuba Missile programme, said "The Yank still poorly?"

"Yes Miss Pofford. He ain't gone out today neither," said Iris, "missed his classes and all."

"Take him some of them sprouts and potatoes and a bit of ham."

"But they're two days old, Miss Pofford."

"Uncle eats 'em! They ain't killed Uncle!"

"Yes, Miss Pofford."

"And give what's left to the cat."

"Yes, Miss Pofford."


In his darkening, room -- Cyril and the whole day long gone -- Andy, from his bed, drowsily watched The Blind Girl tap the way to her wall meter. She inserted a coin, and returned to the door where she stopped, turned towards him, whispered, "No visitors tonight, dear?"

"N-No, ma'am."

"Good luck with your Russians, dear."

"Th-Thank you, ma'am." Andy listened to Gladys the Blind Girl's gentle, tapping retreat up the basement stairs. The silence was deafening -- Uncle and his dogs must have been out for a walk or sleeping soundly. Andy marvelled at the patience shown by nearly everyone for errant Iris who neglected her duties causing severe hardship for the aged and handicapped and who had, it seemed, no manners at all. Unless one were a gentleman. Andy lay back, coughed loudly for a moment, closed his eyes and saw himself in a swimsuit on a sandy, sunny California beach with a surfboard under his arm. He had never in his young life had a surfboard under his arm! Why was he imagining these things now? Were these imaginings, these delusions of some he-man-healthy, sunlit grandeur to be the last sane thoughts to visit his deteriorating mind?! "Don't go all cinematical on us, Andy" said Granddad so softly Andy nearly missed it .

"Sorry, Granddad, I'm... I'm poorly.  Granddad, do you think I'm nuts?" There was no answer.

# 13

Andy lay awake. Granddad's comforting voice was silent. Andy knew he must think of other more pleasant things than tearing himself apart. He must change his pre-midnight attitude if he hoped to sleep at all. So he thought about Cyril of the bloodshot eyes. Cyril was a 'jolly good bloke.' Had said so himself and his concern for Andy was yet another beau geste notch on Andy's shiny sickbed belt. Enough beau gestes and Andy could retire as a well-liked, confident bon vivant! Like Cyril? Like Yves? No. It must come from within. So there was, Andy was convinced, no hope. Because within, he knew, he was as empty as a kettle drum. This was no help at all. Why had he thought 'kettle drum' in the first place? This image was as strange as his phony surfboard! Oddly, he finally began to doze but was immediately awakened by pounding on his door accompanied by Uncle's yapping dogs. Uncle, who was either out or sleeping soundly, had nothing, to say about it.

Andy's door was flung open, his light went on and Charlotta, known as 'Charlie' entered. She was the formidable friend of Regina, the woman who had stumbled over him after he'd tripped on the four dead rabbits in the hallway, "Sorry!" she said, "I thought you weren't in!"

"I was s-sleeping!" said Andy, who felt justifiably testy but would never have said such a thing if he hadn't been dozing and 'poorly' as well.

Charlie answered in kind. "I said I was sorry!"

She turned away, marched to her wall meter, wound in many coins, snapped over her shoulder, "Stay away from Reggie."

"R-Reggie?!" said Andy -- perhaps righteous anger was the solution to his dilemma?! "R-Reggie?! Who's he?!"

Charlie eyed him intently, "*She*. Regina. Don't play innocent with me, old son. Stay away from Reggie. She's suggestible. In the corridor, remember? She smiled at you. Stay away from her. She's suggestible."

Then, with more than a hint of menace, Charlie said yet again, "Stay away from Reggie. She is suggestible."

Andy coughed, nodded. "I've been s-sick," he said and

coughed again, "Very s-s-s-s-sick."

"You a Yank?"

Andy nodded again. Coughed again.

"I've heard about you Yanks," said Charlie and scowled malevolently at him.

Andy nodded once more. He must be friendly. Maybe Charlie could somehow be added to his list of beau gestes. Damn it! Lay off the beau gestes! thought Andy, this beau geste thing really is insane! He summoned up a genial smile and nodded enthusiastically to this new intruder -- possible new friend, said "All good? What you've h-h-heard about Yanks? All g-g-good I h-hope?"

"Regina is an architect but she occasionally lacks emotional judgment" said Charlie, "Been ill or something? You look gutted."

"I've b-been p-poorly," rasped Andy, and coughed loudly as undeniable proof.

"Jee-sus! What a fucking awful cough! You've been what?"

"P-P-P-Poorly. Isn't that what you s-say over here? P-P-P-Poorly?"

"Oh. Yeah," said Charlie, clasping her hands together. She cracked her knuckles with two great thwacks, "I suppose it would be. Yeah. P-P-P-Poorly. Then it was you, coughing? Crikey! We can hear you at the top of the house! Can you keep the fucking noise down?"

Andy complied, covered his mouth with a corner of his sweaty sheet, coughed again -- the tiniest cough he could manage. Charlie softened, approached and extended her hand. "Charlotta. Call me Charlie. We're not heartless or anything, Reggie and me, but we do need our beauty sleep. I'm in construction. Tarmac, you know. Asphalt, you Yanks call it. That sort of thing. I'm a commercial development architect I suppose you'd call it. Not quite accredited but that's just around the corner, isn't it?"

"If you say so," said Andy.

"I do indeed."

Andy coughed another tiny, polite cough under his sheet,

then nodded enthusiastically again. Charlie continued: "They took the last bloke away on a stretcher," she said, cracking her knuckles again. "I suppose you've heard all about that?"

He had.

"It's this swamp air. Oxford is built in a bloody bog. It's worse than Cambridge! Could use a fair bit of tarmac, it's sinking like Venice. In a hundred years our 'dreaming spires' will be gurgling spires -- below sea level," she said, starting for the door, "if they're not blasted to holy shit by early next week!"

I would be very, very s-sorry about that," said Andy. "I haven't seen 'em yet."

Charlie paused, caught her awry image in the cracked glass of Andy's wardrobe mirror, smiled at herself, grimaced. "Broken mirrors are seven years bad luck, old son," she said, pausing at the door, "If we've even got seven years left which doesn't seem bloody likely after Kennedy's speech. Get some wool knickers or move out of this grotto. That's my advice. And stay away from Reggie. G'night to you then."

Charlie was out the door before Andy could answer.

"Who's out there?!" shouted Uncle, this time through the din of his dogs.

"Charlie, Uncle! Your old mate, Charlie!"

"Goodnight to you, Charlie!" shouted Uncle.

"Goodnight to you, Uncle!"

Charlie was up the basement stairs, no quieter than Iris ever managed it. Uncle's dogs at last quieted down and Andy sat dull-eyed, numbed from the noise and his cold. Charlie didn't seem to care what she said. She was brutally frank, his old art teacher Mr. Bateman might have observed. Would being like Charlie mend Andy's nerves, ease his anxieties? Maybe even grant him a welcome victory over many of those words that refused to behave? No. He was not like that. He could never be like Charlie. He cared too much about pleasing people, making them like him. Dear Grandma used to tease Andy that their family was descended from a long line of courtiers, courtesans and court jesters -- bred by their maker to please others in one way or another. But Andy's need to please was overpowering

105

and a miniature horror to be faced every day. Why did he care so much what other people thought? It was madness! All this ever accomplished was more insecurity, more doubt, more scrambling, stubborn words to chase around his stuttering tongue. He could never have been a court jester! His thoughts began to race, unstoppable, shifting jerkily back and forth, round and round.

Andy studied his awry face in the cracked mirror on his half-unhinged wardrobe door. His distorted split-image was an accurate picture of the fumbling, uncertain, coughing, wheezing, sneezing, stammering individual who now sat shivering in his bed. Alcohol wasn't the answer or was it? Nor posing like a stuck-up English gentleman when he returned to California. (He could never ever mimic an English accent!) Particularly where confrontations with the Law were included. This was perilous and impossible. Being a bull in a china shop like Charlie was not his way either. It went against the grain. Ha! Against what grain? Did he actually have a grain? If he had, he hadn't found it. Not even the cowardly beginnings of a grain. Meanwhile, he'd try hard to imagine himself as his own heroic Leander -- swimming. After a moment or two of this, his Hellespont myth usually eased him. He loved to swim. The idea of water was soothing. Particularly the warm water of that particular part of the world. He'd go to Greece one day, forsake the swimming pool for the azure Aegean. Leander Riley himself had never offended Aphrodite and provoked her tempest. He'd be safe there. But no. Greece would no longer exist. The coming conflagration obviously made planning for the future difficult. But if the Aegean was still around he would go there. He now felt just a little better so he rose shakily from his bed, pulled on his thickest sweater, set the volume low and placed the tone arm on Sheila's radio-gramophone.

*When I'm gone, my love*
*There will come a day*

sang The Mellow Four as Andy, coughing discreetly to assure

106

the comfort of Charlie and Reggie in their respective beauty-sleeps at the top of the house; one woman almost scarily confident, the other suggestible. He got out a pen and an airmail letter pad, climbed back into bed and began.

*Dearest Mother, I've got the flu or something or I would have written sooner. Could you send me some effervescent Vitamin C? Effervescent C is very expensive over here and I don't think I can afford it. Incidentally, could you send me my little Uncle Sam figure? I'd like to give it to my land-lady who collects dolls of all nations. You'd love my room…*

Andy stopped writing, looked about his run-down, shabby ice-box of a room: the confused ivy twisting from the splashing, rain-sodden light-well, the wall of nearly inaudible buzzing, quietly clicking meters, the wounded Chair, the worn carpet over the more worn linoleum floor, his distorted image in the cracked mirror of the wardrobe, those roots, white as an albino chicken! -- he'd tended chickens for his dear, departed Grandma. But these actual roots, growing through and from under the floorboard were now up and almost over either side of the little gas fire! Had they grown since he came here? In so little time? Was he imagining this?! Were these roots crazily stimulated by the alien, new heat of his borrowed kerosene stove? Nobody here noticed! Or minded! "G-G-G-Goddamn it!" whispered Andy into his blankets and laughed how goddamn-it felt strange in his mouth, particularly under a blanket. His laugh became a heavy fit of coughing which he dutifully muffled as Uncle's dogs began to bark.

Dearest Mother, wrote Andy, the English are different from us... But not in a necessarily bad way, his mind went on to say, lest it offend the forty-five million or more British people whose island he'd recently begun to share. Wonderful people, the British, he declared in his head for good measure, in case God or a hovering, surreal anglophile happened to be listening. And just as nice as any American person could ever hope to be! He added, to be on the safe side. Was this the beginning of acute paranoia?! "God! I h-hope not!" he said aloud. "Who am I afraid of? W-What am I afraid of? M-M-M-Missiles!" he shouted beneath the bedclothes. "Russian atomic f-f-fucking m-missiles! That's w-what I'm f-f-fucking afraid of!" And he seldom said 'fuck', at least out loud.

Andy's electricity meter whirred to zero, clicked and the 'Mellow Four' stopped singing and his light went out. Just like the millions of other lights that would soon be going out all over the world. Some schadenfreude comfort here -- he knew the exact meaning of this wonderful word too, damn it! Why must he defend himself from himself?! Granddad once had friendly relations with a kind German lady and learned a few German words which he gladly shared with Andy.

Andy's family on Granddad's side were members of an illustrious family only temporarily in decline but their vocabulary was and would remain top-notch. Just like The Blind Girl's hearing! Andy's family, he knew would all rise again somehow. Whether the coming conflagration allowed it or not! Andy also knew he was not making sense just now. Even in his present semi-sickly state he knew he was bluffing. Nothing could or would survive! He did not have to switch on the radio for this gruesome truth. Anyhow, the radio wouldn't work with no electricity.

Andy put away his airmail paper, sat warily in the dim light of the strange, nearly-root-encircled gas fire, whispered, "Goodnight, dearest Mother," and shielded his mouth and coughed yet again -- another small, unnaturally controlled cough that gave him little relief. But he preferred to battle a wrenching tickle in his throat rather than risk being a nasty midnight bother to others. If he was a bother, they would not like him.

God! Does it never stop raining?! Andy hunched listening to the gushing, overflowing rain gutters lining the light-well just outside his window. A window that could not ever -- for the intruding ivy that grew through its not quite closed top edge -- could not ever be completely closed and the mad, missile-crammed world beyond could never be thoroughly shut out. Not never, not no how. Not unless one took a machete knife and savagely cut away the ivy and slammed the window shut -- a contradictory deed for any gentle, desperately self-conscious, tall, string-bean individual like Leander Riley. But the world would soon change, and desperate times called for desperate measures! Being able to wield a machete knife would be an 'added plus' -- as Granddad used to tease him -- in this new, violent world – what was left of it. But Andy instinctively knew he would instantly, though accidentally, awkwardly, cut himself on this frighteningly unfamiliar weapon against his upstart ivy.

The little gas fire failed as his gas meter now clicked off. A sixpence didn't go very far. Maybe he should use a shilling next time? The 'paraffin' fire had long ago given up. But a streetlamp cast the palest glow into his rushing, rain-swollen light-well. Andy closed his eyes and dozed. His last waking thought was about machete knives. Would they be necessary? Could he take a course on handling them? Not enough time. And time -- Granddad had always told him -- time was of the essence.

# 14

Iris's flushed, red face was again far too close to me for comfort so I backed my head as far as possible into my two lumpy pillows.

"Miss Pofford is ever so upset!" said Iris, slamming down Andy's breakfast tray, "She don't like foreign devils in her premeeses. She seen a foreign devil which came out of the bathroom at Number 12 after bathin' this morning! Oh, she was ever so upset! A foreign devil, she says to me, in my premeeses!"

"F-F-Foreign devil?!" I said, and pulled my head back into my pillow till it smacked the ever cold, ever perspiring wall.

"A Frenchie! A Frenchie he was! Bon Joore! he said, the cheeky devil, Bon Joore as big as life! The cheeky foreign devil!"

"F-French?" I said.

"Yes. And that's foreign and if you laid him on a sheet you'd know he'd been there! Here he was, bathin'! Bathin' in our bathroom just like he belonged there! It wasn't even his bleedin' bathin' day! That foreign devil!"

I covered my mouth, coughed gently, said "I'm f-f-f-foreign too, Iris."

"It ain't the same," said Iris, finally pulling her face away from mine and straightening up and scratching in the armpit of her blue nylon uniform, "It ain't the same. You're a Yank. You Yanks are almost like us."

"Are w-we?"

"Almost."

"How d-did he get in?" I asked as this could be a problem. I halfway wondered if this foreign devil was Yves. He was French and he'd been here. And maybe, this time, you could tell it by the sheets if... He might easily have gone out the back door, through the nettles and taken a bath. If there was any hot water. This did not seem at all likely but lately I was beginning to think that anything that possibly could, probably would happen here -- twice! Everything seemed, just like the hostile world outside, to be in a scary flux. I didn't like flux.

Iris just stood there, a finger to her lip, looking exceedingly puzzled. I tried again. "How d-did he get in, Iris?"

"Miss Pofford thinks it's that Irene woman here at Number

13. The one which models in 'er altogether. Shockin' 'n' it?! That Irene woman and her Frenchie was in the bathroom cavortin'. Miss Pofford heard 'em! She didn't know what he was doin' nor sayin' as she don't speak their lingo! They used up all the hot water we got hotted up for Uncle as it's his bath day! They used up all the poor Blind Girl's soap which she left behind by mistake as she don't see, you see, and didn't view it! And there was the stinkin' smells of alcohol lingerin' in the steamin' air! Miss Pofford was ever so upset! She says to me, I-rees, she says, there was a foreign devil in our very own tub bathin' and drinkin' and if you laid him on a sheet you'd know he'd been there! Oh, Miss Pofford was ever so upset!"

It was then I seriously wondered if Miss Pofford had ever said even half as much as Iris reported. Iris looked thoughtful, scratched again at her armpit, dropped her arm and shot a small whiff of her body odour my way. I took a big swig of tea to counteract it and coughed mid-swallow. My mouthful of tea sprayed over the bedclothes and was extremely embarrassing and Iris leaned close again – too close as usual, and grinned.

"We're havin' our Outin' today, Andy. Miss Pofford and me and The Boy and The Blind Girl and old Uncle. It's ever so nice. They send us a special auto from the garage in Boar's Hill and we go tourin'. It's ever so nice, tourin', as Miss Pofford says. Pity it's rainin'. No schoolsy-woolsy, then? Poorly then?"

"P-P-poorly," I said, and sneezed and felt dizzy. My razor cut finger throbbed. Now I had two lousy fingers to deal with. One shaking. One aching. It almost made me laugh to think about it, specially in rhyme.

"What you need is wooly knickers, Old Andy."

When, I wondered, did I become old Andy?

"The gentleman as was here before you had wooly knickers but was rushed out on a stretcher all the same. Died in a ambulance. Which is lucky for you as you got his room, you see, you bein' late for term and all. Miss Pofford says you was lucky bein' late and all, as you got the dead gentleman's room and not only that but you got the poor bugger's bathrobe and umbrella as well! You was lucky!"

"Even if my room is below s-sea-level?" I said and I knew right away I shouldn't have said this because Iris gulped and her eyes shot daggers at me. "Who said that?!"

It was not a polite thing for me to say under the circumstances. No one is completely comfortable below sea-level. I sure wouldn't be! Not unless I was surrounded by mile-high dikes. Iris was just trying to tell me that I was a lucky guy. Even if I didn't think so. But I felt 'poorly' so I added, cruelly, I am ashamed to say, "A qua-qualified architect s-s-said" – Charlie's architectural credentials were just around the corner so it wasn't a total lie – "that this room is below s-s-s-sea-level."

This was too much for Iris and she exploded! It really scared me because although I was at least a foot taller she had bigger arm muscles than I did!

"It is no such thing!" she yelled, "Who said that?! Who said that this room is below sea-level?! Who?! Who was it, then, said that?! Who?!"

I whispered "I am not r-revealing my s-s-sources." I did not want to get Charlie in trouble and I was certain that Iris could make things tough on someone she didn't like. But I was unable to stop myself -- I was feverish -- and I added: "This p-p-person also s-said that Oxford is built in a s-s-s-swamp! Like Cambridge!"

Iris's eyes went wide. "Oh, if Miss Pofford ever heard them awful words she'd be ever so upset! Us livin' in a stinkin' swamp and all. Like Cambridge even!"

Iris suddenly looked exceedingly sad and I felt rotten. Is this what happened when you asserted yourself? If it was I didn't want any part of it. Better to be like a reed in the wind or even a floor mat. People would like you better if they could wipe their feet on you, and if you didn't insult their homelands or start fights with them. It was more comfortable. At least for a nervous coward like me with a crazy little finger. And another finger rotting off like some mad bastard! Very awkwardly put, Andy!

"I'm s-sorry, Iris," I said, "I c-can't tell you who s-said it but I talk to everybody. Everybody comes down here at night to put s-s-s-shillings in their meters. They all s-say you l-lose their m-meter m-money at Bingo tables in Little C-C-Clarendon s-s-street."

This just popped out. I was nuts! I was not able to stop myself! I felt more rotten even than my infected finger! But it just popped out. It was my feverish, run-down physical condition. I coughed quietly a few times to sort of cover up my shame and maybe even earn a little sympathy. Dear Granddad would have been chagrined. I felt really awful to be so – I don't even know a word to describe behavior so disgusting. Maybe a sneaking sonofabitch or something equally as awful? Isn't that just like me? Not having the right word? Even if I had the word I probably couldn't get it out of my goddamned mouth. Here I was, mentally swearing! Anyhow I felt exceedingly rude and now I knew it was not just due to my cold or flu or whatever it was. I had discovered I was not a nice person. Plus I was losing my marbles.

"Who said that?!" said Iris, "Who said I lost their shillings and sixpences at Bingo?!"

"Is it t-t-true?" I asked as I now suddenly began to go overboard for poor Iris and wanted to give her every opportunity to defend herself because I knew just how she felt. I feel exactly that same way many, many times a day -- insecure. Especially now in these uncertain times. I thought that if I did not stop thinking about this I would start crying. This was terrible. So I coughed again, very careful to muffle my mouth under a sheet so as not to disturb Charlie or Regina. But they had already gone out to work. I heard them! I heard their footsteps right over my head!

So what is it with me? Am I crazy? Have I become a Freudian Nightmare? My dear Grandma once called my dear Granddad a Freudian Nightmare because he had a distant cousin who really was an authentic Freudian Nightmare and was confined in a mental home -- that's what Grandma called it -- a mental home and not a 'Funny Farm' or an insane asylum as she did not want to rub it in. Anyhow, Granddad was not very happy about it because he felt that insanity might actually run in our family and it hung over his head, he said, like Damocles' Sword.

Grandma apologized later to Granddad and said that she loved him more than life itself and that she was convinced by her research that no one else in our family had the least possibility of going nuts and I believed her. So did Granddad as Grandma never told a lie to my knowledge. She was only influenced by that film, 'Spellbound.' It starred Gregory Peck who played a guy who was totally nuts, and my favorite actress of all time, Ingrid Bergman, who played his sensationally fraught lady-psychiatrist. Even if Miss Bergman, in real life, was married to one man and simultaneously had a child out of wedlock with another and was thrown out of the good old USA she was still my favorite actress. She probably got thrown out only because she had earlier played a devout nun in that corny Bing Crosby film, 'The Bells of St Mary's' and the USA Congress strongly felt that devout nuns should not have illegitimate babies so they passed some crazy immorality regulation and threw her out. Anyhow, she remained my favorite actress of all time. Possibly because she looked a heck of a lot like my own extraordinarily beautiful Mother, Marian Jane, who might even have been more beautiful than Ingrid. That is saying a lot!

I always thought this terrible scandal was Miss Bergman's husband's fault because he knew very well she was pregnant by another but he wouldn't divorce her and allow her to marry the Italian movie director of her choice who knocked her up. I always take the ladies' side for they are the weaker sex, said my Granddad. I also feel deeply for girls in trouble. So did Grandma. She always gave money at Christmas to the Salvation Army because they support the accidentally pregnant. Grandma knew what that meant. Granddad did too. He made me promise to never mention it and confided in me once that he had almost got a girl pregnant out of wedlock but they were married just in time. They would have been married long before but their whole town was marooned in the worst blizzard in the history of Kansas and people were trapped in their homes for nearly a month. I knew that this girl was Grandma herself, due to what Mother told me, and that the baby turned out to be my poor old dad who never had any advantages in life because his older cousins always picked on him and he did not finish the fourth grade but had, according to my Granddad, the brains of a Nobel Laureate. I cannot honestly vouch for this because I never knew my father as he was around only long enough to inseminate Mother and was immediately drafted from his war-plant-guard job and shipped overseas in the last months of WW2. He died somewhere in the Pacific. A hero's death. At least somebody in our family was a hero. Besides Granddad who was involved in a hush-hush incident in the Panama Canal Zone and came out smelling like a rose. Though I am not familiar with the details. It was Top Secret and Granddad was never a divulger of Top Secrets. I like to believe that dear Granddad was a counterspy for the USA and was too heroic to admit it. I always felt they should have given Granddad a bigger pension for all that undercover work.

But I digress. Iris was still here and staring at me like I was crazy and still hurting from my harsh and callous remarks.

"The Russian ships has surrounded Spain," said Iris and took a butter-stained envelope from her blue nylon uniform pocket and handed it to me. "Your post," she said, "And Miss Pofford says you're to have sprouts and potatoes and a bit of ham later as you're poorly. Free of charge, she says to say. Nothing due with the rent. Free of charge. Miss Pofford said that. She said for me to say that. To you. And I did."

"And I th-thank you and Miss P-P-Pofford."

*Leander Riley, 13 Wilton Street, 'by hand'*

I opened the butter-stained envelope as Iris, accompanied by the awful racket of Uncle's curses and barking dogs, clomped up the basement stairs. She didn't stay because she already knew what was in my letter. As usual, she'd read it. The butter stains and forced envelope-flap were mute testimony.

*Dear Leander Riley,*
*Strictly as a matter of mythological/legendary interest,*
*did you know that your name, "Leander", derives from*

115

*an ancient Greek myth in which you, Leander, against*
*seemingly insurmountable odds, i.e., a torrential storm and*
*gigantic waves, attempt to swim the "Hellespont" to be*
*reunited with your beloved, the high-priestess "Hero"? You*
*are, of course, drowned in this attempt and your lover, the*
*aforementioned high-priestess, kills herself. It is, of course,*
*all the fault of the madly-jealous, "Aphrodite." If you care*
*to know more about your namesake, please do not hesitate*
*to contact me as I am a classical scholar determined to one*
*day become a  permanent fixture in Ancient Mythological*
*Academia.*
*Yours, in the ever bursting bosom of finer things,*
*Marcella Fisk-Barrett-Smyth,*
*Lady Marian Hall. Oxford.*

*Ps.  I sat four places to the right of you on your first and, it*
*seems, only day of Life Drawing at the Rossetti. I hope you*
*have not been inordinately ill and shall return to us rather*
*sooner than later. Further, do not construe this letter as*
*flirtation, as some might do, i.e., that Sheila woman. I am*
*desperately interested in individuals from other nations,*
*particularly in these especially stressful times and am*
*seminally drawn to individuals whose names are celebrated*
*in ancient song and story.*

*For your information, I wore a turquoise blue angora*
*cardigan and green and yellow American-Indian beads and*
*a heavy Tweed skirt and long, extra-coarse, wool stockings*
*-- not necessarily stylish but warm indeed and unquestion-*
*ably practical at this impossible latitude.*

*Do you like poetry? I have recently founded a poetry*
*reading group at LMH. We meet every Friday afternoon.*
*Interested?!*

I put down the letter, drank some tea and stared for a very
long time at the now wrinkled yolk of a fried egg Iris had set
beside me. I remembered Marcella embarrassing me by shouting
my name at the Rossetti immediately before she began arguing

with Sheila over the use of a vacant easel but poetry readings sounded interesting and Marcella might, as a determined classical scholar, shed more detail on my mythological namesake. I was open to all new ideas as long as they weren't upsetting. Or too loud -- and when I didn't feel inordinately jumpy. But I seriously wondered if I was ever going to be able to summon the physical, and most of all, mental strength to leave my cold, dark, dank, but safe little room. I was beginning to think I was on the verge of becoming seriously obsessed!

# 15

"I-REES!" shouted Miss Pofford through the thinness.

"Coming, Miss Pofford," echoed from somewhere in the house. I heard the back door slam and wondered if nettles ever hindered Iris in her daily duties. Had wondered earlier, before the reality of them stared me in the face. There really were nettles there to hinder ones approach to the back door of our sister-house, Number 12, and its exceedingly basic bathing facilities.

I am too gullible. That is one of my multi-numerous character defects. I guess there is no remedy for gullibility but getting more experience in life -- if the terrifying international circumstances permit it. I needed to be, as Granddad used to say, tempered by fire. Maybe we would all be. Not only tempered by fire or even, as Walter Pater said, burning with a hard, gemlike flame. No! We'd all be scorched to a sodding crisp! And soon!

There was a knock at my door. Not exactly a knock, more of a sliding-thump.

"C-C-Come in." I said in a very friendly manner considering my present subterranean mental circumstances. There was no answer, so I opened the door and there was Nola sitting on the last basement stair gazing up at me with a terrible frown.

"Are y-you all r-right?" I said, as I helped her into an upright position. She glared at me "Of course I am all right. I was restin'. My knees gave out."

"M-May I help you up?"

"If you must! Where's my stick?!"

"Your w-w-what?"

"My stick!"

Nola was extremely annoyed! She pointed to her cane just out of reach on the floor beside her. I was happy to have this mystery solved so soon. "Oh," I said, "your c-cane!"

"If you say so, dear," she said, calming down a little bit. "Be so kind and hand it to me, please."

I handed her 'stick' to her and said, "This is what we c-call a c-c-cane."

"Well, it's a stick! You can help me up now, duckie. I'm ready."

I got Nola back on her 'stick' and she saw and headed directly for The Chair but I intervened and led her to the only other chair in the room. I then had a terrible attack of coughing. Nola squinted at me for a moment and seemed concerned. It was comforting to think someone might care even in this brusque way.

"The last boy lived here died. Or was it the old man just before him died? Yes? No! They both died! One after the other with hardly a decent interval between. That was it, wasn't it? Sad, that."

"Very s-s-s-sad," I said, as I totally agreed with her and hoped that this was not to be my fate too. I coughed again for emphasis.

"You were very kind to me and Vera, the other day when we were in distress. But now you see as how it's all happened again and Iris has reverted to her robber's ways. Oh, but I do apologise, Andy, I was very rude just now, wasn't I? I just see red when Iris behaves like this to Vera and me with our knees. I become the devil hisself!"

Nola pulled a handful of shillings from her cardigan pocket and handed them to me, "Could you do the honours, love? Divide them like last time between the gas and electric so Vera and me can have our cosy fire and some reading too, after the sun goes down. As you so kindly came to our rescue before, we did not dare to call on you again in our distress. So Vera and me drew straws and I lost. But I paid for it, didn't I ?" she said, massaging by turns her heavily cotton-stockinged knees.

I pushed the shillings into their gas and electric meter boxes and they clicked to life and Nola let out a great sigh of relief. "Bless you, dear! Vera will be so pleased. She's waitin' to light our gas fire as we speak!"

"I t-told you before that I w-would be very happy to f-feed your m-meters for you, N-Nola. Anytime. I'd be v-very happy to..."

But Nola wasn't listening. She was gazing sadly around my basement bed-sitter. She pointed at The Chair where I sat shivering, subtly balancing myself on its three legs.

"That is my chair," she said, "the chair you are sittin' on. Or rather it was my Floyd's chair. A heirloom, it was, and in his family for at least fifty years and my Floyd gave it to me on our wedding day."

"I-REES!" suddenly exploded through the thinness! I jumped, The Chair flipped, exposing its broken leg and dropped me on the floor and Nola began to cry. "It was such a beautiful chair then! All four legs functioned like they was clockwork! It was my heirloom!" she sobbed.

"NOLA! Is that Nola?! How are your knees, love?!" came pouring sympathetically from the thinness.

"I am sorry to say there has been no change, Miss Pofford! None whatsoever!"

"Well, keep your pecker up, dear! If you see Iris tell her she's in trouble and will get no pink cake for one week!"

"S-S-S-She's not here Miss P-P-P-Pofford!" I volunteered into the thinness, "But we'll be s-s-s-s-sure to tell her!"

"What did you say?! Speak up, boy!"

"I s-s-s-said we'll be s-s-s-sure to tell her!"

"Thank you! Get well, Andy!"

It was very nice of Miss Pofford to comment on my rapidly declining health. Nola dabbed her eyes and blew her nose in a hanky and moaned when she saw her split reflection in the cracked mirror of my broken wardrobe door. "That wardrobe was my Floyd's too! And these carpets, what's left of 'em!" She scuffed her bedroom-slippered foot over the ragged carpet. "I could weep with shame."

I was hoping she wouldn't. Not so soon anyhow. I was depressed enough already. But it is our duty as human beings to listen carefully to the woes of others and comfort them when we can. If we're lucky they will do the same because we will all soon need each other in the worst ways. I well remember my school's Atomic War Survival classes.

"My only consolation is that my Floyd is not alive to witness this. He passed away a week after we were wed. We were like ships that passed in the night but dear Floyd left his cargo with me. Our Dennis was born exactly nine months after Floyd died.

Floyd's been gone for donkey's years but our Dennis is a great comfort to Vera and me. Though Dennis never married."

Nola's eyes shifted to the light-well where the rain continued. It was now torrential, gushing over the rain gutters and down the ivy covered bricks. "When they brought me here to live I came with all of Floyd's family's furniture which was stored here in this very basement and which has over the years been pilfered away. Piece by piece. Iris is a clever one and no mistake! I think she sold it on the black market!"

"I'd be happy to take c-c-care of your m-meters for you..."

"She lives the high life, does Iris, on her shady Bingo winnings from our meter money. Ill-gotten gains, I call it! Blood-money sucked from the miserable suffering of our poor knees, me and Vera's! Blood-money!"

"L-Leave your m-meter m-m-money, Nola. I'll m-make sure it's..."

"Oh we couldn't do that, love! Iris has always put the money in the meters, hasn't she? When she does, I hasten to add. She always has and that's that, ain't it? Iris is a poor foundling and must find joy where she can."

"I s-s-s-suppose s-so," I said. I was stymied.

"If you'll do the honours, duckie, and see me out?" I helped her up and out my door and Uncle's dogs started to bark. "Who the hell's out there?!" shouted Uncle through his door.

"It's only Nola, Uncle."

"Hello, Nola, me old love!"

"Hello, Uncle!"

"How you keepin' girlie"?

"They haven't buried me yet, Uncle! But they could bury my goddamned knees and I wouldn't give a toss!"

"Let me know when they do, darlin' and I'll be there!"

Nola laughed merrily and Uncle's dogs began again, this time howling too.

"Belt up, you puking bitches!" bellowed Uncle and they were quiet. I insisted, despite my horrible cough and weak condition, on escorting Nola to her door. When I returned to my room "Andy! Andy!" came sailing through my window.

# 16

Andy coughed several times into a heavy sweater, pulled it on and went, in his sagging underwear, to the window and looked up. There at the top of the light-well, leaning against the iron railing in the pouring rain was Sheila.

"I didn't know you were ill until today!" she called down, "I've been up to London with Daddy. I made him buy me a stereo gramophone. I've missed you so! God! Let me in! I'm perishing, darling! I'm positively drowning!"

"I'm p-poorly! I'm in b-bed!"

"No, you're not! I can see you perfectly! You're in your underpants! We've no Life Classes today. Irene is laid up. Someone said she was at the Radcliffe for tests or something. They couldn't find another model so here I am completely at your disposal!"

"Th-Thanks for coming over," called Andy up the light-well, "I'll s-see you when I come back to The R-Rossetti!"

Andy was terrified she'd rip off her clothes and jump straight into his bed again. He wasn't up to it. He hadn't yet properly learned how to handle this possibly glorious event and he felt too ill to try just now.

"Let me in! It's pissing rain! Pissing!"

"I'm p-p-poorly! I m-might infect you!"

"What?!"

"I'm p-p-poorly! S-S-Sick!"

"I know that! that's why I'm here, you imbecile! To care for you! I'm bearing a bloody heavy care-package! I've got pork pies and custard tarts and…"

"I'm p-p-p-poorly! The world is about to end! P-P-P-P-Please go away!"

"Leander! You b-b-b-bastard!" She turned on her heel and splashed into a puddle, cursed, slammed through the little iron gate that could have used a good rust treatment, thought Andy, and a lick of new paint.

On towering heels Sheila, cursing, clacked up Wilton Street through pouring rain to flag down her father's chauffeur who had pulled over for a cigarette. Andy wondered why she'd worn such inappropriate shoes considering the weather, and decided this was a cruel thought – she had only wanted to help him. But by throwing his immaturity in his face?! Well. He felt guilty for the next five minutes anyhow. But he also felt that this post puberty dilemma with a female had at least kept his mind off you-know-what. But referring to the Crisis as you-know-what, was nuts in itself and he knew it.

Andy was on the edge of a 'sensationally' personal nuclear melt-down! Too much had happened in too little time and he knew he was too immature to assimilate it all. Sheila had revealed himself to himself! To top it off, he was poorly!

Suddenly, from the corner of his eye, Andy was certain he had seen one of his tiny floorboard roots confidently stiffen and move closer to the ornate, iron-edged top of his gas fire for a snuggle. Who wouldn't have? It was warmer there!

Iris watched Sheila's noisy departure from the second floor where she stood hoovering Irene's empty room. She hoped Irene might stay away, might take her foreign devil with her and never come back. Foreign devils in her premeeses made Miss Pofford ever so angry. When Miss Pofford was angry, Iris got swatted. It wouldn't do to have Miss Pofford too angry for too long. It did sting a bit but far less than Miss Pofford knew because crafty Iris always pretended that it was worse than it was. Miss Pofford was always sorry afterwards and gave Iris that pink cake with strawberry filling, sometimes even ice cream. After the strawberry cake Iris would trot herself down to Little Clarendon Street and gleefully lose no less than four shillings-sixpence from the meter money. No less than four shillings-sixpence! Every bleedin' time! She smiled into the rain spattered window. It was almost worth it. No. It was worth it. Sometimes, though not often, she actually won four shillings-sixpence. And she never, ever wasted her ill-got gains on meter money for anybody. Anybody at all! Revenge was sweet. But not for poor Gladys. The Blind Girl was Iris's usual victim because she would never tell on Iris.

From the rain-spattered window just above hoovering Iris stood Regina, the red-eyed, tear-stained 'Reggie', wondering too, if it was worth it – her stormy relationship with Charlie the almost accredited asphalt-architect. Regina had come home early. She half-thought she'd pack her clothes, disappear, and that would be it. But she couldn't just yet. She hadn't made up her mind. So she sat down, stared into the rain, saw Sheila as she stumbled out the little gate over watery cobblestones and into her chauffeur's car in those inappropriate shoes with Andy's 'care-package.' Reggie had heard it all -- lifted her window a crack and heard everything drifting up from Andy's light-well. You couldn't miss it. What on earth was wrong with Andy? Sheila was a dish! Indeed, a dish fit for a queen! Curly blond Andy was dishy himself in an astonishing, tall and bony sort of way. Funny he didn't seem toknow he was attractive -- but attractive, of course, for that very reason.

Charlie had better, if I do decide to stay, thought Reggie, Charlie had better keep me away from the Yank! I've a penchant for Yanks. Especially blond, dishy, very young, tall, gangly and totally unaware Yanks. "I'm suggestible!" whispered Reggie. "Says Charlie!" She laughed but was suddenly stunned by her anguished reflection in the streaming window and whispered "I love only Charlie in the whole wide world! Why do I torture her? I don't mean it. I never mean it!" She wiped her eyes, frowned at Iris's noisy hoovering in Irene's room below. It was never quiet here! That alone was reason enough to flee. She knew she now made enough to live on her own, just. She hoped Irene was all right. She liked Irene. Irene was an attractive woman. Reggie chuckled, wondered if... dropped it, turned from the window as she heard Charlie bounding up the stairs. Why was Charlie here and not at work? Of course, Charlie had rung Reggie's office. Was it time, now, for their confrontation?

Vera and Nola, their four gammy knees exposed in a tight row, sat reading before their gas fire, Vera, a very serious novel, Nola, a newspaper faithfully brought up each day by the friendly news agent just over the road before he opened his shop. MORE RUSSIAN SHIPS HEAD FOR U.S. BLOCKADE! blared the headlines. "Oh my," said Nola, holding up the first page for Vera, "We're for it now."

"Not to worry, dear," said Vera looking up from her novel, "We'll win. We always do. After a bit."

"We're in a pretty pickle if we don't," said Nola, "with our notorious infirmities!"

"But you've lovely, tiny feet, Nola. Lovely, tiny and surprisingly strong feet. You could walk to the end of the world on 'em, dear. You must take comfort in that."

"Oh, I do, love! A very old friend once asked if my tiny feet had been bound at birth in the ancient Chinese fashion as nothing else could account for their delicate design. His exact words."

"I know, dear," said Vera behind her book. "You've said."

"I have?"

"Yes, and I'm not at all surprised," said Vera, "It is quite true. Your feet have always been a tiny wonder. "

"Thank you, Vera, how very kind. That gentleman slipped letters through my slot for a year. Until he was run down by a lorry and died instantly. His sister, who was with him at the time, wrote that she herself escaped without a scratch but lost a shoe. I suppose I've told you that as well?"

"Yes. What a sad but lovely remembrance it is." said Vera.

"But incomplete. I cannot remember the poor man's name," added Nola. "Or his grieving sister's.

"Nor can I," said Vera, "It's been donkey years."

"And now we've nothing but war, war, and rumours of war! Intercontinental atomic missiles to boot!"

"Not to worry, love," said Vera, "We've got our own missiles. Quite a few if I'm not mistaken. We've also got the Yanks and they've got even more and isn't Andy a lovely boy?"

"Oh, yes," said Nola, "So helpful and polite for a Yank."

"He's masses more considerate than your Dennis, isn't he, love? Or my darling Herbert was, rest his shady soul."

"My Dennis is a good boy. He loves his Mum!"

"Oh, I wasn't saying he didn't love you, Nola. I only meant

that he's not as thoroughly considerate as he might be, considering our health and all."

"Now that, I will grant you," said Nola, with a tiny frown, "That I will grant you."

A steaming tea beside her, Gladys The Blind Girl, cosily tucked up in her bed and smiling all the while listened to The Archers on her almost new radio, a gift from Irene who'd found it at an Oxfam thrift shop whose manager owed Irene a certain favour. Then the flame in her gas fire sputtered, hissed out. Yet again no money in the meter. Iris had been warned before by Miss Pofford and should be, by Gladys's reckoning, clearly at the end of her tether. Never mind, Iris would be back soon to collect the breakfast trays. Gladys would spring it on her then, through appropriate threats of revealing all to Miss Pofford. In vain, of course and which she firmly knew she would never do. Iris knew this too. Besides, Gladys even preferred now to do it herself since the young Yank had come. It forced her from her room of a rainy evening and a couple of words with the boy was a tonic.

Truth be told, Gladys's fate hung directly in Iris's hands, not Miss Pofford's. Gladys was wise in the ways of these two houses, 12 and 13. She knew precisely on which side of her cold, dry toast the butter lay and who else would bring her steaming cups of tea and even the occasional wedge of pink cake or a biscuit when she didn't feel up to joining the others in the telly room? Of course, if Iris continued to be remiss with her meter-monitoring, Gladys might now, in extremis that is, when poorly, depend on the polite young Yankee boy. Andy was about the age her own boy was when he died at Normandy on D-Day. It would be nice to depend, however briefly, upon another boy who might, had fate allowed, have been her own.

Uncle, a grossly overfed, clogged-eyed mongrel on his lap, sat sprinkling flea powder behind its floppy ears. After each application he pressed his mouth close and blew the powder deep into the thick, shiny black dog hair. The other dog, scratching now and then, watched anxiously, as though she knew it was her turn next.

Iris had a tender spot amidst her rough bravado. It was reserved for The Boy whom she now bathed with a touch so gentle it might have come from an angel's hand; certainly not the work-hardened, dirty-nailed fingers of Miss Pofford's dogsbody.

Charlie stood in the doorway. "Reggie?" she said, "Reggie, love?"

Reggie didn't speak, wiped her eyes, then, after a moment, "I came home early. Had a headache. Came home early for a rest."

"I rang your office," said Charlie, now sitting at their small desk. After a long moment Reggie answered, "I know."

"I love you, Reggie," said Charlie and rose.

Reggie rushed into Charlie's arms and was lifted high in the air and dropped on their bed.

"I'll never leave you, Charlie, never!"

"I know, love," Charlie smiled, sat on the bed close beside her. "I know." Charlie cracked her knuckles twice. They laughed.

The Honourable Mr. Cyril Lemmington, he of the bloodshot eyes and occasional Forence Nightingale demeanour, stood combing his lank, long, brown hair in his rain-streaming window. He too had heard Andy's altercation with irate Sheila. One could hardly have missed it, especially one so attentive as he to the goings-on at Number 13 Wilton Street. Particularly when he was bored shitless. He too had experienced similar recent altercations with two equally irate young women and at least one young man whose name he couldn't recall just now but which was often at the tip of his only occasionally forked tongue. He was at heart a good Samaritan and there were, too, occasional fringe benefits.

He splashed from a hand basin into his eyes, hoped cold water might ease those intricate scarlet-webbed patterns – they weren't attractive.  Not that he cared -- but he did. He knew drink was the culprit and the only solution, abstinence, which he was not inclined to practise. One needed willpower to lay off the sauce. He knew himself. Willpower wasn't an option.

Cyril wasn't worried about the impending world war. Alcohol saw to that. Best be blotto when bloody bombs battered ones bum to bits. He loved his whimsical way with words, and wondered if he might just be a wee bit more clever than he thought. This cheered him. For a moment. Because he didn't actually believe it. Only wondered. It was good to keep an open mind. He smiled, snatched a small, flat bottle of gin from beneath a stack of greyish, white underwear, unscrewed it, partook. Partook again. And yet again drank up the last of his rent money. But Mummy and Pa were generous. His gas fire flared and hissed out. He swore, decided on a trip downstairs to Andy. How was the Yank -- who owed him a couple of shillings for his meter -- faring?

# 17

"I wanted to th-thank you again for looking after m-me the other night," said Andy.

"Think nothing of it. You owe me two shillings, meter money."

"In my p-pocket," said Andy, "On The Ch-Chair. There's a whole bunch of s-s-sixpences."

Cyril helped himself, wound four sixpences into his gas meter, and took two of Andy's cigarettes from a packet on the floor.

"Mind?"

"N-no."

Cyril lit up, offered one to Andy who shook his head, said, "They'll s-s-s-start me coughing."

Cyril stuck the other cigarette behind his ear for afters. "Regina molested you yet?"

"She's s-s-suggestible," said Andy and coughed, would have smiled but it hurt.

"Wild horses couldn't have dragged her off me. Charlie has got her hands full, never mind the gender. Regina's appetites are universal. Watch out for Charlie, too. Though the object of her affection is more focussed, she lacks judgment and will defend Reggie with her life if need be. A winning, though risky combination, that."

Cyril sucked on his cigarette, exhaled through his nose and lay back in The Chair, nearly upsetting it. He righted himself and took an envelope from his pocket, "This came through the door this morning. You do look a bit better."

Andy coughed again, said "I'm n-not. I don't think I'll leave this p-place alive."

He meant it, thought Cyril, but he said "Well whatever. I'm going upstairs to shut my eyes. Got in rather late last night. Knock me up if you feel like a coffee later."

"Knock you up?!" said Andy.

"'Wake me up'. By the way, who is this Marcella bird?"

Had Cyril been reading his mail?!

"Don't look at me," said Cyril, "Iris was reading this in the hall a moment ago. See the butter stains? She's got to read aloud to understand what she's reading. I always listen. Two letters in one day. Crikey! By hand! Who is this Marcella bird?"

Andy coughed again. Was *everything* possible here?! Every-bloody-thing?! Was simple, decent privacy a forgotten word?

"I d-don't know her."

"He doesn't know her?" said Cyril, "Two by-hand letters in a day from the same young person and he doesn't know her?"

"No, he d-doesn't," said Andy as gently as he could and coughed yet again, "I've n-never really m-met her."

"Not doing badly, are you, in your first three or four days in the mother country, having hardly set foot from your grotto. Ah, well, hands-across-the-sea. The one who screamed at you? I reckon she was here before? Monday night, I make it. What's your secret with the birdies?"

"If you are r-referring to g-g-girls, I...I..."

Andy began to cough, thought for a horrific moment he'd bring up his breakfast.

"Well?" said Cyril, rising and taking a last deep drag then stubbing out his cigarette in a spot on the wall uncomfortably near the thinness, "Your secret with the birds?"

"S-S-Secret?" said Andy and suddenly, in an odd, almost delirious way, feeling full of something alien that might even be himself -- for the first time in months, maybe years, proclaimed "I am a Y-Yank. And y-you, y-you s-s-s-sir, y-you are n-not!"

It just popped out. Andy enjoyed saying it. A lot. It just popped out, well, almost. Though it very probably was a little rude. Was he suddenly becoming...fearless? Or only rude and careless? It happened and it surprised him and he knew, which was very comforting and a sure sign of encroaching maturity, that Cyril could easily take this sharp little reversed-jest in his stride. After all, Cyril was a gentleman. Andy grinned as Cyril, chuckling, left the room.

Andy now felt the tiniest bit encouraged and proud of his surprising frankness and coughed quietly into his blanket. Then, suddenly inspired, threw off the blanket, grinned, opened his mouth as wide as he could in his sickened, straitened circumstances and delivered a fearless, hawking, shrill, and deeply satisfying though painful cough directly into the ceiling. This enormous, near mythical noise took flight on the chill, damp air and crackled through the two houses. Miss Pofford, on the kitchen side of the thinness, was so startled she dropped a dish of pink cake she was about to hand to Iris as restitution for a swat. "What the hell was that?!" she snapped, cocking her ears. For this was no ordinary sound, the sound of a truck thundering along cobbled Wilton Street or the rumble of bathroom plumbing, or even Old Uncle hurtling, once again, down the basement stairs. This was a sound she had never heard before. It was the rare noise of a staggeringly unsure young alien attempting to assert himself. It was the sound of Andy at the fragile edge of the beginning of his coming of age.

# 18

Andy sat for a while enjoying his wondrous release from self-imposed servitude as he successfully fended off a myriad of tiny arrows of guilt that struck at his new, though paper-thin, armour. After worriedly inspecting his reddening single-edged razor cut and bandaging it, he settled down to read Marcella's latest:

*Dear Andy (if I may call you so),*
*I had hardly got to my tutorial after delivering my previous*
*note to you, when I remembered that our poetry reading*
*evening had been rescheduled for tonight! Sorry!!! Mea*
*culpa! Mea maxima culpa!!! You are cordially invited.*
*We meet at the Cadena on Cornmarket for tea, circa 4.15,*
*continue from there for a delightful walk through the*
*Parks (opposite Keble College -- I'll be your personal guide*
*-- bring your umbrella!) then on to my lodgings at Lady*
*Marian Hall for readings and additional refreshments (by*
*my own hand). We often roast bread on my electric fire and*
*we've masses of homemade strawberry jam! You needn't, of*
*course, reply to this note. Just be at the Cadena (circa 4.15).*
*Yours, in haste, Marcella. PS, We wonder if you would care*
*to discuss 'A young American's reaction to the currently*
*terrifying Cuba Missile Dilemma'?*

Andy wouldn't. And what the dickens was mea maxima culpa? He knew it was Latin, he'd seen the film, 'Quo Vadis', but that was all he knew of Latin. He put down the note, was startled by a sudden sheet of rain that slashed its way through the window gap and spat on his cheek. He wiped it off on his thickest sweater's sleeve, grateful there were no witnesses to this breach of etiquette, and thought for a moment. A very peculiar moment. Then suddenly, with an almost audible crash, his self-doubt returned and whined in his ears. Whined and moaned! Nothing in his experience had equalled this! He was...poorly! He was below sea level! He was cowering in a murky cavern, imprisoned by ill health, imperilled by an international situation tragically out of control! He was deserted by his drawing ability -- his very only advantage in life! The brief confidence afforded by his revolutionary cough had disappeared like a spray deodorant. And of course it would, thought Andy, as he was actually, just gangly, skinny, flighty Andy of the nervous, spinning, left little finger, being paid back in aces by Fickle Fate for having grown, a bit too soon, a bit too big for his britches -- legendary cough or no cough! Andy had momentarily risen above it all only to be slapped down. Slapped down by himself! Repeat, Andy, now listen! -- slapped down by yourself! That's me, thought Andy, that's me all over! Know thyself, Leander, late of the Aegean sea! Paddle back to your own primitive little bathtub!

After the briefest moment Andy knew he had to cough again, could not control his raw, cold-savaged throat. After all, he was poorly and on death's bed. He was true to form in this singularly lethal subterranean venue. It was to be a big cough, a huge, basement rattling cough destined to reach Charlie and Reggie on the third floor and a lead-pipe cinch to again invade Miss Pofford's kitchen through the sinister thinness. And so it might have been, but wasn't. It was now delivered against a pillow under at least three blankets and a sheet. It was silence itself. For shame, Leander. For shame!

It had been quiet today, rainstorm and the usual random dilemmas excepted, no major disturbances from Iris, or even Uncle's dogs who often went for walks with Uncle. No atomic missiles. Yet. Number 12's Outing had been called off because of car trouble, and everyone, Andy was luckily not to know, had gathered around their telly next door and the news from Cuba was as exciting as it was frightening. But Andy left the radio off. He didn't want to know. He knew he wasn't strong enough – because cowards like himself can take weeks to recover their always suspect strength, even after his brief cough bravado, his intimate epiphany. Andy also knew that cowards die a thousand deaths, and brave men, only one. That's what Granddad says, isn't it? Via Mr. Wilde, of course. Andy well knew where he and his juvenile cowardice stood in that equation. He wondered why he hadn't got a letter from Tom. Now that was the height of stupidity! Tom is in emergency training for his flights over Cuba, maybe even Russia! I think such idiotic selfish things, he thought.

Then, in a scary reprise, and this thought was 'exceedingly' horrible; he knew  he would never be able to leave his basement until The Crisis was over. He couldn't. "I can't swim," he whispered into his blankets. "I can't swim, not in the real world -- only in swimming pools. I'll drown!" It was just then that everything began to go cock-eyed. His brain rocked in his head and when he coughed he felt it thump against the inside of his skull! His cut finger, redder than ever, throbbed. He coughed again. Where was his welcomer, Yves and his bottle? His comforting, calming welcomer, Yves, with the bourbon whisky?

# 19

He was anxious, ill and confused, but Andy slept. He didn't awaken till the rich girl, in her shabby but fasionable old fur, stood by his bed in the twilight holding over his head what appeared to be a small pile of old newspapers.

"Fish and chips," she said, "Fish and chips direct from the best shop in Oxford. I'm starved. Iris let me in. God! You look awwwwful! Hungry? Hope you're hungry. Hungry?"

Andy wiped his eyes. Didn't know where he was, who she was. It was dreamlike. Further evidence that he was losing touch. Was he actually at the Rossetti? Was he in England? Was everything that had happened in the last few days a dream? Had the horrifically thinkable occurred? Had he and every-one else on earth been incinerated in a peppering deluge of atomic missiles? Was he now but a woeful, curious spirit? And Goddamn it! His cut finger was sore!

He had been convinced he was recovering. But no, maybe not. His thoughts were scrambled eggs. That clenched it. Reality would soon fade in and out until it disappeared altogether amidst the twitching of one finger and the increasingly painful disaster of another.

Sheila knelt beside his bed, laid the fish and chips in their plentiful newspaper wrapping on the small bed table where Iris always set his breakfast. Andy watched for a moment, puzzled, but slowly focussing. Sheila! Yes, that's who she was! She was real and intact, real in his room and…pretty. Very pretty. Very, very pretty. He said, "The n-newspaper…?"

"Yes, darling?"

There it was again, 'darling'. Shouldn't the word 'darling' mean something special?

"Yes, darling?" she repeated.

"The n-newspaper the f-fish…and the French fries are w-wrapped in…?"

"French fries?" She laughed. "You mean 'chips', darling, We call them 'chips'." Sheila gazed at him, tolerant, forgiving, "The newspaper?" she repeated tenderly, intimately, "What about the newspaper?"

Andy coughed, again careful to cover the cough lest he disturb Charlie and Reggie. His new 'independence' be damned! Those women must by now be home from work and possibly even preparing for an early night's sleep. He couldn't disappoint them. They wouldn't like him.

"This n-newspaper the f-fish is wrapped in," said Andy, scanning a section that read, up to its wrinkled fold, 'RUSSIAN SHIPS ARE...' "Is this n-newspaper c-clean?"

Sheila, who was now laying the fish out on two paper plates, looked up, laughed, "You Yankees! Of course it's clean!"

"Then," said Andy, "Nobody's r-read it?" Was he being unreasonable? No, It was important. Everything is over-important to a raving maniac, the crazy person lying just now in his own deathbed.

"Of course somebody's read it!" snapped Sheila.

"If s-s-s-somebody has r-read it then they've t-t-t-touched it."

"Of course they've touched it, you idiot. You can't read a fucking newspaper without touching it, can you?!"

"Th-Then the newspaper is n-not clean, is it? N-Not hygienic."

"Look, goddamn it! Are you hungry or not?!"

"Yes," said Andy, "I g-guess so. I g-guess I'm hungry."

Sheila began to fade before his eyes until she took a steaming piece of fish from the oily newspaper, brought it to Andy's mouth, slowly slipped it in, her fingers playing at the inside of his lips. "You are hungry, aren't you?"

Andy wasn't sure. He supposed he was. He should be, shouldn't he? She was...pretty. He'd had no food since breakfast. The promised sprouts and potatoes and a bit of ham hadn't appeared. Iris was probably deep into a Bingo session in Little Clarendon Street and the nocturnal visits to his subtly clicking, clunking wall meters would soon begin again.

From her rain-wet wicker basket Sheila took a bottle of wine. "Voila!" she said, "Good stuff. Expensive. Not Spanish Graves rubbish! We brought a case. Thank God for Daddy's chauffeur!"

Andy peered sleepily at the opened case of wine under his work table as Sheila uncorked her bottle with a foldable corkscrew and in the picnic basket found two small crystal glasses, filled each to its brim with fragrant, expensive wine and handed one to Andy who had just swallowed another large bit of fish. The wine was wonderful, so soft and easy to drink that he gulped it down like water. It would be good for him. Soothing alcohol would kill all the germs that were gearing up for their final, fatal siege, as well as calm his rapidly growing, and as rapidly receding, anguish -- his ping-pong terrors. Sheila was such a comfort to this globe-trotting teenager who was ever so poorly and half-mad yet somehow lay in Andy's bed eating fish and French fries! No, Andy! Fish and chips bought and brought by a lovely girl who mysteriously calls him darling and whose name must surely be Sheila. Fish and chips served from filthy, used newspapers.

"You are supposed to savour a fine wine, darling," said Sheila who smiled and topped Andy's crystal glass with a fine wine that Andy's dear Grandparents would have understood and enjoyed. Especially as it was being served in cut-crystal glasses. Andy drank greedily, gratefully, extended his glass again as the horrors that had risen earlier in the evening diminished. Andy was now perfectly in tune with his childhood friend's alcoholic mother, her various blue bruises and all.

"M-M-May I have s-s-s-some m-more, p-p-please?" he asked, extending his glass yet again.

"Certainly, Oliver. My little Oliver Twisted!" laughed Sheila and poured Andy another crystal glassful.

# 20

I felt warm and wonderful! Sheila was beautiful and I hadn't coughed for twenty minutes – make that twenty-five. Sheila was good for me. Now. Could I be good for her? I hadn't thought of vitamin C for – I didn't know how long. A day? The food she brought, even if it was served from old newspapers, was a whole lot nicer than the English lunch I'd had on the train from Southampton; greyish boiled potatoes and over-boiled stringy meat. I felt easy and calm and friendly. I knew it was the wine. I felt the same when Yves gave me bourbon whisky. Where was Yves, the welcomer? He was nice too. In a different way. I was delirious. I knew that I was sick even if I hadn't coughed for – now it was nearly a half hour. Delirious. Yes. Why couldn't other people see this as they faded in and out before my eyes? Why couldn't they see what I saw?

"God, you are swilling it!" said Sheila, pulling out another other bottle. She sat on the edge of my bed, said, "Have you seen a doctor, darling?"

"N-No, darling," I said, taking another glassful of smooth, wondrous wine. Fine wine, I knew, was something that denoted culture and class. Granddad and Grandma always praised the virtues of finest wine though they couldn't often afford it. They liked the finer things, my dear grandparents did. This comforting loop of memory wound faithfully around in my head and repeated. It was familiar, therefore wonderful. The finer things were hard to come by on Grandma's sewing teacher's salary. Granddad's naval pension didn't amount to much. It's a pity the old United States senatorial-genes of my family tree had petered out and not branched more firmly into our small Southern California twig. Senators got huge pensions. Granddad assured me this was the case.

"Shall we call a doctor?" said Sheila leaning firmly against me.

"N-No," I said and began to feel strange. It was almost like when I put my hand on myself. I was getting hard. How could I be so sick and woozy, yet get so hard? It could be embarrassing if Sheila noticed. I drank down the last of the last of my wine and

Sheila kissed my forehead and I became even harder. It almost hurt down there. I knew Sheila could see it now, my boner, my loud lump under the blankets. I was exceedingly embarrassed! Sheila stood and began to take off her clothes. I didn't know if I should watch her or not. What could I do? I closed my eyes and thought of England.

When she was naked she slipped into the bed with me. It was very crowded but it felt good. She moved up against me and pulled down my Y-fronts then sat on me and grabbed my boner and stuck it inside her. I'm glad she did because I, myself, wouldn't have known precisely just where or how to stick it in there. But I pushed deep as it seemed like it was the right, though embarrassing, thing to do -- the gentlemanly thing to do. To push as deep in as I could. She said something like "Ehhh!" and rolled over, pulling me with her. She grabbed my butt and pressed me in even deeper and it was very soothing. A great comfort in a terrible time of need. I hoped it was nice for Sheila too. I had no idea if it was because she didn't say anything specific. She just moaned a lot and made odd little noises between her teeth and scratched my back hard. By accident, I suppose. I thought I might have hurt her. Then it was over and it felt fantastic and absolutely every bit as good as when Tom and I masturbated each other in the trunk of Tom's car when our girl-friends were smuggling us into a drive-in theatre in San Diego. Maybe it felt even better. Both of my fingers had calmed down, possibly soothed by an excess of alcohol. I just lay there and I was getting really sleepy and sweating a lot and Sheila leaned over me and poured another glass of fine wine for each of us. She looked wonderful now. A lot more beautiful than when she was naked in my bed on Monday night -- what was wrong with me then?

We drank our wine for a while and I coughed a lot every few minutes, very careful to keep the noise down for Charlie and Reggie. What a coward I am! Stifling such a basic human need as coughing! I'm so considerate I make me sick! Then Sheila leaned over me and switched on the radio and yelled "News! News!" And I switched off the radio and she said, "Your side will win, for God's sake! The Russians will back down!" I said I didn't want to know because, well, because I just didn't want to know.

"Then we'll listen to your Mellow Four!" And she put on my record. Sheila was really a good sport!

"You travelled to a star…" sang The Mellow Four.

"Did we just travel to a star. Andy?" she said, climbing back into bed.

I said, "I th-th-think so," and she said, "Th-Thanks a fucking heap!"

Then Uncle's dogs began to bark and he yelled at them. There was a soft knock on my door and an even softer "Gladys Charlton, Andy." When I didn't answer, The Blind Girl quietly opened my door and tapped her way to her meter and wound a coin in and whispered, "Lovely music, Andy. American, is it?"

"Y-Yes," I said.

"I have an American cousin once removed. Sorry to have disturbed you, dear. I'm afraid it's Iris yet again. She has forsaken me. "

"You c-could leave the meter m-money with me, Miss Charlton. I could put it in f-for you."

"Oh my, no, my dear!" she said and looked very upset. "It's always Iris puts the money in. I couldn't offend Iris. I'd never get my tea and toast." She tapped herself to the door and stopped. "Sleep well, dear. Your lady friend too."

She let herself out, gently pulled the door shut. Uncle's dogs began to bark. "Who the hell's out there?!" yelled Uncle.

"Just Gladys, Uncle, tapping her way to heaven."

"Hello, Gladdy, me old love," said Uncle, "Let me know when you get there, girlie, and I'll meet you for a cuppa."

"Sleep well, Uncle," said The Blind Girl.

"That I will, Gladdy. That I will."

"We've got to get you out of here," whispered Sheila, "You'll go berserk! I've got Daddy working on it."

"I l-l-like it here."

"No, you don't. That's absurd!"

"I do. Th-This is a f-funny place," I said and I was beginning

140

to feel strange again. I mean *exceedingly* strange. Was it the wine? I pictured myself falling down hundreds of times and bruising my elbows and knees and losing the key to my exquisitely carved liquor cabinet and not minding it a bit. Even though my psychiatrist had given up on me and my disillusioned wife and frightened children had deserted.

"Is it?" said Sheila, "is Oxford a funny place?"

I began to cry. It was so fucking embarrassing! I couldn't control it! I was going crazy! I couldn't stop myself. I wanted to shrink to almost nothing and join the assault of the tiny albino roots on my gas fire! I wanted to disappear under the damp-linoleum-frayed-carpet-covered-floor so no one could ever find me again! And my inflamed cut finger began to hurt like hell!

"Crikey!" said Sheila, "You were a virgin. Oh, goddamn it. I'm sick to death of sniveling Oxford virgins."

I kept crying. I couldn't stop for love or money. Sheila put her arms around me and hugged me and said in an extremely tender voice, "Don't cry, baby. Mummy's here," just like Elizabeth Taylor had said it to Montgomery Clift in 'A Place in the Sun.' 'Mummy's here' should have been soothing but only made me cry harder. Then I remembered what Tom said about virgins -- that they always cry when they lose their cherries. Even if this applied to girls-only it was a very practical and comforting thought. Because I had just, in a way, I guess, lost mine. Although it seemed a lot more like I had gained something than lost it as I was relaxed. Even with my damned cut finger I felt relaxed! So I guess I was just crying from relief. Then a small stone knocked a pane out of my window, and a horrible high-pitched voice shrieked "Leee-annnnnnnder! Leee-annnnder!"

"Jesus Christ!" screamed Sheila, and sprang up in bed, "Who the fuck is that?!"

I wiped my insanity-tears on a hanky and pulled on my dead man's robe and stumbled over to the window. "W-W-Who is it?!" I yelled, surprised that I should be so dizzy and weak and unsteady on my feet. But I remembered too, that I had just spurted out my manhood and, like Samson with all his hair cut off, I was weak. It was to be expected. An odd little thrill of accomplishment raced through me even though I was tipsy and sick in mind and body and my fucking finger was infected. But the giggles of my uninvited window-breakers continued so I took a deep breath to clear my head and  yelled again, "W-Who is it?!"

"Marcella and Alasdair, Leander! I'm afraid we're sozzled! Let us in! It's raining cats and dogs!"

What a miserable time for visitors I've never even met! Especially directly after my embarrassing, bawling in front of Sheila. "You b-broke my w-window!" I moaned and grasped my work-and-dining table to keep from keeling over.

"Wasn't me, Leander!" yelled Marcella, "Alasdair did it and he's terribly sorry and he promises never to do it again! Tell him, Alasdair! Tell Leander that you're terribly sorry and that you promise never to do it again!"

I looked up and could just make out through the rain this little Alasdair guy, leaning over the iron railing. It looked like he was about to fall into my rain-flooded light-well. Marcella was hanging on to him and they were both pretty drunk as they kept weaving back and forth. "I'm terribly sorry, Leander, for breaking your window and I promise never..."

"Never to do it again," prompted Marcella.

"Never to do it again," said Alasdair.

"Let us in!" yelled Marcella, "It's raining cats and dogs! We've masses of plonk!"

I turned to Sheila, "P-Plonk?" I said.

"Cheap wine!" hissed Sheila like a striking cobra.

"Alasdair wants to read you a poem!" yelled Marcella.

"Yes," slurred Alasdair, "A poem."

Alasdair unzipped his trousers and in the dim light from my broken window, pulled out his little pink dick and stuck it between the iron fence rails at the top of the light-well and began to pee. There certainly wasn't any danger that this little pink dick might get stuck between the iron rails although that was not a very nice thing to say about anybody's dick. Big or small. Dicks are private affairs and should be left alone. It is like rudely discussing the size of women's breasts -- it is discourte-

142

ous and vulgar and an unpleasant reflection on the background of the ill-bred person who does it.

"Tell them to piss off!" yelled Sheila.

"Alasdair!" cried Marcella, "Stop that! It's disgusting!"

"Tell them to piss off!" screamed Sheila, louder.

"He is p-p-pissing! First he b-breaks my window then he p-p-pisses on it!" I yelled and suddenly found myself sprawled on the floor by the window, my naked butt in the air for everyone to see!

Marcella giggled. "What has she been teaching you, Leander?! And you, Alasdair, you are disgusting! Zip up your trousers and behave!"

"He's a Yank, isn't he?!" yelled Alasdair spraying a thin thread of pee down the light-well at my window. "The Yanks are pissing on us and I am pissing on them! Go home, Yank! Go home, Yank!"

Sheila clambered out of bed, threw the sheet around her and screamed up the light-well, "Piss off, you horrid, jumped-up little twit!"

"We're sorry!" cried Marcella, "But we are sozzled and wet!"

"You too!" screamed Sheila. "Piss off and take your mini-lout with you!"

"Really!" cried Marcella.

"Yes, really!" screamed Sheila.

"But we've masses of plonk!" cried Marcella.

"Stuff that cheap rubbish up your posh little arses!"

"Come Alasdair!" huffed Marcella, "Put yourself away and come! We are not wanted here! Our company, therein, is not desired!"

"Not desired," said Alasdair. He tucked in his dick, zipped, cried "Owwww! I've caught me hair!"

"Alasdair, you are hopeless!" laughed Marcella. "Goodnight, Leander. Sleep well! If she'll let you!"

"Fuck off!" screamed Sheila.

Marcella and Alasdair, hoisting their clinking bottles of 'plonk' between them in a canvas bag, fumbled open the little iron gate at Number 13 and started up Wilton Street. Marcella's large umbrella, which she struggled to hold upright in her other hand, was no match for the wind-driven rain that pelted them and pounded into puddles at their feet. "He's with that Sheila woman," called Marcella into the howling wind, "I'd know her Medusa quack anywhere. She'll turn Leander to stone."

"To stone?" slurred plump little Alasdair, "Leander doesn't turn to stone, Leander drowns."

"Horrid, isn't she? That Sheila?"

"Horrid."

"She's a nymphomaniac," said Marcella. "She's had a baby."

"A wee babe? "

"It's common knowledge. They took the baby away from her, of course. Her family had it adopted out or something. It was all over the gutter press."

"Poor little blighter," slurred Alasdair as a great sheet of rain struck him squarely in his round, pink face.

"I believe she wanted to keep it," said Marcella, "Keep the baby."

"Keep it," slurred Alasdair.

"Her family simply wouldn't allow it as she is a practising nymphomaniac."

"Obviously," slurred Alasdair.

"She'll suck Leander dry and spit him out like pomegranate seeds!"

Marcella paused in the rain, smiled happily, said, "Excellent, n'est-ce-pas? Pomegranate seeds?"

"Excellent!" managed Alasdair, well aware of the importance of the pomegranate in ancient Greek mythology. He was slowly beginning to sober up but was still content to bask in what seemed to be, as he was only just eighteen himself, Marcella's aura of mythological expertise.

Marcella shook the huge, sagging umbrella which had begun to gather more water than it cast off and she and Alasdair continued through the rain to Beaumont  street where shelter might be found in the Star Bar at the Randolph Hotel if they were allowed in. Which was doubtful, even though her posh

Mum had won a small ownership share in the Bar as a party favour.

"He b-broke my window and p-peed on it," I said, pulling myself up from the floor. "He p-peed on my w-window because I'm American."

"Don't be paranoiac, he'd pee on anybody's window if he got the chance. He's a posh little shit. That's precisely the sort of thing stupid, posh little shits do," said Sheila, "Come to bed."

I stumbled, muffling my coughing, toward the bed and felt awful that someone would do such a rude thing. I'd never even met Alasdair. How could a perfect stranger do something like that to you? My entire family would have been shocked. Especially Granddad. There were things one did and things one didn't. "Why did he p-p-pee on my w-w-window?" I said, falling into bed.

"He thought it was clever," said Sheila, pulling the blankets closer around us.

"C-Clever?"

"Darling. In Oxford there are many individuals who would believe that's clever."

I began to cough again. I also thought I might vomit. Too much wine in too little time. Why was it that everything here always happened at once? It was me, of course. All my fault. Then Uncle's dogs began to bark.

"How can you possibly sleep with that fucking kennel next door?!" said Sheila. "Daddy has lovely spare rooms in Isis Street. No dogs allowed."

"It's only old Uncle's d-dogs," I said and climbed out of bed so fast my head swam. I swayed back and forth. I knew I was going to vomit. I said "I th-think I'm going to v-v-vomit!"

Sheila sprang up, "Shall I come with you?!"

But I was already to the door, naked, attempting without success to pull on my dead man's robe, hoping I could make it to the toilet on the landing in time. I was about to open my door when someone tapped on it and Uncle's dogs went berserk. But The Blind Girl had already been here tonight. Why was she

145

coming again?! At such an inopportune time?! I opened the door and Regina, grabbing my naked body for support, fell into my room. Sheila was naked too and right behind me. Regina took it all in, screamed and scrambled to her feet and rushed up the basement stairs. From somewhere above I heard Charlie shouting "Baby?! Reggie, baby, are you all right?!"

"Belt up, you hairy bitches!" yelled Uncle, over the dogs, "Who's out there?"

"A-A-Andy, Uncle," I yelled as I stumbled, naked, up the stairs as fast as I could.

"Go on up, Baby," yelled Charlie to Reggie, "I'll take care of him!"

Charlie stood in the hallway directly in front of me, blocking the door to the toilet, "What the hell do you think you're doing?!"

"V-V-V-Vomiting!" I cried and threw up all over her bright red plaid pajamas. This was exceedingly embarrassing.

# 21

It was morning, still dark and cloudy and raining harder. Andy, in his sepulchral bathrobe, crouched on his bed watching anxiously as Charlie puttied a pane of glass into his window. Would it soon be broken again? Would his window be blown in or sucked out by a massive atomic explosion?! Would his damp, frigid walls, glow, disintegrate and drift in the radioactive air for a thousand years? Would those healthy, white floor board roots shrivel and vanish? Or would they mutate into monstrosities able to leap tall gas fires in a single bound? Would he himself be but a scorched smudge on a charcoal floor as swirling clouds, many times the temperature of the surface of the sun, circled the globe in opposite directions to finally meet in a cataclysmic explosion that split the earth's crust from pole to pole? His left little finger twitched violently and his razor-cut throbbed anew, worse than ever. This was the kind of day it was and it was impossible to subtract it from his life. Now he must live it, minute by eternal minute. He must live it or leave it!

Was the whole volatile world out to get him, in league against him? 'In league against Leander?!' He'd heard that from Granddad. How he missed Granddad. Especially since Grandma died. Granddad and Andy's extraordinarily beautiful mother meant the whole world to him. And there was dear Aunt Graycie, Aunt Fran, Aunt June and Aunt Dot. And there was, of course, dear Tom. And Mr. Bateman. And little Tinker. Would they survive?

"You gave Reggie quite a shock last night," said Charlie, "She dropped all our shillings somewhere. We reckon thieving Cyril got them. We had to spend the night without heat. Are you in the habit of answering your door bare-arsed and vomiting on innocent passersby?"

"I d-didn't mean to s-scare Reggie," said Andy, "I thought it was The B-Blind Girl. I was about to v-vomit and you wouldn't let me pass."

Charlie turned from her window work, grinned, "Reggie said you were entertaining a lady friend. She was starkers too."

"I d-don't think I was very entertaining," said Andy, "I've been p-pretty m-messed up the p-p-p-past few days. I th-think

147

I'm going crazy."

Charlie ignored this, said, "we've got to solve the meter money caper some other way. I wouldn't trust Iris with a pot to piss in. But as much as I detest the lying, prying thieving little wretch I'd not want her horsewhipped by Pofford. Got any ideas?"

"I could collect the m-m-meter money and…"

"Not on," said Charlie from the gas fire where she was about to cut back the roving roots with her putty knife.

"N-No!" yelled Andy, "I l-like them! They're b-brave and symbolic! They s-s-stand for a better w-w-w-world!"

Charlie, unfazed, shrugged, went back to the window, surveyed her glazing with an expert eye, said "Iris would hold us hostage if we commandeered the meter money. She counts on a hunk of it for entertainment, poor cow. Got any good ideas?"

Charlie put a sweeping, very professional finishing touch on her window glazing, laid down the putty knife and dropped herself into The Chair, swayed merrily, said, "I thought you Yankee boys were innovative."

"N-Not this one. N-N-Not now."

"Poorly, are you?"

Andy winced. Of course he was poorly! Wasn't it obvious? He looked terrible, felt terrible, had been to the Rossetti exactly once in his first week, and would probably flunk out. It was an existential problem. His Mother, Granddad, favorite aunts, best friend Tom, and his dog, were all about to die in an atomic confla-gration. Perfect strangers broke his window and peed at him -- yelled go home, Yank! People brought him whisky, wanked him and were never heard from again. They jumped into his bed naked without prior warning. Spied on him, read his mail, resealed it with butter and eavesdropped through the thinness. To top it off he was probably dying of blood-poisoning from a single-edged razor-blade cut. He was going nuts at seventeen! How could he not be poorly? "J-Jesus!" muttered Andy, "Jesus C-C-C-Christ!" and immediately felt double-guilty for taking the Lord's name in vain. Yet here was this helpful, self-assured woman he had showered with vomit the night before. Here she was, repairing his window and not complaining about the vomit, that horrible, purple wine vomit. He was a fiend!

So he'd lost his virginity. Was that what was really troubling him? His fucking virginity? God! Was he some kind of religious freak?! Virginity? Virginity?! Boys weren't meant to be whining little virgins! Boys fought to lose their so-called fucking innocence! It was a mark of manhood. They should love it. Had to, to propagate the fucking world. But did the world need more people? Never mind, they'd be thinned out, culled, and how! Any day now. Soon! This minute! Tonight! Tomorrow at the latest! Charlie stared at Andy. Did this boy have problems! He hadn't said a word but everything he thought went zipping in flashing neon across his fever-cheeked face. "That's all right, kid," she said, "I know how it must be for you. Us Brits are an odd lot, aren't we? Can't be much like where you come from. Where did you say you came from?"

"C-California. S-Southern C-C-California".

"California. That's the long, skinny one on the left, isn't it? It's huge."

Andy brightened, pumped up that image of himself with his fantasy surfboard under his arm, standing in the knee-high surf of that sunny, warm, impossibly beautiful, beach in La Jolla. Yes, La Jolla shores! "Y-Yes," he said proudly, "C-California is the l-long, skinny one on the l-l-left. They c-could fit th-three Englands into it."

"Crickey!" Charlie grinned, "I wish they bloody would! I hear the weather's wizard! I'd be there with bells on! It's a bleedin' paradise screaming for more asphalt to park their billions of cars on." Charlie got up to leave and The Chair, relieved of Charlie, tipped on three legs, swayed and fell on its back with a great thud. "Blimey!" she said.

"What was that?!" screamed Iris from the kitchen through the thinness.

"Me," yelled Charlie directly into Andy's side of the thinness, "Charlie!"

"Miss Pofford says to say that you're a week overdue on your rent, Charlie! There'll be no butter for your toast tomorrow!"

149

"So be it!" yelled Charlie.

"Miss Pofford was ever so upset!"

"I'm devastated!" yelled Charlie into the thinness.

"What's that m-mean, 'Blimey'?" said Andy, lighting up a woodbine and coughing maniacally into his blanket.

"Damned if I know!" said Charlie, "See ya!"

She was out the door -- but immediately slammed it open and tossed a small white bag at Andy. "This was hanging – pardon the expression – on your knob!" Charlie was gone before Andy could thank her.

# 22

Andy stubbed out his cigarette, coughed softly twice, and opened the bag. In it were three custard tarts and a note.

*Hope these goodies find you mending, Andy from Lemon Gulch , California. Would have brought them in myself but you seemed occupied. See you in class on Monday? Hope you're well by then. Love, Irene -- the tall, naked broad in that fabulous, red silk kimono.*

Andy took a bite of tart, knew he must somehow immediately thank Irene and Jean-Francois for the paraffin fire and the custard tarts. It wasn't like him. Oh yes it was! He had now feverishly stumbled into some despicable, discourteous limbo and would be incinerated before he had a chance to right his many wrongs! Not a merry prospect! He took a bite of tart just as Cyril entered.

"Don't you p-p-people know how to knock?" Muttered Andy through the custard tart crust.

"I heard chewing," said Cyril, "What have you got in there? Andy held out the paper bag. Cyril snatched a custard tart, broke it in two, slammed half into his mouth, said "Tah, a gift from not too mysterious Marcella?"

"N-No," said Andy, "Irene."

"Jesus! Yet another slave in your Harem. Second floor, our side. Soon to be removed from the prem-eeses as I-rees says Miss Pofford says. But it's possibly only I-rees says."

Andy's mouth dropped open. "Irene th-thrown out?! F-For what?!"

"Fucking."

"F-Fucking?! Is th-that illegal in Oxford?!"

Andy imagined himself being jailed for a situation he had no control over – sexual intercourse with Sheila. His heart was in his throat. Wasn't this a free country just like the good old USA?

"Illegal? Depends," said Cyril, slamming in the rest of the custard tart. "Depends on who you are and whom you fuck.

Seems our Irene fucks frogs."

"F-Frogs?! Our Rossetti nude model f-fucks f-frogs?" gulped Andy, imagining an odd, European sexual practice he'd never heard of and was not prepared to actually believe. She seemed like such a nice, naked woman. "F-Frogs?!"

"Frenchies, Leander, French blokes! By the by, who feeds you? Besides your Harem?"

"Iris, w-when she r-remembers."

"Sprouts?" said Cyril.

"Irene is an angel, She has a p-p-perfect right to f-fuck who ever she p-pleases!"

"Whomever she p-pleases."

"That's what I s-s-said!"

"So" said Cyril, sensing Andy was not to be badgered at the moment, "Sprouts was it?"

"Y-yes. A lot of s-sprouts. L-Lots of sp-sprouts."

"And potatoes."

"Y-Yes."

"A lot of potatoes."

"I like p-p-p-potatoes."

"And a bit of ham?"

"Y-Yes."

"Pity my Pa's on tour. He's a noted chef. He'd treat you right. No peasant garbage for you! What amazes me," said Cyril, who grabbed out another tart, stretched languidly, unconsciously balancing in The Chair as he munched. "What amazes me is that we're still alive. Any of us. You are familiar, young Yankee creature, with what is occurring on the surface of our wayward planet just beyond the mouth of your cave?"

"I sh-should be…home."

Suddenly through the thinness Iris's voice rang clear, almost sweetly: "Today is May Day, hoo-ray for May Day…"

"Sh-Sh-She likes you," said Andy.

"Everybody likes me, Sunshine!"

Cyril rose, went to the thinness, shouted, "I-rees!"

Instantly: "Yes, Mr. Lemmington?!"

"Tea and cake for Andy and me!"

Instantly: "Right you are, Mr. Lemmington!"

Cyril turned from the thinness, "Leander, you are far too egalitarian. You care too much about what people think of you. And they will use it to your disadvantage. I don't give bung-all what people think of me. The world ain't gonna end if you don't say thank you to an inferior! God must have loved the inferiors 'cause he made so many of 'em! But I know where I stand and I damn well let them know where they stand. It's the fucking eternal hierarchy. This is basic stuff, dear boy. Keep it that way, my Yankee-doodle-dandy. God is in his heaven and all is only semi-right with the world. World without end! Amen! It never gets any better than that."

"Except for the w-war that will b-blow us to smithereens about five m-minutes from now! What an awful thing for you to s-say! Everyone knows that all m-m-men are c-created equal!"

"Equal to what? Atomic missiles? We live in troubled times. Face it. Read the papers, listen to the radio. Even to be at cross purposes with your own tribe is dangerous! I may be forced to defend your rear from attack. Speaking of which, who was that dishy frog in your room the other night, that tasty Frenchie?" Cyril stuck a finger in his right nostril, plucked idly, "That smooooth Frenchie! You can't trust 'em. He had a lean and well-hung look."

"H-He was on a s-s-student welcoming committee. He wants to be a w-writer/actor," said Andy.

"Amongst other things," said Cyril who tugged something from his left nostril, rolled it between forefinger and thumb, examined it then flipped it into the gas fire where it was consumed with the tiniest hiss. Suddenly Cyril's face twisted, darkened. "I've been sent down."

"S-Sent down?"

"Rusticated, excommunicated, expelled, kicked clean out of Oxford!

"Jee-sus! God, I'm s-s-sorry, C-Cyril! Why?"

"Passive Resistance. At three A.M. in Carfax."

Andy knew that the Carfax intersection was the geographic centre of Oxford. He'd read it in his Dreaming Spires booklet.

Cyril frowned, looked about, continually dismayed at the unspeakable shabbiness of Andy's basement room. "If I lived in this sodding cellar, I'd kill myself. I'd put a hose up me nose from your pathetic little gas fire and squat against a crumbly wall and smoke your filthy Woodbines till I was either put away, put down, or blown up."

Cyril glanced at Andy who had hidden his face behind his hands. "No," continued Cyril, "I'm not clever enough. That's why I'm getting the boot. I'm actually quite stupid. In my splendid stupid way."

"N-No, you're n-not stupid," said Andy from behind his hands. "You're at Oxford! and you've got sensationally keen repartee!"

"Sensational...keen repartee?! Christ! How would you know?!"

Cyril winced and rose from The Chair, knelt on the floor beside Andy's bed. Andy did not remove his hands from his face, turned away. "God, I'm sorry, kiddo," said Cyril, "Forgive?" He pulled one of Andy's hands from Andy's face. Andy was streaming with tears.

"Andy, love. It's me, got axed, kiddo, not you."

Yet again Andy went overboard for his fellow man. "I'm s-s-s-so sorry, Cyril!" he sobbed, "Y-You being a gentleman and expelled."

Cyril was moved at such raw emotion in someone he hardly knew. He got up from the floor, sat, and stuck his finger up his nose again, probed, "That's not the worst of it. Pa's enrolled me in a Hotel Management School. That's not even the worst of it! The school is in Paris. Paris, France. I hate Paris!"

Andy wiped his eyes, "H-How can anyone p-p-p-possibly hate P-Paris? I've always wanted to go to P-Paris. P-Paris is the Art capital of the world."

"Glitters, does it? Why not Florence, Madrid or Barcelona? Or even Rome?! My God! Anywhere but Paris, that bloody parvenu frog pond! They're rude! I'd be bored shitless! They refuse to speak English! Even when they know teach it!

"C-Cyril," Andy finally managed, "Oxford isn't the only

place in the w-world."

Cyril exploded. "How could you possibly know?! You've never been to Oxford! You've spent your first week here hiding out in a rat hole! Much as I hate to say this, Leander Riley, you are in Oxford rather than at Oxford! You attend a noteworthy art school that happens to be in Oxford! Whilst I, at Trinity College, am at Oxford – or was at Oxford. The difference should not be hard to grasp, even for an American. Andy, your soul resides in a shiny skyscraper, peering out over waving fields of toothpaste and hemorrhoids billboards!"

Then, wonder of wonders to Andy, Cyril too, began to cry. He was full-out shattered, didn't bother to hide it. He twisted up his face in a frightening way and cried like a baby -- cried with abandon, just as Andy cried -- in a great, grieving gulps and rasping suckings of air. Were they really so different? thought Andy who began again to sob recklessly -- sat there, under his blankets, sobbing away, joining Cyril who sobbed, sighed, stamped his feet, rocked perilously back and forth in The Chair till he looked peculiar and jumped up, rushed to the window, slammed the bottom pane open and fell to his knees vomiting energetically into the light-well. Then, raising himself with a giant sigh he stood, heaved in a massive breath of air, pulled a hanky from his pullover sleeve and daintily wiped his mouth. He returned to The Chair, sat and smiled sweetly at Andy as though he hadn't been bawling or vomiting or even momentarily out of control. Andy sealed Cyril's smile with his own. It was to be their silent blub-pact, never to be broken. What a comfort to witness in the flesh, another human being who cried so wholeheartedly! So energetically! So fuckingly cinematically!

Iris, to the racket of Uncle's dogs and old Uncle's assorted curses, swooped suddenly through Andy's door with a tray of tea and pink cake. "Here you are, Mr. Lemmington, tea and your favourite pink cakey-wakey. "How's the Yank?" she said to Cyril without glancing at Andy, "Still poorly?" She ploughed on, "Them Russians took photographs of all the American cities they was fixin' to bomb! The photographs was on the telly this morning. The Yanks has got us in a tight spot this time! Miss

Pofford is ever so upset! Miss Pofford's niece, you see, she's on holiday in America. Bloomington, Illa-noise, which is in the middle of…" Iris stopped abruptly, stuck her stubby nose into the air, sniffed, "Who's been sick?! Who's been sick, eh? I smelt it from the stairs too! I thought it was old Uncle's doggies. But it ain't, is it?!" She slammed down the tray of tea and cake and, arms akimbo, strutted sniffing, directly to the window, looked out and cried "Aha!" and marched triumphantly to Andy's bedside, stood there accusingly. As usual, too close for Andy's comfort. "Miss Pofford'll be ever so...

"Wasn't Andy, 'twas me. I killed Cock Robin."

"Oh, Mr. Lemmington," said Iris, suddenly pink as the cake she'd just fetched in, "The Yank'll tidy up then as it's his room."

"No," said Cyril, "You will – and quickly -- or I shall be sick again! Begone, wench! Fetch your accoutrementi! Act! Before all this rain washes all my sick into the drain and it clogs and the stench lingers for weeks!"

"Right you are, Mr. Lemmington! Miss Pofford'd be ever so upset if it stinks in her premeeses!" cried Iris and flew out the door and up the stairs to fetch pail and mop.

"I've got some books for you, Andy," said Cyril, pitching another ripe bogey at the fire, "Won't need 'em in grey Paree. Can you read?

# 23

"I-rees! You, I-rees!"

"Coming, Miss Pofford!" The front door slammed with a crash.

"There you are, I-rees! Do you know what time it is?! Where the hell have you been?! In Little Clarendon Street, you wretched Iris?! Bingo was it?! Playin' Bingo again?! Was it?! Was it?!"

"No, Miss Pofford! You're mistaken and no mistake!"

"Liar! Where's our tea?!"

"'Have they invaded?! Miss Pofford?!"

"Has who invaded?!"

"Them Russkies! Have they invaded Spain?! You said you'd shout if they'd invaded Spain! I thought you was shoutin' that the Russkies invaded Spain!"

"Cuba! You I-reees! The bleedin' Russians is invadin' Cuba!"

"Same thing 'n' it? Have they then? Invaded Cuba?!"

"No they ain't! The Yanks is defendin' us. The Yanks is een-vin-ceeble. They said so on the telly. Een-vin-ceeble!"

"I'm ever so glad they ain't invaded, Miss Pofford. You'd be ever so upset if they'd invaded."

"What?! What?! Me upset? Me upset?! For Christ's sake, you stupid girlie thing! When have I ever been upset?! When have you ever seen me upset?! The Yanks is een-vin-ceeble, you I-rees! They said so on the bleedin' telly!" cried Miss Pofford stretching stealthily from her chair toward a suitable vase.

"I'm ever so pleased, Miss Pofford!" cried Iris leaping quickly out of Pofford's striking range and adding, "Your Yank's still ever so poorly, Miss Pofford."

"What Yank?" said Miss Pofford, wrenching one spectacled wall-eye from the telly, "Had 'em here for the war! What Yank is that?!"

"Our Yank," said Iris, "Our Yank, Miss Pofford, in our basement at Number 13. He's ever so poorly."

"I'm not surprised! In that bleedin' Black Hole of Calcutta! Give him extra bacon tomorrow with his breakfast. And double-butter for his toast!"

"Yes Miss Pofford."

"Free of charge."

"Yes, Miss Pofford."

"Nothing extra due with the rent."

"Yes, Miss Pofford."

"Stop hangin' about, my girl, and fetch us our tea! You're late!"

"Yes, Miss Pofford."


"You don't seem very excited, Andy. Daddy went to a hell of a lot of trouble to find the proper digs for you." Sheila straightened her heavy pullover, sat down on the bed beside Andy, and began to slip into long wool stockings – she'd long given up her fancier kit. The rain was relentless, had been so the entire week. "Well, darling? What shall I tell Daddy?"

There it is again, thought Andy, the 'darling'. He hardly knew Sheila – and this struck him with the greatest awe – he'd now slept with her twice. Completely. Despite his shattered health he had, by any measure, managed an authentic sexual intercourse. A 'jolly good' sexual intercourse, she'd said. Maybe 'darling' was appropriate after all?

"P-Please tell your f-father I like it here."

"You like it here?! How is that possible?! How can anyone like it here?! Why didn't you tell me that before Daddy went to all that trouble?"

"I d-did tell you th-that."

"God, you're rude!"

"I'm p-poorly!"

"Darling! That's precisely why we must get you out of this death trap. You'll die here."

Sheila took a swig of wine, was slightly tipsy and more than slightly irritated. "I have it!" she declared slamming down her wineglass, "You feel safe here. Underground. That's it, isn't it? You are a tiny grey mole. A frightened little underground critter. You won't listen to the bloody news. You're not…whole!"

Andy turned away, pulled the bedclothes over his face. He knew she was right, he wasn't whole, and he was getting exceedingly nervous again and the wine didn't help. Not this time. He knew he was being unfriendly when all his resources should have been at the disposal of this beautiful, generous, caring girl – more of a woman than a girl. He was a cold-hearted fiend! No. Of course he wasn't. He had no idea at all about what he was. None.

Sheila quaffed the rest of her glass, "For your information the world is in crisis," she said, casting a fistful of coals-to-Newcastle into Andy's lap, "Honestly, you're certifiable. Are all Americans like you? They must be. That's probably why we're at the brink of annihilation."

"It's not my f-fault," mumbled Andy from beneath the blankets and coughed, twice for good measure, though he could have made it in one. His body was disintegrating, his mind was a mess and his immortal soul was in mortal disarray.

"I shall be trite, darling, so you will understand -- it's everybody's fault!" said Sheila, ripping the blanket from Andy's face, "Everybody's! Bloody hell! You come over here and just because you're a bloody, fucking American you think everybody's going to fall all over you!"

"W-What's that got to d-do with Cuba?" cried Andy in a tiny voice so he wouldn't disturb Charlie or Reggie. Sheila was wrong. He had no intention at all that everybody should be falling all over him! That would have been terrifying!

Sheila was not receiving. "You think just because you're the all-American boy all the girls will be after you!"

"I'm n-not the all-American boy. I'm anything b-but! I'm a m-mess! I'm a s-s-s-sissy and a coward, and I'm p-poorly, and I can't even f-f-fucking draw any m-more!" cried Andy and pulled the blanket over his head again but not before he'd glimpsed and suffered at his distorted, hollow-eyed reflection in the fractured wardrobe mirror. He was now...a wraith! A fragmented, disappearing wraith! She'd said he wasn't whole! He agreed.

"All right," offered Sheila, "all the girls are not after you!"

"Y-You are," said Andy from beneath the blanket and instantly regretted it. This sort of talk was not usual for him. It just popped out. This was odd, things popping out so often. It was usually a struggle to get anything out. Anything at all.

Now it was a struggle to keep rude things in!

"You ungrateful bastard! I gave you my radio-gramophone! Not to mention my body! Twice!"

"I d-didn't ask for your b-b-body even once! Or your r-radio-phonograph -- You can have it b-b-b-back!"

"I don't want it b-b-b-back! I could buy hundreds of gramophones! The point is…Oh, fuck the point! You don't respect me, do you? You're trying to make me a monster. I am not a monster!"

Andy lay quiet in the relative safety of the blanket over his face. He knew Sheila wasn't a monster. He was the monster. But he couldn't have spoken just now even if he'd had something soothing to say. Even if that soothing something had made its way out of his mouth from a normal tongue, a more dependable organ, that might have successfully relayed his most tender thoughts.

Things had now abruptly stopped popping out. Suddenly it seemed he had no thoughts at all. Nil. Confusion and wine had flushed all order from his head and he became nearly speechless.

"Go on," said Sheila, "say it!"

Andy just managed a tiny "S-S-Say w-what?"

"You don't respect me."

"B-But…"

"You don't respect me because I tried to fuck you the first day I met you and you'd never been fucked before. You should be fucking flattered!"

Andy suddenly became his namesake, battling treacherous waves, sucked beneath them into whirlpools of emotion he'd never experienced. He was dealing with a real woman and he was far from being a real man -- the man he'd hoped one day he'd be. If he didn't drown in the attempt or was pulverized in the coming nuclear onslaught. What, really, was she talking about? What, really, had happened? "But didn't I f-f-f-fuck you?" he managed softly.

"You can say that again, boyo!" cried Sheila, "You fucked me all right! Leander who swam his f-f-fucking Hellespont!"

Was this what it was like swimming a Hellespont? He'd just thought it and she'd said it out loud. It was crazy fate. It was his destiny to drown as he sought his heart's desire. There was something heart-throbbingly correct about that in a Hollywood sort of way. For Andy, like many seventeen-year-olds, his life was tragic. He knew he would never find fulfilment. Certainly not while one finger twitched and another pumped poison into his weakening body while the world itself threatened to self-destruct. He had lost his single advantage in life! It now seemed he could not create a convincing stick-figure! How tragic was that?! But back to the business at hand.

"Everybody can't be a bloody virgin like you, 'Leander'! Marcella's not the only one who can read, you know! Prattling on all week about your namesake and Aphrodite's stupid, fucking absurd revenge! Who the hell do you think you are? Just because Lady bleeding Marcella is at Lady bleeding Marian Hall doesn't mean she's a goddamned goddess! I'm only an art student but my father could buy and sell five Marcella's! She slums when she takes classes with us! Looks down on me and you! That posh cow! I'm not a monster. You are trying to make me a monster. I am not a monster!"

Andy continued to flounder in this sea of misunderstanding with an authentic woman. He could have laughed at his image – would have, had he not been 'poorly' and too many wines along and utterly 'at sea' and dying of blood-poisoning into the bargain. He did not understand women -- women nearer his age. Women who expected something very specific of him. But particularly this beautiful woman, whom he had either just fucked or been fucked by but who later insisted that she'd fucked him first then somewhat later that he'd fucked her. Was this simply an English/American language dilemma? An international misunderstanding? God knows it wasn't at the only one! The room swayed on cue.

"So what is it with Marcella?!" said Sheila.

"Sheila, I d-don't even know M-Marcella. I've n-never actually met her. P-Please tell me w-what this is about."

"Nothing," said Sheila, now fully dressed and jamming on a

second sensible shoe, "It's about a big mistake I almost made."

Sheila jumped up, rushed to the gas fire, grabbed a root, "Jesus Christ! What the fuck is this?! Tree roots?!"

"L-Leave them alone!" said Andy who had ripped the blanket from his face and was now sitting up in bed.

"They'll eat you alive!" screamed Sheila.

"Not if you get him first!" came thundering through the door. Uncle's dogs exploded into their traditional yelping barks.

"Who's out there?!" yelled Uncle.

"Cyril, Uncle! Cyril visiting the sick Yank!"

"Tell the boy to get well, Cyril!"

"Right you are, Uncle!" called Cyril and knocked loudly at Andy's door.

"Jesus!" cried Sheila. She rushed to the door, opened it and Cyril said "Is it safe to venture in? I could not help but eavesdrop. The volume was overwhelming."

"Jesus Christ!" screamed Sheila.

"It's pushing midnight, Cinderella," said Cyril, "There's a turnip waiting for you up yonder on the street."

Sheila grabbed her coat and umbrella, cried "Another bleeding posh prick! Where do you find 'em, Andy?! In the woodwork? Under one of your filthy carpets?!"

Sheila thrust Cyril aside. "Oh, do stay," he pleaded, "I'll stand in for poor, sick Andy and you can shriek at me."

"Piss off!" cried Sheila and slammed out Andy's door amidst the usual cacophony of Uncle's dogs. "Belt up, you hairy bitches!" screamed Sheila.

"Who's out there?" yelled Uncle.

"Sheila, Uncle!" screamed Sheila, "It's fucking Sheila!"

"Sleep well, Sheila, me old love," said Uncle.

Sheila bounded out into the rain with a great slamming of the front door as Cyril poured himself a glass of wine, sipped it, said "My, my, my! This purple fruit juice ain't plonk!"

"Th-There's a whole case under the table. Her father had it s-sent over."

"Glasses too," said Cyril pinging the glass with a well-manicured finger, "Crystal glasses! Don't be reckless, dear boy.

Could you not reconsider your arrangement with this newly disaffected though startlingly affluent and drop-dead-gorgeous female? Nay? You simply won't be bought?"

Cyril drained his glass and poured another for himself and Andy, sipped delicately, said "Now what was that all about?"

Andy scratched his head and coughed. "M-M-Marcella, I guess."

"We're being fought over, are we?"

"I d-don't even know M-Marcella!" Andy winced, he knew nothing. He had no idea about what had just happened so he said "I'll visit you in P-Paris, Cyril. I p-promise. I've always w-wanted to go to P-Paris. I'll hitchhike."

"Don't threaten me," quipped Cyril and laughed. "You do that, Yankee boy."

Cyril poured the dregs of this exhausted bottle into his glass, quaffed and took another bottle from the case under the table and uncorked it. He poured himself another, offered it to Andy who declined. Cyril sighed, sipped, slumped back in The Chair, sighed again, said "I blame it all on the decline of the Church."

"W-What?"

"Our present difficulties, every goddamned one of 'em. That's what Pa says. He's a vicar."

"I th-thought you said he was a f-famous chef. Or was it a d-doctor? I th-thought you said..."

"So I did. He's apparently a vicar. Cheers, Yank."

Cyril raised his glass, grinned, "Cheers and a hearty welcome to…"

A softly chattering meter whirred to a stop, clicked and the lights went out. The room was now dimly lit by the gas and paraffin fires until another meter stopped and the gas hissed off. Two more meters clicked off and Cyril said "Those'd be mine and I've got no money. No money at all though I believe you owe me a fortune in sixpences."

"There's a b-bowl of s-shillings on the m-mantel."

"Ach! An embarrassment of riches!"

"Help yourself. They're c-compliments of Sheila till I'm on

my f-feet again. Her f-father keeps a big brass chest of 'em. She calls it f-funny money."

"There is nothing remotely funny about money," said Cyril, "I'd suggest you salvage some equitable arrangement with Miss Sheila, given the parlous state of the world. Celebrate, my boy! Life is nasty, brutish, and …Blow me! I forget the rest."

Cyril grinned, swayed from The Chair and took a handful of shillings from the funny-money bowl. He fed the meters and the lights came on. He lit Andy's gas fire, rushed upstairs to light his own, returned and flopped into The Chair and took up his wine. "Welcome, I was about to say before we were so rudimentarily interrupted, welcome to Merry Old England! It is nineteen hundred and sixty two and we're counting down!"

# 24

Cyril left with a couple of bottles of my fine wine under his arm and I coughed – quietly – about seven times. I felt guilty as hell about poor Sheila who had trusted me, given her complete and total self to me and been betrayed by me, the horrible-American-crazy-sonofabitch-child. I was like Montgomery Clift when he shoved Shelly Winters out of that canoe in 'A Place in the Sun' and she drowned in a moonlit lake. It was different of course. I was a mere boy attempting to do a man's job though in another way I felt ancient. Like a one of Nola's old chairs or something. I had lost my virginity twice – if you could say it that way. Sheila called me darling and said she loved me. She seemed, really, to love me. This should count for something very important. But in my shallow, childish way, if it did, I didn't know how it did. So I lay there and went completely overboard for Sheila and poor Cyril who was to be sent away from his wonderful old Oxford and the Dreaming Spires that he loved. Oxford, which he was at and not -- like me -- only in. But Cyril was wrong. On my Official Scholarship Admission information from the Rossetti it stated:

*UNIVERSITY OF OXFORD,*
*THE DANTE DOMINIC ROSSETTI*
*SCHOOL OF DRAWING AND FINE ART*
*Founded in the University*
*by Dante Dominic Rossetti in 1869*
*for the study of Fine Art*

So I was at Oxford too, and on a scholarship, *as it were!* Anyhow, Cyril could also have said I was under Oxford as well, in my dark, subterranean rectangle from which I had no intention of emerging until they carried me out in an oblong wooden box and...

Oh shit! But I was still me and sick with God only knew what and poisoned by my cut alien finger and in direst peril. Like everyone. But the excess of wine had lessened the  bite of Sheila's righteous wrath. Poor beautiful Sheila. It was I who was

165

a monster. Of the very worst kind.

Of course, I felt sorry for myself. What monster wouldn't?! I was a poor guy who didn't belong anywhere except maybe playing chess on the veranda with my Granddad or drawing or painting pictures that I stored in a garage even darker than my present digs! And my drawings or paintings were immature and would have never been more than amateur -- until my Art instructor, Mr. Bateman, had visited, seen them and made me believe in my abilities. All of this was enough to make anybody cry. But just now, though I needed to and usually would have, I couldn't. Because I heard a voice calling down my light-well.

"Leandair! Leandair Riley! Are you zair?!"

It was Yves and I could just see from my bed the shining bottom of a big bottle he was wagging in the rain at the top of the light-well. I put on my bathrobe and for the first time I noticed that it smelled dank. Then I pulled up and smelled my T-shirt and it smelled dank too. Then it occurred to me that my whole room smelled dank and I had become as dank as my room -- and just as depressing. Now I was not only a monster, I was a dank, foul-smelling monster! My own dear Granddad would have hated me!

But the roots that grew from the floorboard and now wound almost completely around the top of the gas fire were applauding me and flourishing and about to become entangled with a loose brick. They were thriving on the powdery mortar that had sifted down and sprinkled a tiny white beach at the bottom of the shiny red-painted brick mantel. A tiny 'beach', that had I been tiny enough, I might have explored with my phony surfboard under my arm, pushing my naked toes through the fine warm brick-powder. These were not sane thoughts.

"Leandair?!" called Yves, "Leandair Riley?! Are you zair?!"

"C-Coming!" I yelled, pulled on my Y-fronts and coughed quietly several times though I knew that Charlie and Reggie had gone out a few hours before and hadn't returned. I was familiar with Charlie's clomping footsteps which were similar to Iris's only vibrated more because Charlie was twice as tall. But Iris had big muscles in her arm and muscles are always extra-heavy.

166

"Leandair! It is veray wet out here!"

"C-Coming!" I repeated and slammed dizzily out my door and up the basement stairs to the barking of Uncle's dogs. "Who the hell's out there?!" yelled Uncle.

"It's Andy, U-Uncle!"

"Sleep tight, don't let the bed bugs bite!" Laughed Uncle.

"Christ!" I said as I puffed swampy air into my failing lungs and hobbled up the basement stairs, "have we got bed bugs here too?"

But we hadn't.


Yves poured a second bourbon into Andy's glass – a crystal wineglass, courtesy of recently departed-in-a-huff, but exceedingly beautiful nonetheless and wrongfully punished, Sheila. Andy was relieved to be drinking this soothing bourbon with Yves. It would extend his freedom from Sheila-guilt. Sweet escape! And Yves had no claims whatsoever on him – would not force him to relocate his digs and had no desire to jump naked into his bed and confuse him. A comforting thought. But was it?

Andy loved the warm glow Yves's bourbon whisky brought – like bathing in some ancient Ionic-pillared, vaporous bath. The alcohol fumes were soothing, reassuring and allowed Andy to forget the woes of permanently threatening, earthly violence and with it, his immature, inferior, possibly terminally ill and cowardly-for sure- self. He pictured the fabled Leander floating on his back on a still, glass-like sea. No churning, storming Hellespont here. No beautiful women, thus no scary challenges.

Andy thought with pleasure that lately he'd not been as dependent upon mundane things like water-soluble vitamin C. Maybe it was because he hadn't time, with all the new and strange experiences that clustered around him. His mind had mysteriously  creaked open to a wider, even more confusing world. And this new world was much less frightening inside a second crystal glass of bourbon. What to do?!

"Your cold is bettair now?" asked Yves.

"A l-little," said Andy, downing the bourbon and feeling a stab of pain in his infected finger -- He had smothered it in several band-aids and willed it to go away as there were other things to ponder, far more important things. But after one and a half crystal glasses of bourbon he couldn't remember what they were. Did bourbon actually taste better in a crystal glass? Andy was certain Granddad would have thought so and had probably commented on it though Andy could not just now guess what Granddad might have said. Was this good or bad? Was alcohol killing his brain cells one by one? Or maybe two by two? My God! Maybe three by three! Andy coughed several times and said "How is your w-w-writing going?" realizing yet again that he had not been giving Yves, the bourbon-bearing welcomer, the courteous attention he deserved.

"I 'ave decided me that the Love is more important even than the Death," said Yves, "I am exploring eet. I weel write of eet. I no longer wish to be an actor, only a writer. To be a writer one must live for thee sensations. One must 'ave experiences, live thee life of thee drab, thee whore!"

"Thee what?" Andy was certain he hadn't heard right.

Yves stretched his legs to balance the precarious Chair. "Love," he sighed, "I shall explore and discover all of thee maneefestations of eet! All of eet's fascinating fa-cets!"

"Love is a m-many s-s-s-splendoured thing," sighed Andy, as a shimmering, meltingly lovely, though properly pensive Jennifer Jones stood tall in his mind's eye, waiting for young, handsome William Holden on a high and windy hill overlooking Hong Kong in the 1956 film, 'Love is a Many Splendoured Thing.'

"Just so," said Yves, marvelling at Andy's romantic acuity, "You must 'ave another drink, Leandair," he said, "We shall experiment with several manifestations of the Love."

Andy was game, said, "W-Why not?"

They toasted their crystal wineglasses, quaffed and set them down.

"Now," said Yves, unzipping his own trousers, "Remove your penis from your underpants and we shall engage in mutual masturbation."

Andy was severely disappointed! This was nothing new. He

and Tom, had done this. Several times, in fact. Though it was exceedingly satisfying, it was by no means full of splendour. Lovely Jennifer Jones would have been mightily disappointed. Not to mention young William Holden.

But Andy's already interested, and not necessarily obedient, penis had already removed itself from his Y-fronts as requested. He gazed down at it as Yves moved closer and revealed his own growing erection and placed Andy's fingers around it and took hold of Andy's. Through his pleasant alcoholic haze Andy noticed that Yves's penis had not, like his own, been circumcised. This was somewhat alarming as Andy had never encountered or handled an uncircumcised penis before. It felt squirmy as he moved Yves's foreskin up and down. Tom's penis was almost like his own – and not at all squirmy. This alien French penis was somewhat disquieting. But the alcohol and growing pleasure as Yves expertly manipulated Andy, quickly dispelled any strangeness at all.

Yves then removed all his clothes and climbed into the narrow bed where he took Andy's penis into his mouth and, after several soothing sucks, asked Andy forthrightly if Andy would kindly have sexual intercourse with his, Yves's, bottom. Andy was not in a strong position to resist, even if he'd wished to. The alcohol, weakness from flu, or whatever, and Yves's expert lips and tongue on his boner did not allow resistance. It was the first time anybody had put his or her mouth on Andy's boner. It was experience. Life Experience.

So, willingly, utterly exhausted and sick as a dog, Andy acquiesced and fucked Yves in his bottom. Much as he'd fucked Sheila in her vagina. It seemed, as with Sheila, far superior to mutual masturbation.. Love was indeed a many splendoured thing.

They lay there later, Andy dozily wondering how this sexual encounter had actually happened. It had started as any inno-cent, universally popular, mutual masturbation would. But one thing led like lightning, to another. He had never met anybody so frank and forthright as Yves. But wait! He had! Sheila was easily as frank and forthright as Yves! Maybe more! Andy had succumbed to both.

Yves's naked body felt every bit as warm against his own as had Sheila's. These two acts of intercourse seemed almost alike, with the exception that Yves was tighter to enter and had reached back and placed Andy's hands on his squirmy uncircumcised penis and soon shot all over Andy and his sheets. This was not at all convenient. Andy would have to sneak his sheets to a launderette before Iris saw them. With a shudder he also imagined the frightening prospect of some meter-feeding nocturnal visitor who hadn't bothered to knock!

"Ees some thing wrong?" asked Yves, turning in bed to reach a glass of bourbon.

"N-No," said Andy.

"Bon," sighed Yves and drained the glass, "C'est bien."

Then Uncle's dogs began to bark and Uncle yelled at them. Andy put his finger to Yves's lips as the door opened and The Blind Girl tapped her way to her meter where she wound in a coin, tapped her way back to the door, whispered "Goodnight, Andy. And goodnight to your gentleman friend as well."

Gladys closed Andy's door as softly as possible.

"Who's out there?!" yelled Uncle over his yelping dogs.

"Gladys, dear, tapping her way to heaven."

"Tell 'em I'll be along soon, love."

"Perhaps we all shall, Uncle, dear, Every Jack and Jill of us."

"Sleep well, Gladdy."

"I shall, Uncle, dear, I surely shall."


An hour later, Yves kissed Andy on his forehead, rose from the bed, dressed, said, "Merci, Monsieur Leandair,"

"Merci, Monsieur Yves" said Andy drowsily and coughed as Yves quietly let himself out. Luckily, Uncle and his dogs were at last asleep.

# 25

With her usual clomp and clang, Iris arrived the next morning with breakfast, slammed it on the small table by Andy's bed.

"Today is Mayday, hooray for Mayday!" she sang, as usual poking her head as close as possible into the sleeping Andy's face. One by one he blinked open his eyes, stared at her. Who was she? Was she really, as Yves had said, a She-Devil? Where was he -- Yves? He who was so recently here, naked and warm by his side.

"No school today?" said Iris, pressing her face ever closer to Andy who had now retreated, as usual, as far as was  possible against the glacial wall at the head of his jerry-built bed.

"No s-school," said Andy. "I'm p-poorly."

"You've missed a whole week then," said Iris, "A whole bloomin' week."

"I'm, p-poorly," repeated Andy.

"I seen a foreign devil exitin' here at Number 13 at two in the morning whilst I was up for my wee-hour wee," stage-whispered  Iris. "That Irene woman is for it! Havin' foreign devils in her premeeses at two o'clock in the morning! Miss Pofford'd be ever so upset if she ever seen a foreign devil evacuatin' in her premeeses at two o'clock in the morning! Ever so upset!"

Andy knew she meant Yves, not Jean-Francois. He had to put it right. He did not want Irene blamed and thrown out – and he must remember to thank them both for the paraffin fire.

"Are you s-s-sure he was a f-foreign devil, Iris? I had a f-friend visit me, the s-s-s-son of the American ambassador in P-Paris. He looks F-French because he's lived in F-F-France so long. He s-s-speaks French too." said Andy, and coughed several times to ease the guilt of his out and out lie then compounded the lie with "I g-guarantee he is one hundred p-p-percent American. He left about t-two am. Are you s-s-sure it w-wasn't him?"

Iris placed a stubby finger to her chin to ponder, said "Maybe it was! Are you sure?"

"I'm s-s-sure. Irene w-would never have anyone in s-so late, foreign or not. Miss P-Pofford would be ever s-s-s-so upset."

171

"Did Irene say that?"

"As g-good as," said Andy, crossing fingers under his blanket.

"Then I'll tell Miss Pofford it was that American ambassador's son from Paris, France. Miss Pofford'll be ever so pleased!"

Iris left, singing and clomping up the basement stairs to the usual uproar of Uncle's curses and yelping dogs as Andy settled down in his sickbed to have breakfast. The tea was warming, particularly as he had not yet lit his paraffin fire and the room was colder than usual. Should he see a doctor about his inflamed finger? He dismissed the thought. What was the point? He'd be dead soon anyhow. Everybody would. He coughed, sang softly to himself "Bless us all, Bless us all, Bless us all, the long and the short and the tall!" and sipped his tea thoughtfully for a moment. He felt a little 'cuckoo' for a moment more but it passed quickly. He didn't even question it. It felt so 'normal'.

What had happened with Yves was only mutual masturbation. It was excellent. Due, obviously, he thought, to the excess of bourbon that oiled the wheels of his 'perpetual reticence', a term he was familiar with from dear Grandma in her psychoanalytical period; compliments, of course, of Ingrid Bergman's depiction of that fraught psychiatrist in Hitchcock's 'Spellbound.' which had sent Grandma directly to the library for nearly a week of research.

Mutual masturbation was such an ordinary thing. They called it 'wanking' over here. Everybody did it. No. Husbands and wives had their own exceedingly suitable, almost sacred and blessed by the 'Book' rituals to achieve sexual relief plus replicate. Hallelujah! One day, Andy, you'll be married! He laughed crazily, feeling at that moment his heart thumping painfully, at the very tip of his slightly swollen finger.

But this sexual intercourse with Yves's bottom was not an ordinary thing. It was not something about which he would immediately write a letter to Granddad. Or tell Tom. Maybe he would tell Tom. Tom had mentioned something once as they wanked and Andy hadn't known quite what he meant. But Tom had a girlfriend and he loved her and had a heck of a lot of excellent sexual intercourse with her. So Andy must have

172

been, thought Andy, wrong here. Would they both survive long enough to ever discuss it?

Andy coughed softly several times, was reassured, knew that his 'influenza' was an excellent cover for insanity -- a perfect excuse for secluding himself below street level. Though, rather than end his days in a TB sanatorium he might well find himself locked up in a Funny Farm. He laughed aloud at this Americanism. Could an 'idée fixe' actually land him in a Funny Farm? But who would defend him, protect him from those sadistic creatures who invariably ended up washing bedpans while perpetrating unspeakable deeds on the poor, nutty individuals they were meant to care for? Olivia de Havilland in 'The Snake Pit,' was utterly at the mercy of a tribe of these corridor-crawling, sanatorium louts. But she did get an Oscar nomination at the end of it all. A poor guy like himself in that crazy condition needed his champions to defend him. Andy's champions, Tom and Mom and Granddad and Aunts; Graycie, Fran, June and Dot were nine thousand miles away either sitting on their respective verandas drinking iced tea or already 'safely' underground somewhere. How could they help him? More important by far was how could he help them?! He couldn't! He was, as usual, a total zero. Furthermore, he doubted the English had ever heard of iced tea. Now that was crazy! But he was crazy now, cuckoo, goofy, and nutty as Aunt Fran's fruitcake! As deranged as Olivia de Havilland's pursuers. He was a toy train on the wrong track.

How he missed Granddad and his wisdom. Granddad who had a tried and true saying for nearly every philosophical complexity that ever intruded into the lives of ordinary persons, especially his dear grandson's. Dear Granddad, who wished only to live and let live and give excellent advice. Granddad, who was the best of the best. There was comfort in that. Comfort that even the shivering adolescent presently lounging in his bed might partake of. And did.

Uncle's dogs began to bark but became quiet and Uncle never said a word. He was watching missile reports on the telly at Number 12. Andy heard voices, a lot of voices on the stairs just outside his door. A brief knock, the door opened and there stood Iris and The Blind Girl and, this was a big surprise, Vera and Nola on their canes, or 'sticks', and with those knees! They all had the very saddest looks on their faces. Tragic looks. Every one of them. And Andy wasn't being cinematical.

Was the unthinkable now thinkable?! He should have been paying attention! Had the USA been summarily erased by hydrogen bombs? What was it?! This was the only tragic thing that might have brought Vera and Nola and the others, to his door. To seek shelter!

# 26

I hunched over in my bed and coughed as quietly as I could and stared at them as one finger twitched and the other throbbed a message that it was due for removal one day soon. I'd ask Cyril to make an appointment with a GP.  But not now. I couldn't say a word. It was worse than ever. Not a syllable would come out. My tongue was slack and sleeping like my dick right after I'd shot. It worried me that I was thinking so much about my dick lately, me being so sick and poorly. I seemed to have a shocking interest in sex. Any sex at all. First I was afraid of it. Then, after a few drinks, I'd do anything! This was not The American Way. Grandma always said I was too impressionable and easily led. I put my hand on my forehead. I was sweating. I had turned into an teenage, alcoholic, European libertine...as it were! To top it off I could hear myself speaking when I thought I was only thinking.  But I had no idea what I was saying *or* thinking.

I did my best to focus my eyes. Maybe missiles had not yet been loosed upon my homeland?! And all of these people standing in my doorway had simply brought shillings for their meters. Was it only a courteous coincidence that brought them all to my room at the same time?

The Blind Girl came in first. The others stood at the door watching her. I thought they're going to take turns feeding their meters. How thoughtful! Was this only a polite way to fill all the meters at one time to not disturb me by coming in late at night, or calling down the stairs for me to help them as had Vera and Nola? After all, I was poorly. But it looked too, as if Vera and Nola were both crying. Had Harry died? Even Iris looked sad as she scratched thoughtfully at her blue nylon armpit. I'd never seen her like this. Only an hour ago she was singing her May Day song. Oh shit! I thought. I was right! Today *was* May Day and the Russians had attacked and the good old USA had been obliterated and these people were, in fact, coming to my basement room to find shelter from the inevitable second rain of missiles! I couldn't say a word. My limp tongue was locked behind my teeth. I was going crazy but was frozen solid as

Gladys, The Blind Girl, tapped her way toward me. Why was she coming toward me? Her meters were in another direction. "Gladys?" I said, "W-What is it? W-What's happened? W-What's wrong?"

It was like a dream. The Blind Girl didn't say a word but just held out her hand and said "We are very sorry, Andy."

In her hand was a folded piece of paper. I took it and read: 'we as live here are very, very sorry for your loss. typed by william the boy.'

I looked up, saw Iris, fumbling with an envelope, still scratching, and Vera and Nola -- leaning on their canes and weeping – it must have been terrible for them to come down all those stairs to my room. I saw that Gladys was now crying too.

"S-S-Sorry, Gladys?" I said, with my left little finger wobbling like there was no tomorrow and my razor-cut-one assuring me that there wasn't. "S-S-Sorry for what?!"

Iris shoved through the others into my room as Gladys, silent and sniffling, tapped her way back to the door and waited there with Vera and Nola who, those sad, scary expressions on their faces, wiped their eyes and looked lovingly at me. Then Iris handed me a butter-stained letter. "Your post, Andy," she said, "Just come, poor Andy, fresh from the postman. Fresh from the postman's hands."

I took the letter which did not look fresh at all, but had been crudely opened and read and reread and clumsily resealed. It was from my mother. My dear Granddad was dead. He had shot himself. He said in a note that he had died when Grandma died. I knew what he meant. I knew exactly what he meant. That's how I felt about dear Granddad. Now I was dead too. I heard the crash of death first at the center of my forehead. It spread as I sat there frozen in my own deathbed. Scary thoughts of the wicked world beyond my smudged windowpanes had to wait for another day, or even for a week if earthlings were allowed a week. My dearest, dear Granddad was dead. I didn't give a damn about the Cuban Crisis. Or the wicked, fucking -- as Sheila said -- world. Fuck the wicked world! Fuck it and everything

176

in it! I was now using execrable language. Granddad would never have approved! Everything now moved in slow-motion. Even the voices seemed to be playing at the wrong speed -- like Harry's lesson record. Dear Granddad would... Fuck Granddad! Fuck him too! Him too! He'd just killed himself! Who needed him?!

I said, just loud enough for all of them to hear, "P-Please g-go" and "I appreciate your c-c-c-caring," and "Th-Thank you. I'll be okay, I'm f-f-f-f-feeling better. I'm not so p-p-p-poorly now."

I had to be polite. Granddad would have wanted it. I had forgiven him already. How could I not have? I loved him. Good breeding was a favourite word of his. As we were, my dear Granddad and I, descended from a noble United States senator. I had to be polite. I had no choice. Even 'in extremis'.

They left: Iris, who first promised some sprouts and potatoes and a bit of ham; The Blind Girl, softly crying for me -- she knew what it was for a loved one to die violently, away from you, in another country -- Iris had told me about Gladys's lost son; Vera and Nola with their knees and canes would struggle back up the basement stairs with two flights more to painfully accomplish. These were labours of love. I appreciated it. A multi-beau geste package. I had slowly begun to think again. But it wouldn't bring Granddad back. Or Grandma either. Or me. I was dead too.

Death crashed in my head again -- loud and long. Spread down my legs to my feet. I wondered if Charlie and Regina had heard it on the third floor. They hadn't gone to work today. I wondered if they were poorly too. Or maybe they were arguing and weren't getting along well. I hoped they could work it out somehow. People should be unhappy as little as possible -- all of them. Or maybe Charlie and Reggie had hangovers. I'd already had two horrible hangovers and they were probably almost worse than my childhood friend's mother's must have suffered. I hadn't fallen down yet and bruised my elbows and knees or got a big blue lump on my forehead. But that would happen today. I would fall down today. I was falling now. I could hear the wind whistling by in my ears. The two crashes in my head were me, shattering my way through the double doors of Hell. I'd been to Catholic Sunday School once when I was seven.. I knew now exactly what I had to do. Hell -- or 'Hellespont' -- was waiting for me and only a mortal sin could stop the ridiculous pain of losing Granddad who meant everything in the world. But my eyes were dry, not a tear in sight. Maybe, when there is something really important to cry about, tears don't come at all. My adolescent reservoir of cheap emotion was bone dry. I shouldn't have been aware of this at just-turned seventeen. I was now lapsing into total insanity!

# 27

I washed my hands of it all! Everything and everyone could now go straight to hell! My beautiful Granddad is dead. So fuck the Russians and their bloody missiles and the Americans and their bloody missiles! And fuck me! And fuck Art! Art is a phony substitute for Life and Life is now meaningless! In all my profound, post-pubescent glory I declare Life meaningless!

These thoughts made no sense at all. These creepy, idiotic ideas were coming from my root friends who curled heroically from beneath the mouldy floorboards!

The roots now embraced Andy's helpless gas fire. He saw them move! Roots that stealthily clutched and dusted everything with a white, sinister powder that wafted from their feathery micro-tendrils. Poisonous white powder, "wisping where it would," added Granddad 'sotto voce' -- and Andy heard! -- these roots that whirred and clicked, like the ominous wall meters, from beneath the edges of damp, decaying linoleum and layer after layer of evil, decrepit, purloined carpet. Just ask Nola! Or her long dead husband Floyd's family. Or Floyd himself! He must be available *somewhere*.

Or was it only the meter boxes whirring? Not the roots?! Goddamn this devilish room! It had killed two innocent souls already, maybe more. It was evil! How could Andy, a young, alien coward know what was really happening to him? Every thing lied! What a silly, little room it was! A gas fire and a blessed kerosene stove weren't enough to drive dingy death from the air and the fine white root powder had powers this ignorant room could only dream of! Were they both to be partners in the mortal sin of Leander Riley's untimely but well-deserved demise? Every painful pulse of his swollen poisoned finger confirmed this. And he wished it luck. Maybe Dame Nature needed a push! The verdict was in. He winced again at his thin, split face in the cracked, mirrored wardrobe's awry door. He wanted to cry but didn't, couldn't. He needed his remaining strength to turn and throw himself, as ordered, directly into the deadly tsunami rising behind him.

I went to my window, dropped myself on the floor, and slammed my spine against a cold, paint-flaking wall. I stared for a moment at the eternal rain slashing down the ivy smothered light-well and tried to clear my head of the myths and lies and terrors that surrounded me. Fuck the Pre-Raphaelite Brotherhood! Fuck the Mona Lisa! Fuck The Louvre where she hung behind the crucial six-inch thick glass to keep her safe from eight billion desecrating vandals! Why did I leave Granddad way back in California? I knew he was suffering from the terrible loss of dearest Grandma. I could have helped him -- eased his loss. The loss I feel now. What kind of loving grandson was I to him? But what kind of suicidal traitor was he to me?!

I was scarily dizzy. My razor-cut finger was agonizing now, throbbing and swollen, demanding a solemn promise I would never again sharpen a charcoal pencil with a single-edged razor blade. I laughed! Had I ever before received an ultimatum from an infected wound?! In league with this mad room it was! Of course I'd never sharpen another charcoal pencil. I'd never draw, or paint another picture either. Not in this life! Anyhow, my work was now shit! And I wasn't sure if there were any other kind of life. I hoped not. I couldn't bear to wake up, even in paradise, and be forced to relive this unbearable burden of loss. There was only one escape.

I began to cough. I didn't care a damn if Charlie or Reggie heard it at the top of the house. Who did they think they were compared to my grief?! I was Swamp-Boy, slathered in muck, smothering in poisonous white root powder, and soon to be shunted off to nowhere!

Sheila was right. The roots would devour me. Eat me alive! They were already chomping at my rotting finger. I didn't mind. They were my saviours! Let them kill me! When I died, and I hoped it would be soon, I was ready and waiting below sea level. The roots could easily dive into my decaying guts and whisk me under the crumbling carpets, warped floorboards, and basement walls into Oxford's sacred, ancient earth. I was eager manure for whatever tall and graceful tree my devoted root-friends preferred. I would become a quivering, cowardly leaf with a tree-top view! I could at last see The Dreaming Spires. Where were they when I needed them?! Who cared? As it were?! There was no comfort. I was finished dreaming and drawing and freezing and fucking! The end was nigh! Bring it on! I'll have it! Let me be dismembered by a million missiles too!

I squinted open one eye and saw the roots excitedly waving goodbye to me. They were impatient for my prematurely corrupted corpse, entranced by my precocious libertine litheness. "Woe is us!" they called! Suddenly I saw a gigantic billboard with massive neon-lit letters high above New York's Time Square! It read:

*'SWEET SEVENTEEN, HE'LL NEVER BE MISSED!*
*BET ON IT!'*

It was now time to cry and I went overboard. As I bawled, my ivy-smothered light-well instantly filled with rainwater and a rushing torrent spilled over the window gap, ripping away great, stubborn tangles of ivy. Jealous Aphrodite's tempest had begun and I, naked Leander, found myself swimming for my life in that ancient storm, swimming for the life I no longer valued or wanted or needed! As I swam, each monstrous wave pounded scary ideas into my mouth and forced me to swallow terrifying thoughts of Granddad's last grieving minutes when he so clearly remembered every loving moment with my dearest Grandma, Granddad's, own immortal beloved. He called her his own immortal beloved especially when Grandma played the Adagio Sostenuto from Beethoven's Moonlight Sonata on their old Upright piano.

Granddad said that when we died, our lives, if we were drowning, passed before our eyes. But why was it Granddad's life, Granddad's grief, passing before me? Didn't I have a life of my own? I began to cry harder, to bawl and howl and scream and strike my fists through the swirling water. Now I was in a slow-motion movie. It was my car crash on Mount Palomar in

Southern California. I was sixteen, trying out my new driver's license and as my car began to skid off the rainy road everything seemed to slow down, finally stopping as I tilted at the edge of a thousand foot ravine. I remember clearly a choir of far away voices singing. Granddad said later that it was The Voices of the Spheres welcoming me into the valley of the shadow of death. But it wasn't my time then. Of course it wasn't! My time was, is now!

There is no heavenly choir, only the whoosh of water. Every time I open my mouth for air it is filled with cold, foul smelling, seawater. I struggle against each huge breaking wave with numb arms until I am sucked under, and swirled over and over, tangled in seaweed. This is what I get for living below sea level! Charlie was right! Now, and I have no idea why, a crazy jingle bounces right into in my craziness! And I follow the bouncing ball and say!

> Listen! Listen! The cat's pissin'!
> Where?! Where?! Under The Chair!
> Quick! Quick! Get the gun!
> Ah, shucks! It's all done!

All done. Almost but not quite.

# 28

My own life's passing now began. Quietly. Charlie and Reggie swam by just above me in thick, cotton underwear and Sheila swooped over my head in all her naked glory – I would never draw or paint her now. She breast-stroked elegantly away followed closely by naked, uncircumcised, dark-haired Yves who sized me up from the corner of his eye, and winked in a casual, Gallic manner.

Far above, flopping on the surface of the rushing water splashed Cyril in a 1930's swimsuit like Granddad's. He was face down, grinning at me with his bloodshot eyes, and caught in a powerful current that swiftly carried him away just as Tom came swimming in full U.S. Air Force dress, saluted, smiled and dived out of sight into a whirling cloud of bubbles. It must have been difficult swimming fully clothed. But if anyone could, Tom could. Then Gladys, cane-less, in a flowing grey dress that matched her grey, short-cropped hair, drifted near humming a melody I'd never heard. She grinned happily to herself as though she had some wonderful secret and passed beneath me.

Now I saw the rocking bottom of a rowboat and could just make out, above the surface of the water, Iris in her light blue nylon uniform rowing in circles with one powerful arm. In her other hand she was waving a butter-stained letter and singing 'Today is May Day!' as she rowed toward a faraway shore where stood the grieving Vera and Nola who could never have managed a swim. Not with those knees. Miss Pofford stood there too, beside Vera and Nola, shrieking at Iris's approaching rowboat but I couldn't understand a word.

So it was finally May Day, my own, long awaited, May Day. But no birdies sang either. Then, after a moment when thousands of bubbles made it impossible to see anything, the lovely Irene swam through them toward me, smiling and swirling in her beautiful red kimono. Behind her swam -- his T-shirt said – 'The Loyal Jean-Francois'. I had terrible pangs of guilt because I had never thanked them for my kerosene stove. I would never have the chance now. I was a goner. It was sad, soggy curtains for me.

Though Granddad had said that your whole life passes before your eyes I found for myself that this was not always the case. All of these swimming people, not including Tom, reflected only the last week of my life. Was I being cheated by fate, even at my own death? Life wasn't fair. But death was worse! I was now dying and sane enough to know it. My swollen right arm and rotting, painful, cut finger seemed to light the water around me.

I got sleepy then sleepier. I couldn't move my arms or legs now but only floated. I took a deep breath. This time it wasn't water that gushed into my mouth. It was swamp air. I took another deep breath -- I couldn't help it. It seemed I had to breathe – but why? I was dead. I took another deep breath and another and I saw dear Granddad climbing through my window. But it couldn't have been Granddad. Granddad was dead. Dead like Grandma. Dead like me. "Hello, Granddad," I said, just in case it was Granddad. "Welcome to May Day, Granddad!"

"Today is May Day! Hooray for May Day!" sang Granddad. Suddenly here was Grandma too, singing to Granddad, "Where birdies sing and everything and you shall marry me! Damn you! In spite of the weather!"

And that was that. That is how I died.

# 29

Andy lay on his back and Yves, from the top of the light-well saw him on the bare floor directly below his window. Sleeping, Yves thought, and dropped himself into the light-well, to surprise Andy. Yves easily slammed open the window and climbed through but Andy didn't move.

When Yves saw Andy's swollen right arm which culminated in a flaming red index finger as round and thick as an over-fried sausage he ran up the basement stairs and pounded on the nearest door crying " Mon dieu! Mon dieu! Andy is dead! Leandair is dead!"

Cyril, whose father may or may not have been a medical doctor or a vicar or a famous chef -- sailed into Andy's room with Yves, swiftly took in the situation and yelled through the thinness. "Somebody call an ambulance! Andy is dying!"

"Right you are, Mr. Lemmington!" cried Iris, who wasn't surprised, through the thinness and a mouthful of pink cake.

Iris slouched at the doorway of Number 13 scratching absently at the only faintly fetid armpit in her blue nylon uniform. She watched eagerly as Andy was wheeled through the tiny garden's rusting iron gate into an ambulance and whispered to herself "Miss Pofford'll be ever so upset," and wiped a tear, or was it sweat, from her flushed and much too red cheek.

# 30

When Andy woke, an awfully nice nurse in a starched, white uniform with a large cap that resembled a white bird spreading its wings, said "Welcome to the world, love. You're at the Radcliffe. You've had severe blood poisoning. Doctor caught it just in time! Without treatment in another hour you'd have died."

She smiled and of course Andy, always a fool for a smile, liked that -- a nurse telling it like it was. No-nonsense-Grandma would have loved it. It was exactly the sort of nurse Grandma would have made. Had she been a nurse.

Andy's mind was nearly clear now with only a trace of crazy, seawater flashes and he began to wonder what all the fuss was about till he noticed his hugely bandaged right hand and the tube in his arm and the nurse said "We're feeding you antibiotics. You might have died without them. Many have." Andy felt it wasn't crucial for her to say twice that he could have died. Especially if he nearly had and could vaguely remember having wished it.

"What a terrible coincidence, blood poisoning and walking pneumonia at the same time. You might well have died," said the awfully nice nurse. Andy thought he could hear his dear, frank Grandma laughing and he joined her and the nurse was puzzled. This was no laughing matter.

Then it hit him again, with a blinding thud. His dearest Granddad was dead -- a bullet from an old gun Granddad had kept for a year in a drawer under his socks Mother had said in her letter. So what did Andy do? What else? – cry-baby that he was, he burst into sobs and bawled uncontrollably like the lunatic he had briefly been.

"That's it, dear," said the nurse, "Cry it out. Severe blood poisoning affects the whole body, the mind, everything. Your walking-pneumonia didn't help. You were terribly weakened by the time the blood-poisoning slotted in. Doctor told you all about it this morning. I don't believe you were listening." Andy could not remember much till now and he continued to bawl.

With great, gaping, gasps for air he bawled with impunity like a child in a tantrum. As he and Cyril had. The nurse did not realize that Andy was simply a cry-baby and, humouring him, went on "Your friends have gone for lunch, love. They've visited every day."

"Every day? How long have I b-been here?"

"Four days and a bit, love. It was touch and go."

It was then Yves came in, closely followed by Cyril who, after meeting Yves, had abruptly changed his opinions on 'frogs' and Paris.

"It's r-r-r-really considerate of you to c-come," whispered Andy and attempted to sit up as they entered, but was gently motioned back on his pillow by the nurse.

Cyril and Yves told Andy the story of his rescue and he could only hazily remember the two attending him. But the thought of it summoned up happiness of such unbearable proportions that Andy lay silent, overcome with gratitude and, typically, unable to express it. He was forced to call upon all of his remaining strength to keep from bawling again. The nurse seemed to understand his predicament. "He is too tired to speak just now, boys." When they'd gone she brought Andy a hot milk and said she'd give him something to help him sleep if he needed it. He didn't. He finished the milk and was just dozing off as his tiny, new self piloted the nurse's white-winged cap into the blue sky above the even bluer Pacific with its several hundred surfers riding as many soon-to-break waves.

But Andy was sleeping by now, oblivious, even, to the colourful conclusion of this, his own restful dream.

# 31

Upon his return from hospital two days and three or four visits from Cyril and Yves later, Iris presented Andy with a butter-stained, re-sealed letter from the battleground that had not yet become a battleground, his homeland. It was from Tom who said only how sorry he was about Andy's Granddad and how the family knew that Andy couldn't be there for the funeral and for him not to worry but knew he would anyway. But not to. Tom was not much of a letter writer. Andy also had letters from every one of his four favourite aunts. All of the envelopes were witty though butter stained, one with a perfect oily thumb-print from he knew who. She could be arrested over this he thought, and her thumbprint filed!

The next morning after a long, restful sleep Andy woke to see more torrents of rain gushing into his light-well and Cyril lounging in The Chair smoking the last of Andy's Woodbines. Beside him on the floor was the small box of books he had promised Andy.

"Congratulations" said Cyril, the very second Andy's eyes opened. "You've won, their ships have turned back, they'll remove their missiles -- every last one of the beggars, and Kennedy has sent a gob-stopper to every Yank in Oxford. Here's yours."

Cyril leaned back, dug deep into his dingy cords and pulled out a small colourful sphere of hard candy known in America as a jaw-breaker. He tossed it to Andy who, surprising himself, handily caught it then seemed for a moment he'd cry yet again at this new completely spontaneous gesture of kindness but suddenly laughed, jumped out of bed and pulled Cyril up from his chair and hugged him. Cyril seemed pleased. But one never really knew with Cyril.

Uncle's dogs broke into their traditional cacophony as Iris crashed into Andy's room with two rattling breakfast trays. "The Russians has sailed away from Spain, Mr. Riley!"

Where had this 'Mister' come from?! Andy, was stunned. He and Cyril, mutually awed, glanced at one another.

"Sailed right away!" announced said Iris, "And they ain't

to missile bomb no cities neither! Not one! Not even Oxford! Miss Pofford was ever so pleased! Miss Pofford says you're to have Sunday lunch today whether you're poorly or not! Are you still poorly, Mr. Riley?" Iris slammed the two breakfast trays on Andy's bedside table and slapped her small, rough palm on Andy's forehead. "Still poorly, are we?"

"N-No," said Andy, "I'm n-not poorly now, Iris. I was p-p-poorly in h-hospital but that was a m-millennium ago."

"You what?" said Iris.

"I'm n-not poorly now, Iris," repeated Andy, "n-not n-now. Not anymore."

"Miss Pofford'll be ever so pleased, Mr. Riley."

There it was again, thought Andy, 'Mister.'

"Will you be takin' your brekky-wekky with Mr. Riley, Mr Lemmington? I brung your brekky-wekky down here to Mr. Riley's room to you as I thought you was here in his room as you wasn't up there in your room. And you was!"

"A singular deduction! I shall breakfast here, Iris, with Mr. Riley, if you please," said Cyril, "In this very chair."

"Right you are, Mr. Lemmington!"

Iris took up the other breakfast tray and slammed it into Cyril's lap nearly toppling him as The Chair tilted to its side and Iris's mood changed abruptly. She glared at Andy. "What have you done to Miss Pofford's chair, Mr. Riley?!"

"Mr. Riley has done precisely nothing to this execrable wreck of a chair, Iris. It has been this way since the Boxer Rebellion!"

"You what?!" cried Iris as though she'd something to which she must instantly take exception but wasn't certain.

"Desist and be gone, wench!" cried Cyril.

Iris grinned -- she adored being called a wench especially as it was a gentleman said it. It brought to mind the buxom Maureen O'Hara beauties in her favourite Pirate films. Something tickled her about it that she couldn't put a buttery finger on. Sometimes Cyril did catch her by surprise in the nicest way. "Right you are, Mr. Lemmington!" she beamed, slammed out, shrieked "Uncle! Uncle! The Yanks has won! The Yanks has won!"

"Bugger the Yanks!" shouted Uncle over the barking chorus.

"Had 'em here for the war. Noisy bastards!"

"Miss Pofford is ever so pleased!"

"Bugger Pofford! Where's my goddamned breakfast?!"

"Oh Uncle!" cried Iris, refusing to be brought down from her wenchly high, "Oh Uncle, you are rude!"

"Where's my breakfast?! Goddamn it!"

"Our Mr. Leander Riley's got your breakfast, Uncle. We wasn't expectin' him till tomorrow. I'll fetch another for you! Our Yank's eatin' your breakfast!"

"Stuff our Yank!" yelled Uncle. "How's that boy doin', then?"

"Mending, Uncle, back from hospital. Mr. Leander Riley is doin' just fine. He's not poorly now, our Yank. Not poorly now."

"Good for him!" yelled Uncle through his door, "Now move your arse and fetch me my Saturday tea and toast, and double bacon and egg, goddamn it!"

# 32

Cyril left his small box of books with Andy: Hardy's 'Jude the Obscure'. Andy had the year before read it in his high school English Lit class and had whole-heartedly identified with the tragic Jude. There was also Kafka's 'Castle', Eliot's 'Wasteland' and the first two volumes of Durrell's 'Alexandria Quartet' which Cyril had no intention of ever reading, "Not even," he sighed, quoting his idol, "for ready money."

Cyril was thanked and Andy promised to read every one of them. He later did and Cyril, from afar, assured him that he was well on his way to wisdom -- of a sort.

The next morning found Andy and Cyril under umbrellas in driving rain outside Number 13 waiting for Cyril's taxi to the station and ultimately to the boat train in London. Andy helped Cyril load his luggage and promised to visit him in Paris. "Don't threaten me," sighed Cyril with his wryest smile. As his taxi moved away Cyril refused to turn and wave. His agony was visibly unbearable and to expose it again, definitely 'non-U' though he'd never actually believed in that crap. Not really.

As Cyril's taxi disappeared, another taxi, large and bus-like, arrived just as the front door of Number 12 crashed open and Iris, scurrying under a huge black umbrella, wheeled out The Boy, who was proudly sporting an orange bow tie. Andy rushed to assist the driver and they placed The Boy and his chair in the back of this vehicle as Iris led Gladys The Blind Girl, beautifully attired in a bright blue dress and thick, dark green, wool coat, into the taxi. Then Iris disappeared. Andy wondered if she was not going along with them. The driver installed cursing Uncle just as last but obviously not least, Miss Pofford, smiling graciously at Andy and everyone else in this small world she ruled, swept out in a green-feathered hat, green tailored suit and a primarily orange, thick woolen shawl. When Miss Pofford was comfortably seated, Iris, not to be outdone, returned in her newly laundered light blue nylon uniform with a lavender velvet band of artificial daisies tight around her head and a stunning, far nicer than Sheila's, short, fake-fur jacket. A proper 'wench' she felt even if her Sunday-best, crushed-velvet suit still languished at the dry cleaners for lack of funds to fetch it. She'd lost the funds. Everyone knew where.

As they drove off, all, including Uncle were delighted or at least excited. Even in the rain. It was their long delayed Outing in this brand new vehicle provided by Miss Pofford's twin brother's garage up the Banbury Road.

Yves was now in Paris visiting his father but soon to return. Cyril, too was in Paris, in management training at the same hotel in which his idol, Oscar Wilde, had spent his last, sad days as Sebastian Melmoth. This touch of the literary was a comforting balm to Cyril who still loved history and literature, even after he had partially accepted that he would never claim a crucial role in either.

Cyril's multi-layered 'Pa', actually a prominent investor, amidst so many other pursuits, owned a moderate chunk of this Paris hotel and Cyril found himself graciously welcomed. Cyril was also more amenable to 'Frenchies' since he'd met the also amenable Yves whom he felt could use a bit of mothering. Et-cetera.

Sheila had not visited Andy during his perilous hospital adventure at the Radcliffe, just up the road from Numbers 12 and 13. She had the day before left by ship to California accompanied by a hunky young American Art student she'd met on her stereo-gramophone shopping tour in London. She was to continue her Art studies in Los Angeles where, with lightning speed, Daddy had arranged all the necessaries; transfer of records etc. from the prestigious Rossetti. Sheila had also hoped to grab a bit of California sunshine before, considering the delicate international situation, it was too late.

But all of this was, obviously, more to do with her hunky new American than it was about California, sunshine, or Art. It was also rumoured, possibly by Marcella, that Sheila was again pregnant. How might Andy have churned in his grave had his septicemic, death-wishing finger succeeded and Sheila was pregnant? But she wasn't and it hadn't so he didn't.

The Crisis was resolved whilst Sheila was mid-Atlantic. She needn't have hurried, as she finally wrote to Daddy, but would be eternally grateful if he would allow her to draw upon his California bank a sum considerably larger than they had agreed upon before her departure. Which, of course, doting Daddy did.

Marcella knew nothing of Andy's, and not a lot about the world's close encounter with extinction and continued to have afternoon poetry readings in her room at Lady Marian Hall -- continued, too, to roast bread on her electric fire and often, with her chubby acolyte Alasdair for company, to spread delicious homemade strawberry jam on the toast. Andy was slated, in the near future, to discuss 'A young American's first impression of the city of Dreaming Spires' to be immediately followed by Alasdair playing an arranged-by-himself, flute solo of the 'Largo' from Dvorak's 'New World' -- Andy, being most appropriately from and of this 'New World.' Everyone, by this time, had completely forgotten civilization's, as well as Andy's, razor-thin escape from the abyss.

Andy had also spoken discreetly to Marcella to go easy on the Leander-Hero legend as he felt he and the world had already successfully swum to the other side of this particular body of water. The myth, he insisted, no longer applied. At least not specifically to him, because Andy had returned to the Rossetti where his work was now proceeding more than swimmingly.

# 33

After class and a trip to the bakery for three custard tarts, Andy was on his way through the pouring rain to visit Irene at the Radcliffe, the same hospital he had so recently vacated. He'd been there several times in the last week and he and Irene had spoken at length about his love for dear Granddad as well as her brief 'marriage' so long ago to her Sergeant Ricardito Martinez.

In the hospital corridor his awfully nice, tell-it-like-it-is, nurse remembered and greeted him with "You're looking the picture of health, Andy."

"I was at d-death's d-door," said Andy with a smile.

The nurse grinned and understood perfectly that he preferred not to speak of this any longer. So she congratulated him on his victory over the Russians.

Andy knocked, entered and received a warming look from Irene, her head tied in yet another flowered scarf. She was sitting up in bed reading 'Lady Chatterley's Lover'.

"How lovely of you to come, Andy! You look dazzling, darling! Irene seemed thinner than when he had seen her only the day before though her enthusiasm remained solidly intact.

"Sit, darling," she said, and 'darling' seemed so right, the way she said it. Anything Irene said, thought Andy, would be right.

He handed her the small paper bag of custard tarts and sat. He had loved this woman from the moment he met her as she stood naked and unembarrassed in the bathroom door at Number 12.

"Feeling much better, are you, love?" said Irene, adjusting her flowery turban.

"I s-s-should be asking you that, Irene...d-darling," he grinned. Here she was asking Andy how he felt.

"How is it g-going for you, n-now?" asked Andy.

"As expected. No particularly earth-shaking new develop-ments, although the latest medicine is not nearly so sick-making."

Irene did not know that her doctor had ceased the strong chemical attack on her cancer as it had proved useless and only made her ill.

"Jean-Francois has been a brick" she said. "He comes every day. It has to be quite early. Before he goes to work."

Andy had already personally thanked Jean Francois for his paraffin fire and Irene for arranging it and told them that without it, given the circumstances, he would surely have died of that 'walking' pneumonia. Then regretted having said 'died.' He felt rotten, especially when he had so poorly valued his own life and she was so valiantly fighting for hers.

"Honestly, darling," she said, noting his troubled, young face, "It's not as bad for me as all that. Mum always told me that the worst thing that could ever happen to you was to have your head chopped off and tossed in a ditch. I hardly think that's about to happen!" Irene laughed. "And the ditch part of it wouldn't matter would it?!" She laughed again. "I've certainly felt worse. How are things at Number 13? Iris still losing the meter money?"

Andy nodded.

"I was so very sorry to hear of your dear Granddad's passing. I know what he meant to you."

Andy had kept this sad news from her but such news travels but he knew why he continued to love this woman. With one word, remembering to place the 'dear' before Granddad, she had established herself in Andy's eternal hall of fame.

A nurse came in, said Andy had stayed long enough.

"Pish-tosh!" sighed Irene, but acquiesced as she was very tired indeed. She thanked Andy for the custard tarts but took only one and gave the rest back saying the food at the Radcliffe was outstanding and she didn't wish to ruin her appetite or they might think her ungrateful. Andy took the bag of tarts and kissed Irene on the forehead and left, promising to come the next day after class. He did not mention that her replacement model had now been brought in at the Rossetti.

"I'd love to see you tomorrow, darling," she called after him as he left. Andy never saw her alive again. Irene died that night.

# 34

As Andy entered the hospital corridor from Irene's room he came face to face with Nola and assumed she was here to visit Irene. "This is her r-room," he said.

"It most certainly is not!" replied Nola. "She's down the corridor. I've been there all morning and I've just come back from the ladies'. My, but don't you look well after your seizures."

"Thank you, said Andy, I'm f-feeling wonderful. In top f-f-form! Who's down the c-c-corridor?"

"Our Vera, of course" said Nola, "they brung her in last night. It was all so sudden. I'm sure she'd love to see you. She's been asking after you ever since we got her here."

Andy followed Nola to Vera's room wondering why he had been asked for. As they entered, Nola wiped her eyes and blew her nose into a huge hanky. "She's sleepin'."

"I am not sleeping," said Vera, eyes closed, from her bed.

"You've got a visitor, Vera," said Nola.

"Who, then? The Grim Reaper?"

"It's our Yank, Vera. Leander, whose compatriots has just swam the Hellespont and put the Russian Bear back in his sodding cave!"

"Bother the Russian Bear!" Vera's eyes snapped open and whirled like pinwheels, searching for her new visitor. But otherwise she could move only with difficulty. "Come closer, Andy, so Vera can see you, love."

Andy moved closer, sat, and bent near.

"You're looking absolutely wonderful. So healthy and well! How thoughtful of you to come and see old Vera. She's had a stroke of bad luck," said Vera, with a sly smile. "I don't know what's got into me. Nola, dear, would you be so kind as to excuse us for a minute or two? Possibly three?"

Nola rose from her chair at the other side of Vera's bed. "If that is your fervent wish, Vera."

"It is, dear, just now, but only for a minute or two. Or three."

Nola, unable to hide her hurt fled haltingly on her cane to sit in the corridor just outside as Vera whispered to Andy, "Is she gone, love?"

Andy assured Vera that Nola was not there and was about to add that, to be honest, he'd had no idea that Vera was here in hospital and that he'd actually come to see Irene but Vera didn't give him the chance. She spoke quickly, "Now. Listen to me. Here, take my hand, I've got a bone to pick with you. You surely opened a can of worms being so nice and helpful that day you came up and saved Nola and me from freezing to death." She gave Andy's hand a tug. "Come closer so Nola can't hear. I don't want to hurt that good woman's feelings. She is my dearest friend."

Andy moved closer, "I opened a c-can of w-worms?" He was astonished that Vera, considering her condition could speak at all, let alone be so talkative. "Just listen to what I have to say. I'll get to that later, dear."

Vera was puffing for air as she lay there, eyes flashing. She could have had great success as a public speaker, thought Andy, on any subject she chose. He was mesmerized.

"I'm getting better by the hour. It was what they call a 'mini-stroke'. I couldn't speak last night when they brought me in and look at me now. I can't move completely yet but I'll be movin' all my arms and legs by evening and that's a promise. Watch! She gave her left hand a small weak wave and grinned. Now. I want a promise from you, Andy. Will you promise?"

"P-P-Promise what, Vera?"

"I want you to promise me that you will temporarily take over the care and feeding of Harry the budgie."

Vera's eyes shone with determination. All was going to be just so, just as she ordained it. "Now," she continued, gathering breath, "I would put this in writing but I can't write properly. I shall, I am certain, retrieve that facility by early tomorrow. But I'll thoroughly inform Nola of my decision when she comes back. I don't wish to hurt Nola's feelings as she has been lovely in all this turmoil. And with those knees!" Vera took a very deep breath to catch up with her words. "But I simply will not have my Harry speaking way up here!" Vera raised the pitch of her voice to a shrill squeak. "I won't have my Harry sound like Nola's son, Dennis, who has, in Nola's very own words, mind you, a 'shrill and piping voice' which I find lacking in authority. Now. I know very well that I was playing Harry's speech lessons at the wrong speed on the gramophone. Because, at the right speed the instructor's voice is unfortunately the very carbon copy of Nola's Dennis's. You gave my game away, Andy, by correcting the gramophone's speed. So, partly it's your fault. So that is why I am asking you to do this for me. Now. I know as sure as I'm born that Nola will play Harry's lessons at the correct speed whilst I am absent and when I come home poor Harry will be babbling in unacceptable treble tones! I won't have it! I won't have it!" cried Vera, with such surprising new vigour that Andy jumped. "It will only be temporary," she added, "your care of Harry -- just until I return. And I warn you, it will be soon!" Vera laughed, strained to move her eyes to see Andy's response as he'd moved only slightly out of view. "Promise? Say you promise, love."

"I will p-promise to do my b-best," said Andy, "It w-will be an honour to t-try."

"Good. Now. Where has Nola got to? Could you fetch her, dear, so that, in the nicest way, I can read her the riot act? Will you be coming in tomorrow, love? I'm certain I'll be out of bed by then and dancing a jolly jig with my handsome young doctor. Come and join in! Won't it be fun?! I feel so invigorated! "

"S-See you tomorrow, Vera. I'll be coming to s-see Irene too, she's j-just down the hall."

"Oh!" cried Vera, "What a lovely coincidence! Irene and I are old chums! My God! We all end up here sooner or later, don't we?!"

Andy, knowing well that he too had ended up here sooner than later, closed the door softly and said goodbye to Nola as he left. Vera's grit and feverish valour sang in his heart as he started down the corridor and collided with a familiar looking tall, ravishingly lovely, red-haired girl leaving Irene's room.

"Hello!" said Andy.

She was startled and turned abruptly toward him, said "I'm at the Rossetti too but we've never met."

"Andy," he said, "And y-you're Wendy. I s-saw you scream

and run out of the p-playhouse coffee bar my first day at the Rossetti."

"Yes," she replied, "a close friend was injured in a car crash."

"I hope they're all r-r-right."

"She's doing very well now. It wasn't as serious as they thought." Wendy smiled.

What did Sheila know, anyhow? Why should she say anything like that? Professional martyr, my ass, thought Andy, unless Wendy was some lovely Joan of Arc. Besides, you can't say such things to an English rose! Furthermore, he had himself only just recovered from a near miss at negligent self-martyr-dom. "Irene has told me y-you've b-been to s-s-see her a lot."

"I love Irene," said Wendy and smiled again.

"S-So do I. I f-feel like I've known her m-my whole life. I've just seen her this m-morning."

"I've just come from her, myself. They let me stay only a few minutes. Irene seemed very tired".

Wendy's cheeks and neck flushed pink, the way any normal English Rose's ought to, thought Andy. "Careful, boy," whispered Granddad from behind his ear, "This isn't a movie."

"You've landed on your feet. Irene likes Yanks." Wendy laughed. "So you're our new American, are you?"

Andy nodded. "A bit shop-worn by n- now, I th-think."

"I've heard you'd been seeing a lot of Sheila" said Wendy, with yet another flashing smile. "That might account for it."

"Yes", said Andy," But s-s-she's g-gone to California. Los Angeles, I th-think."

No one could have missed Andy's scarlet blush. But Wendy wasn't looking. She was halfway to the entrance waving goodbye to him over her shoulder.

Andy knew he would see Wendy at the Rossetti on Monday when he would invite her for a pork pie and orange squash dinner for Sunday and maybe Miss Pofford could provide some sprouts and potatoes and a bit of ham -- all due, of course, with the rent.

With my drawing board in my lap I was finishing a very

satisfying sketch I'd brought home to work on. Wendy had left and I was sort of thinking about her and wondering how well the pork pie lunch and potatoes and sprouts and a bit of ham not to mention the very, very orange, orange squash, had gone down today.

But I was wondering, mostly, if it was her smile and dancing eyes, as we walked over Magdalen Bridge -- wondering if it really was Wendy who caused the rain to stop just then and the sun to shine for ten full minutes. Here, over Oxford and several convenient Dreaming Spires. What a sight! Oxford glowing beneath twenty minutes of glorious, gleaming sun! I timed it. I would never forget it!

"You're overdoing it, Andy," said Granddad from nowhere and laughed. Too 'cinematical, my boy! Could get you in trouble."

# 35

I was almost asleep when someone knocked very softly on my door. I knew it couldn't be Wendy because she would never have come to my room at this hour -- it wouldn't be seemly, one of Granddad's favourite words. Granddad is still with me and I listen to him. But I guess in not the same way. The knock at my door couldn't be Cyril or Yves. They were both in Paris. And Sheila was in Los Angeles with her own Yank. Marcella wouldn't have dared, ater her drunken spree, even without Alasdair. Charlie and Reggie had never come during the night since I vomited on Charlie. It had to be The Blind Girl. "Come in, G-Gladys," I said. The door opened and in the dim light from my gas fire I saw Irene's beautiful -- fabulous as she called it -- red silk kimono floating toward me. I thought sleepily for a few happy seconds that it was Irene herself, recovered and returned home but I knew, as my mind cleared of sleep, that three weeks before, we had all attended her simple memorial service. It was Gladys I saw in this far too large, red silk kimono that Irene must have bequeathed her. I sat up in bed. In Gladys's other hand, as she came tapping toward me on her cane, was a very small draw-stringed bag. I said "W-What is it, Gladys?" I was still a little groggy. But not too groggy to pull myself up in bed and straighten one of the wide kimono sleeves that had caught at her elbow. I thought it was sad that Gladys would never see the bright red colour of this kimono that had made Irene so happy in her last days. Of course, cry-baby that I am, it was time again and I sniffled as quietly as I could, hoping Gladys wouldn't hear me. I was wrong.

"You mustn't cry, dear," she soothed, "Irene never cried about herself and neither must we."

What strong women these British people produce!

"Jean Francois gave me these today, Irene's pearls. He said they are not cultured pearls, Andy, but perfectly matched natural pearls. He said Irene wanted you to have them. They're from her long ago Yank husband, Sergeant Martinez. Irene said that as they came from a Yank they ought to go to a Yank. Jean

Francois said that Irene thought you could use them for your Art education. He said something about Irene stealing water, dear, but I didn't follow what he meant."

I took the little velvet bag from Gladys and knew exactly what Irene meant. Gladys went to her meter box and wound in a shilling and whispered "Goodnight, dear" and left quietly to not wake Uncle's dogs. But the dogs yelped and squealed till Uncle swatted at least one of them quiet and Gladys said "It's only old Gladys here, Uncle. Only old Gladys, wandering by and wondering why."

"Good night, girlie," said Uncle through his door.

"Goodnight, Uncle," said Gladys and slowly climbed the stairs, tapping all the way though she knew it with her eyes closed -- I didn't mean that as a joke. I suppose she tapped because she might trip over a pile of dead rabbits as I did on my second day in Oxford. Even though she knew that Cyril now lived in Paris and there would be no more bunnies or fowl in lieu of rent for Miss Pofford.

I pulled open the small, velvet bag, dropped the string of pearls into my palm and sat there dangling them in front of my nose and leaking eyes, indulging in what was to be, I hoped, the last blubbing lack of self-control I would ever experience. The subtle perfume Irene used drifted from the inside of the little velvet bag and didn't make it any easier to sleep. It was a long night and I lay there listening to the rain slap the ivy in my light-well and thinking of that day, not so long ago, that Irene had 'stolen' my hot water. What a crazy exchange. A necklace of precious pearls for a few ounces of lukewarm water. But she got my heart too. Was that a fair trade?

The next day, after class, I went to the garage where Jean Francois worked and tried to give the pearls back to him. He wouldn't take them. He said that this was what Irene had wanted so this is what he wanted. I hoped with all my heart that when Irene died she had known what a good friend he really was besides being good sex as she half-seriously described him to me in one of our last conversations. No. There is not a doubt that Irene knew what a fine honest man Jean Francois was, is, and how much he loved her. I am sure when she described him only as good sex she did not dare to appear to love him -- even if she did -- as it would turn her into a cheat. She was leaving soon for where he could not follow no matter how much she loved him or he loved her. That is a terrible thing about love. Even though it is a many splendoured thing it certainly doesn't conquer all! Not by a long  shot!

My dear Granddad knew this and even wrote a poem about it. He showed it me just before I left Lemon Gulch for the Rossetti.

*Love is the Devil's bargain*
*We pay for with our guts*
*To fall in love forever*
*We've got to be half nuts*
*For even if our love's returned*
*In equal measure ...Sigh!!!*
*The Devil's compensated*
*When either of us die.*

Even if you love with all your might, there is a payday. I should have stayed with my dear Granddad. He needed me. 'But such is youth' he used to say. I fitted the bill *in aces!*

# 36

Andy felt, knew, he was getting himself back. He suspected, too, that the self slowly being allotted him would be a bigger, better self than he'd had before. Certainly not perfect but he wasn't the complete freak he had always imagined himself. His freakiness had come from his dearth of experience with the freakiness of others. Particularly all of these English people. They were themselves and most of them didn't care who knew it. Charlie didn't care who knew it. She spoke her mind. Though it might have hurt a few feelings here and there once in a while -- probably more than once in a while -- at least it was honest. Charlie never lied. It was obvious to Andy. Especially obvious to the new Andy. Reggie had crept down his basement stairs one day while Charlie was at work and surprised him. "Andy," she'd said immediately, "I want to apologize."

"What f-for?" he had asked, exceedingly -- though he seldom used that word anymore -- exceedingly surprised.

"I was a little forward the other day (Andy couldn't remember any day that she had been even a little forward) and I may have had some...ideas."

"Ideas?" asked Andy.

"About you," replied Reggie.

"W-What s-s-sort of ideas?" asked Andy who had no idea what Reggie was talking about.

"But everything's changed now," said Reggie, and smoothed back her long, silky hair. "I am deeply in love with Charlie and I was wrong to ever have any other ideas."

"That's good," said Andy, knowing that ideas, particularly other ideas, that he had absolutely no idea of, might easily have been wrong. Or even right. It wasn't philosophically impossible. There was plenty of latitude for wrongness here. Or rightness. The new Andy could not deny this, in view of his recently acquired wider err...perspective, as it were. "Would you like some orange squash?"

"I don't think so," she'd said, again smoothing back her silky hair, "I'd better go. Charlie will be back soon and she might get the wrong idea."

Andy had said okay and that he had enjoyed their talk and Reggie just looked at him. When Reggie was gone he mixed himself an orange squash and ate what remained of a small pork pie from the day before. He liked Charlie and Reggie, especially straightforward Charlie who had replaced the window pane Alasdair had broken and peed on. Even though Charlie told him that Miss Pofford had paid her.

On Vera's return from the Radcliffe Infirmary -- it had indeed been, and fortunately, a mini-stroke -- Andy was invited to tea. Vera looked splendid and almost the perfect picture of health -- leaving out knees. Both women daily fought the good fight against Nature's inevitability, especially concerning knees and various other ligaments, and creaky joints, and sought and received the mutual comfort expected of one another. Though the very tiniest hurt had remained with Nola for almost two days. It was when Vera, at the hospital, had asked her to leave for three minutes whilst she spoke to Andy alone. But when Andy later spoke to Nola so diplomatically about Harry, revealing absolutely nothing about her son Dennis's 'treble, piping voice' this very tiniest hurt vanished -- and what a relief! However, Nola firmly refused to give over the care and lessons of Harry, the budgerigar.

Vera's recovery was as spectacular as she had foreseen it and she retained only the smallest hesitation moving her left hand. She was right-handed so this posed no problem at all. Certainly, it did not interfere in her new correspondence with a gentleman she and Nola, who also attended, had met in a therapy group at the Radcliffe. Unfortunately, this older gentleman now lived in Aberdeen, and distance, not to mention his nearly complete immobility, made a personal visit improbable. But letters between them were cheering and this gentleman always inquired, however briefly, about Nola's health too, and he often, very often, made kind mention of Nola's tiny feet which always provided a modicum of joy, promoting as it did, the two ladies' already firmly established mutual tranquillity.

Tea was presented, Andy was informed, on Nola's long

deceased husband Floyd's, or rather Floyd's family's, tea service. The only remaining heirloom that Nola swore had not been pilfered away by Iris in her recklessly diligent service of Numbers 12 and 13 Wilton Street. The tea, prepared by Nola, was excellent and Vera, on a rare visit with Nola to Nola's son, Dennis, the day before, had also made a splendid cake in his basement kitchen. Vera had retained the glorious baking skills that served her well as head pastry cook at a moderately sized Lyons Corner House in The Strand, London, until it was buzz-bombed in the last year of WW2.

Andy politely inquired about the progress of Harry's general well-being and language lessons and Vera said, under Nola's watchful eye, that Harry's silence had not been broken by a single word. "Not even a line from the Magna bloomin' Carta," added Nola.

"In fact," added Vera sadly, "his instruction recording was shattered, somehow, into a million pieces."

"By Iris," snapped Nola quickly, "quite by accident, when she took it off its table to set a breakfast tray and laid it in a chair and someone sat on it."

"'Twas me," sighed Vera, "I am  that someone and am guilty as charged."

"And there's an end to the whole story," said the two ladies almost in unison. "Except," added Nola emphatically, "that certain people should bleedin' watch where they sit!"

"Or," added Vera, equally emphatically, "They might bleedin' sit on fragile discs placed purposely in chairs by trusted friends."

"And there's an end to the whole story," said the two again, almost in unison.

# 37

Andy's work was at last making him happy again. At the Rossetti Drawings and Painting Exhibition it was also catching attention from a reviewer for the Swindon News -- 'When this boy gets really serious his possibilities are enormous...' and Wendy, whom Andy was seeing quite a lot of lately and who also had received an excellent comment, said they should celebrate their good news with a Saturday lunch.

"Some potatoes and sprouts and a bit of ham?" said Andy, and they laughed and it was planned for the next day, Saturday, for the two of them with the necessary but minimal intrusion from Iris.

So Iris appeared on Saturday afternoon with potatoes and sprouts and more than a bit of ham and water for the orange squash mix in a beautiful antique pitcher and announced that nothing extra was to be due with the rent as Miss Pofford was ever so pleased with Andy's as well as Wendy's favourable mentions in the Swindon News.

"Number 12 is also celebrating the celebrities as Miss Pofford says," said Iris, "We are having a lunch too, with pink cake! It was Mr. Lemmington's favourite, that pink cake. A extra-large piece of pink cake will also be served later to Wendy and Mr. Riley. Miss Pofford said to say that!" called Iris over her shoulder as she slammed out Andy's door to the extra-shrill barking from Uncle's dogs who had no one to swat them to silence -- Uncle was at the table with The Blind Girl and The Boy and Miss Pofford. Iris was to join them after she had delivered two pieces of pink cake to Vera and Nola who wished also to celebrate Andy and Wendy but were, as usual, marooned knee-wise.

Suddenly, shooting through the thinness like a bugle call, came "I-REES! I-REES!"

"Yes, Miss Pofford?!" screamed Iris as she rushed back through Andy's door to the thinness. "Yes, Miss Pofford?!"

"How the hell can you give our Vera and Nola their pink cake when you left their pink cake here on the bleedin' kitchen sink?! Here on the bleedin' kitchen sink! Eh?! How can you?!"

"I was on my way, Miss Pofford, honest I was! I was on my way to fetch the pink cakey-wakey just now! Honest I was, Miss Pofford!"

"Liar!" shrieked Miss Pofford through the thinness. You get back here, you Iris thing! And fetch this pink cake and take it up to our poor Vera and Nola with their knees! Fetch this pink cake now and take it up to poor Vera and Nola or by God I'll make sure you get none of it for yourself! Do you understand me, girl?!"

"Yes, Miss Pofford!"

"Do you understand me, you I-reees?!"

"Yes, Miss Pofford!"

"Do you?! Understand?!"

"Yes, Miss Pofford, honest I do!"

"Liar!"

"Awww...Miss Pofford!"

"For God's sake, my girl, stop hangin' about and fetch the bleedin' cake for Vera and Nola!"

"Yes, Miss Pofford!"

# 38

As Wendy and I began our potatoes and sprouts and that extra bit of ham I couldn't believe it wasn't raining as was forecast. Not a drop as Wendy and I had walked, taking in quite a few Dreaming Spires, from Magdalen Bridge through Christchurch Meadows toward our afternoon celebration in my Wilton Street basement. Wendy might also have been behind this continued perfect weather because the sun always looked so magnificent on her long red hair. Granddad used to say I occasionally got overly cinematical. I plead guilty. "What fools we mortals be" whispered Granddad from nowhere and chuckled.

Uncle's dogs began barking and yapping again and someone knocked, and through the door said "Andy?"

It was Reggie who stuck in her head, peered curiously around and said "Charlie wondered if you had but I see that you haven't." Then she turned and rushed up the stairs without looking back. I had no idea what she was talking about.

"Who was that?" said Wendy.

"Regina. S-S-S-She'd said Charlie had asked if I had.

"Had what?" asked Wendy.

"I d-don't know. She also said, but I s-s-s-see that y-you haven't."

"Who's Regina?"

"She lives on the t-t-top f-floor with Charlie."

"Who's he?"

"S-She. Charlie is s-s-short for Charlotta. They're a l-lesbian couple."

"Good for them!" grinned, Wendy.

We had just begun again on our potatoes and sprouts and ham when a small pebble came flying down my light-well and pinged against the bright new window pane -- possibly the only improvement my digs had experienced in the last hundred years. There was Yves swinging a whole bottle of bourbon over the little iron fence at the top of the light-well at exactly the point from where Alasdair had directed his penis and peed. Not a pleasant memory. "Leandair! Let me een! Let us celebrate your success of thee world of Art!"

"It's Yves," I said. It put me on the spot because this was a very personal celebration reserved for Wendy and me.

"Bon jour, Yves!" called Wendy up the light-well, and whispered "For God's sake, Andy, let him in, he's got a huge bottle of whisky!"

I was about to start up the basement stairs but Yves had hopped into the light-well and was already at the window sliding it open. I did not forget he had done this once before and I owed him. He was through the window before he noticed Wendy.

"Yves," I said, "this is Wendy."

"Enchante," he said, straightening up. He took Wendy's hand and kissed it and Wendy flashed him her spectacular smile. I felt great and almost jealous. And not sure of whom. But they liked one another and I liked them both. That was the most important. At least for me. That does sound a bit self serving, as it were. And it is. Know thyself.

"Yves d-d-drops in at the R-Rossetti occasionally." I said.

"Welcome, Yves, I've seen you, at the Rossetti."

"Not often," said Yves who had now had other interests to further his writing ambitions though I wasn't sure what they were. Until later. But that's another story.

Wendy asked me for glasses as she graciously took the proffered bottle of bourbon from Yves. At my wardrobe, I very carefully opened the dodgy door which now swung easily! The broken wood had been glued and the hinges were fixed! I took out three of Sheila's crystal glasses -- she'd not reclaimed them yet and Cyril had long ago disposed of the rest of her case of fine wine while I was in hospital.

Wendy set the crystal glasses on my work table and carefully poured a thimble-full of bourbon into each. Yves laughed and sprang from the floor where he had thrown himself on one of Sheila's decorative bed pillows -- thanks again, Sheila!

"Wendy! You must fill thee glasses to thee brim's top! Just as we must fill our lives to thee brim's top!"

So we all willingly quaffed our brimful glasses, laughed

and coughed something awful as quaffing straight bourbon can pack a wallop! Though the Scots say bourbon's far too sweet.

Yves poured another glass each and Wendy and I divided our potatoes and sprouts and those many bits of ham on my one spare dish for Yves and we soon quaffed another bourbon and finished our lunch. Laughing even more, we waited for 'Cyril's favourite' pink cake.


Andy and Wendy now sat on Andy's bed, their backs protected from the frozen wall by two further fancy pillows, gifts of Sheila, in that past life so long, but really only months, ago. Yves, who would one day win one of France's highest literary awards, was sitting on the floor, leaning against the bed near Andy who was holding Wendy's hand. They all sipped lazily from Sheila's fine crystal glasses and Yves rose for a moment to pull the paraffin fire closer to the bed and caught Andy's eye. Andy smiled and turned to Wendy. But her eyes were closed and her red hair was glowing even in the dying light. She held her glass elegantly, too, in her graceful fingers.

"Take it easy, Andy," whispered Granddad from nowhere.

Dark-haired Yves's steady gaze, unblinking and wondering, remained on Andy till Andy, happy on bourbon gazed back. Something else stirred in Andy. Something from somewhere else.

"Take it easy, Andy," repeated Granddad from nowhere.

Wendy sighed, breathed out heavily and seemed about to doze off. Andy took her empty glass, placed it safely on a small shelf by the wardrobe. But something was different. It was his face, for the first time not depressingly disfigured by a huge crack in the wardrobe mirror. Charlie, he now knew Reggie had meant to say, had fixed the hinge on the wardrobe door and replaced the mirror and had wondered if Andy had noticed. Now he had and he thanked Charlie in his head and would soon thank her in person. He had a drawing for her as well. It was of a small Passive Resistance Protest group, lying about, bored shitless, on a seemingly infinite field of Charlie's beloved tarmac. Andy also had a small sketch of the tobacconist's shop for the tobacconist's wife. Her timely gift of a laxative on that first day in England was a godsend. The couple would soon frame and hang his drawing in their shop.

At this angle, on the newly hinged wardrobe door, the faces in the new mirror were three: Wendy, awake now and attempting a drowsy smile, and Andy, who grinned tipsily at Wendy then at Yves who grinned back and covertly clamped his hand on Andy's, jolting him for a cinematical moment into another sort of happiness that Andy would later heroically explore.

In his newly undistorted mirror Andy liked what he saw. He was no longer the whining, worrying, constipated, vitamin-addicted, frightened boy dependent on every chance smile for survival. He was nearly whole and he had no intention of choking to death on ancient seawater for the sake of a mythical high-priestess he'd never met. And he now had an unusually accomplished yet unfinished painting of the wonderful Irene on his easel at the Rossetti. Never in the course of human history, thought Andy, has one 'bloke' owed so much to so many foreigners in such a short time! He had become their 'Our Yank'.

Now and ever after Andy could not wrap his head around the phenomenally good luck that had landed him here in this cornucopia of good fortune, this Numbers 12 and 13 Wilton street treasure! With these splendid housemates. And his two-times-lethal-one-time-almost, damp, cold, dark, rectangular room below sea level that on extremely sunny days at a certain time of year very nearly lay in the faint shadow at least one authentic Dreaming Spire. Was a Guardian Angel lurking somewhere? Did Andy deserve all this? He'd have to decide that for himself. It was he alone who must decide. But he'd need a little time, wouldn't he? The world was no longer in imminent danger -- or no more than usual -- and had now generously offered him that time. There was so much to do! And so much time in which to do it!

Anyhow, here was the familiar racket of Uncle's dogs, and Uncle's "Belt up, you hairy bitches!" Here, too, was the welcome clomp of Iris as his door slammed open and a tray of steaming tea whisked in with a pink cake beside. For afters! *As it were.*

# Afterword

Oxford
Ten years later

"Who the hell are you?!" snapped Miss Pofford.

Her slightly younger sister with whom she now lived had told me this was one of her better days. But Miss Pofford glared at me and spat again: "Who the hell are you?!"

I refused to wilt. Years had passed. The world was still here -- most of it. I had grown up and was not afraid anymore -- I had once been afraid. Of everything.

I was surprised to see the small glass showcase of her miniature doll collection and took out and handed her the tiny American "Uncle Sam" figure in a stars and stripes top-hat.

"I gave you this, Miss Pofford, ten years ago."

The old lady grabbed the tiny doll from me and, trembling, clutched it.

This shrunken, scowling Miss Pofford was no longer the larger than life, reigning landlady of numbers 12 and 13 Wilton Street, Oxford, so ably assisted by her scarlet-cheeked, blue nylon uniformed, lady in waiting, the formidable Iris. Muscular, miniscule Iris was long gone. She scrubbed floors now at the Radcliffe Infirmary and went for group holidays in Spain.

Suddenly Miss Pofford's scowl split. Her fragile body lurched and a fist flew to her mouth to bat away a thread of spittle. She slammed the tiny Uncle Sam to her cheek and whispered "Our Yank, come home to see us! It's Andy, our Yank!"

I took her hand and she squeezed mine so hard it hurt. Suddenly she snatched back her hand, her spectacled wall-eyes narrowed and her fingers raked through her wispy grey hair. The tiny, flag-carrying Uncle Sam tumbled from her lap and one of her eyes slid menacingly back and fastened squarely on me. "Who the hell are you?!"

Also by
Donovan O'Malley:

**THE DELILAH CHRONICLES**
The comic adventures of
a 39-year-old divorcée
doing it <u>her way</u>

**THE IMPORTANCE OF HAVING SPUNK**
A Comic Novel with a twist
to the battle of the sexes,
with a nod to Oscar Wilde

**LEMON GULCH**
Third Edition
of the Comic Cult Classic

**THE FANTASTICAL MYSTERY
OF RITTERHOUSE FAY**
A London tale

**WOMEN WHO LOVE
& OTHER STORIES**

**THE JIMMY JONES SKANDAL**
A humorous bedtime story
for grown-ups,
Illustrated by the author

**LEMONGULCHBOOKS**
www.lemongulchbooks.com

Lightning Source UK Ltd.
Milton Keynes UK
UKHW041949180319
339393UK00001B/16/P

9 789197 918817